DEATH THROWS A BOUQUET

DEATH THROWS A BOUQUET

A REV & RYE MYSTERY

MARIA MANKIN &
MAREN C. TIRABASSI

Published in the United States by Brain Mill Press.

Print ISBN 978-1-948559-95-9
EPUB ISBN 978-1-948559-94-2

Cover design by Ampersand Book Covers.

This book is dedicated, first, to Ann Boulanger, a teacher whose far-reaching view of the world and its possibilities beyond our town changed me for the better in ways I couldn't have imagined at twelve years old. Ann, you are the voice of integrity I hear inside and a compass for justice and action.

Secondly, to the staff of Ryan Elementary, who have given our family so much and welcomed me into their community, where I have found a second home. I'm always happier after a day at school.

Thank you.

—Maria Mankin

DEATH THROWS A BOUQUET

1

Jodi Franklin graded papers for two hours before she took a break to get a cup of tea. She had been teaching for thirty years, and two hours was nowhere near her record. In her younger days, she could mark up essays all day on a Saturday, then drive through the night to visit her younger brother and listen to him sing a solo at church on Sunday morning.

These days her priorities were in better order. Not that she wouldn't still drive to see Daniel when he was performing, but she would never spend her whole weekend working. If a student only spent an hour writing a six-page research paper on the Kennedy assassination, and most of that time was given to coordinating questionable AI input, Jodi was only going to spend five minutes grading it.

At this point, a lot of her job seemed to involve entering paragraphs into plagiarism databases while deciding whether she could make it through one more year of this nonsense before retirement. To be fair, she mostly felt that way in early June, but the burnout had gotten worse. She loved her summers off too much to quit, even when the last of her friends from the old guard had moved to Florida. The fights with administration over teaching to the AP test versus encouraging critical thinking skills, the constant emails from parents complaining about her lowering their children's GPAs with her "overly rigorous" expectations, and those same students failing to follow even the most basic instructions on a daily basis all ground her down.

Teaching had been Jodi's passion ever since she'd first picked up *Anne of Green Gables* as a child. She had managed to keep that flame lit through countless shifts in the educational landscape. Now, though, she was done. In early September, she had negotiated time off to go to the Grand Canyon, and next June she would be on her way to Patagonia to begin her trip around the world. She would never pick up a red pen again.

Jodi glanced out her office window and noticed several of the neighbor boys arguing over their pickup game of basketball. A few went to the local high school, Stoneridge, where she had taught as a young woman before transferring to neighboring Lincoln High in an effort to separate her personal life from her professional one. She recognized all the kids who lived at the Cedars Apartments. Wyatt Eames was often out there, since his parents owned a food truck and were gone for long stretches, and his friend with the expensive haircut was with him tonight. Noah something? It would come to her, probably at two in the morning.

They were up against some newcomers—older than high school, by the looks of them—and those men did not sound happy. Jodi knew, by sight at least, most of the people who lived here, even with families moving in and out all the time. She had called this place home for two decades, but many people saw the Cedars as a stopping point, and not always a happy one. She was used to hearing arguments through the thin walls and passing by all manner of petty illegal behaviors in the stairwell or the parking lot outside. Jodi had called the police more times than she could remember when she suspected the fights were ongoing abuse. That hadn't endeared her to the abusers, the victims, or to the children who saw family members driven away in the back of squad cars, but at least she could sleep at night.

Perhaps being a history teacher made her fond of documentation. She wrote daily about the goings on around her building, thick journals she could produce when law enforcement questioned her about an incident she had reported. Often her decision to track incidents of violence against women with dates and a record of observable injuries made the difference in court. Her corner fourth-floor apartment had the best view in the building. She was 'that person' at Cedars, and she owned it.

She glanced back out at the court, but the basketball players had wandered over to the Eames family's food truck, which must have pulled up while she was in the kitchen fussing with her old kettle. Wyatt and his friend had disappeared, too, probably to the parking lot, which she couldn't see from her window. She could hear shouting, though, and what sounded like someone crying. Her down-the-hall neighbor Jewel had a three-month-old, but Jodi knew little Missy's cries. This sounded like a woman.

Jodi put down her mug and tried to raise the window higher so she could stick her head out. No luck. This rain, along with the blasted heat and humidity, had the old wood swollen tight. She sighed, grabbed her raincoat from the hook by the door, and slid her feet into a pair of old flip-flops. A teacher's work was never done.

2

Dystopian fiction would have readers believe that teenagers were the best choice to save the world, but in reality they were just the easiest demographic to convince to do stupid, dangerous things, which was why Prudence Rye needed to find some.

As vice principal of Stoneridge High School, Rye had a certain clout with kids who were often in her office, while her friend and pastor Wanda Duff, a woman twenty years her senior (with the patience and wisdom to show for it, as well as the occasional gray in her hair) could call in the assistance of youth group members, as well as her live-in nephew, Lance, and his best friends.

Wanda and Rye had become friends a year ago, when Wanda began investigating the suspicious death of a parishioner, Niels Pond. Wanda and Rye had achieved local amateur sleuth fame by solving several other cases together since then, in addition to becoming close friends. Wanda and Lance often joined Rye and her father, Hardy, for dinner, although recently Wanda and Hardy would slip away after the meal and leave Rye with Lance and his friends for entertainment. Rye didn't mind. It was nice to see both her friend and her father looking so happy, and as an only child she enjoyed the chance to boss around a few younger "siblings" now and then.

Today, though, it wasn't the world that needed saving, but a wedding. Was the flooding of the library parking lot the end of the world? Rye would have said no, but the grooms disagreed. Their wedding was in an hour, and Rye and Wanda had been fielding calls from guests all morning—ever since Tony dumped the problem in their laps and told them to fix "this."

Tony Tomeo was Wanda's longtime best friend, Trinity UCC's choir director, and the all-around music guru at the high school. Tony had been an absolute shark in the dating pool until he met Greg Engstrom. Greg, a librarian with sweet cherub cheeks and surprisingly acerbic wit, had won Tony over completely.

"This" was one of several storms of the century that Stone Ridge had experienced this year. It seemed like every other week there were warnings about power outages, downed trees, and, yes, flooding. This storm, which had been predicted to pass north of them, had shown up with all that and more—a tornado warning that had sent the grooms spinning.

"Are you having any luck?" Wanda asked Rye as she hung up from another unsuccessful phone call with the public works department. Wanda pushed her hair off her face. She'd obviously tried to curl it this morning, but it lay sticky on her neck now.

"None." Rye had called her father, the former sheriff, to see what connections he might have to get the sewer grates cleared on the street. The parking lot was a lost cause until Monday, but street parking was available if they could move some of the trapped water. "Dad says everyone he knows is tied up with river overflow and neighborhood flooding or is too old and feeble to risk the weather."

"I don't know what we're going to do." Wanda looked frazzled.

"We'll figure something out," Rye told her with a confidence that was starting to wane. She had a lot of practice telling people half truths as part of her job, but she hated to lie to Wanda. The truth was, if Lance and his friends didn't come through, the wedding might be ruined. "Why don't you go sit with Tony for a few minutes? I'll be on phone duty, and you can work your 'this will all work out' woo-woo magic on him."

"Are you talking about pastoral counseling?" Wanda asked with a small smile. "You know I'm not a fortune teller at a carnival, right?"

"Same, same," Rye said, suddenly much brighter, shooing her toward the library's reference room, where Tony and Greg were getting ready.

A text from Lance had finally come in. Here, it read, with a cluster of emojis she didn't have time to parse. Rye grabbed her coat, a shiny silver number Wanda had convinced her to buy that had turned out to be cuter and more waterproof than expected, and slipped out of her strappy sandals and into rain boots. She dashed outside, pulling her hood up against the wind. Down the street, a Yukon XL rounded the corner. It was followed by a parade of SUVs driven by Stoneridge students and at least one teacher. Mike Nifterick taught PE but was more popular in his role as coach of the track and field teams. Rye hadn't realized he even owned a car, much less an SUV. She had only seen him ride a motorcycle to school before, but here he was, first in line, hopping down to open the back door.

Mike offered a hand to his elderly passenger, then went around the other side to help another woman over the rushing gutter. Under his raincoat, he was dressed for the wedding. Rye realized that though she only thought of him as an occasional running buddy, Mike and Tony must be friends from school. She never would have guessed it.

When Lance had asked Rye why she needed him to find out who drove the passel of high-end, flood-ready vehicles Rye passed every day in the school parking lot, she had sent him a link to the best cars for handling these exact conditions. Why else would the parents of these children have purchased them Suburbans, Wranglers, Land Rovers, and even a Hummer? If ever there was a day to put teenagers to use, this was it, and if their parents had a problem with it, they probably should have bought them secondhand Kia Fortes or Camrys instead.

Of course that wasn't what Rye told Lance. Instead she had tasked him to get those cars out to the hotel where Greg and Tony held a block of rooms, with the promise of as much free pizza as the drivers could consume if they could shuttle the guests to the library. Greg had been skeptical that it would work, but Rye, Wanda, and Tony had enough experience with teenagers to know they required little motivation to take risks like driving in foul weather. Sure enough, plenty had responded, and Rye was glad she'd filled the library's staff room with not only pizzas from A Slice of Pi next door but also packages of cookies and plenty of water and lemonade. Rental cars might not make it through this storm, but the guests would.

She waved to her students as they stopped at the curb. Luckily, Hardy had dropped off the umbrellas Wanda had been collecting earlier in the week, so most of the guests arriving had protection from the downpour. Rye was doing her paparazzi best to get some pictures and videos of this moment (funnier in hindsight, she hoped) for Tony and Greg, but if she stayed out much longer, she was going to be soaked to the bone. Fortunately the last few cars were pulling up, and she spotted Lance with his best friends, Leslie and Nicole, hopping out of the last one. She waved to them, and they all ran up the path together.

The lobby of the library was a joyful tumult when they stepped inside, scented by the lilac branches scattered in vases on almost every surface, as well as a whiff of wet dog. Rye hung up her sopping jacket and turned to see the grooms and Wanda coming down the hall with Wanda's terrier, Wink, wearing a collar with tiny fabric flowers. Wanda may have nixed Wink's participation in the ceremony itself, but that didn't mean he couldn't be dolled up for the occasion.

When the two men were led in, having been sequestered in dramatic despair, a cheer went up from the assembled, dripping crowd of family and friends. Tony burst into tears as Greg wrapped him in a hug. Rye was glad she still had her phone out to catch the moment.

Wanda, in full ministerial mode, stepped to the front and held up a hand for a silence, which she miraculously achieved. "Ten minutes to dry off and chat while we wait for a few more people, but when I ring this bell"—Wanda held up a small replica of a Paul Revere bell—"you'll take your seats, and the ceremony will begin. There will be plenty of time at the reception to catch up!"

"And eat!" someone in the back of the crowd called. Tony whooped in agreement, and the guests let out another cheer.

<h1 style="text-align:center">3</h1>

Wanda was counting Marples.

When a clergywoman is waiting for that single wedding photo she's in (which, of course, will be the last one), and she is in a library with a fantastic DVD collection for Luddite patrons, she has time to compile a mental list of every actress who has played Jane Marple. She began with Margaret Rutherford, of course, and then there was the young Gracie Fields—poor dear, she tried—and on to Helen Hayes and Angela Lansbury, June Whitfield on the radio, Kaoru Yachigusa in anime voice-over, Joan Hickson, Geraldine McEwan, who was quite stern, and finally a few others far too young, which was how Wanda Duff usually thought of herself.

After she and Rye had solved four murders in barely a year in the small town of Stone Ridge, she might well be a Marple-in-training, but she didn't want life to mimic fiction. She fervently hoped that Luisa Suarez was the last murder victim who would require Wanda's self-taught detective skills. She should be counting weddings instead, because she was officiating four more of those in the next month, something unheard of in this era of wedding planner officiants.

Wanda had made it through Tony and Greg's ceremony with minimal tears—more than strictly professional, but fewer than expected when a best friend was at the altar—but now she had been released to stand alone by the cheese spread, trying to look busy without actually eating herself into a brie-induced haze. Her head was starting to hurt, an unfortunate side effect of using her hearing aids at events like this, where there was music and background chatter constantly blurring what she wanted to hear. In the past, she had dulled the problem with a drink or three, but she had been sober now for almost seven months. A couple of Tylenol would have to get her through to bedtime instead.

If she'd brought a plus-one, she might not have noticed the pain. Wanda had waited patiently, like a girl before prom in another era—well, her era—for Hardy Rye to issue an invitation. But no invitation came.

She would have happily settled for the company of a friend, and as it happened many of her friends were here. They were just busy with their own partners at the moment, or, in Rye's case, engaged in a not-so-subtle spy mission regarding her father's plus-one. To be fair, Wanda was in favor of this particular detective work. In fact, if Rye didn't learn something about Hardy's mystery date, Wanda was ready to go full Marple on that situation herself.

It wasn't that she and Hardy were officially anything. Friends. They were officially friends, and he had almost kissed her six times (not that she was counting). They ate dinner together a few times a week, and if those meals were overrun by teenagers, dogs, adult daughters, and the gaggle of people who came with them, all the better! She and Hardy loved a full house. It was another thing they had in common.

He didn't even mind that she was an amateur sleuth. As a retired sheriff, Hardy encouraged it, talking through self-defense techniques and investigations he had been a part of to give her a better understanding of the intersection between police procedure and gut instinct. It energized both of them to have cases to consider, and as tragic as the murders were, they had brought Wanda into a family she couldn't have imagined this time last year.

Maybe she wasn't the romantic lead, though. Maybe she was the best friend instead, she thought, as she watched Hardy and the mystery woman linger over their meals, deep in conversation. After all, she had a nephew she adored, a group of dear friends, and two dogs. Wink, the graying Jack Russell, had fallen asleep at the altar, and Figgy, short for Figaro, a foxeagle with a foxhound's tall legs and a beagle's howl, who had been fostered over the winter and never left. Her life was rich beyond measure. Her house was a mess.

But still there was a twinge of jealousy. This woman was fortysomething instead of fiftysomething, like Wanda. Hardy was in his early sixties and good-looking, with unbelievable cooking skills, a quick but gentle wit, and a presence she felt easy in. Wanda had gone on enough dates after her second divorce to know that those were not characteristics typically found in men her age. She'd usually settled for a sense of humor and something less than complete revulsion at her profession.

Wanda might have spiraled, but as she gazed out at the people gathered for her friends' wedding, she suddenly realized it was chock full of charming gay men willing to dance with a short, aging clergywoman. Tony, known to most as the high school music director, was also the instrumentalist and choir director at Trinity. Between his two jobs, he seemed to know everyone in town, and every gay man in the area had shown up, many of whom Tony had introduced to her as ex-boyfriends. Wanda loved Tony with all her heart, but she knew that he had been a loose cannon on the local dating scene. Although surprised he fell hard for a librarian, she also breathed a sigh of relief.

When she got to know Greg Engstrom better, she was ecstatic. If Tony was the closest thing to a brother Wanda had, welcoming Greg into the family was a dream come true. He was much more reserved than his new husband, but also devastatingly witty, unfailingly kind, and, as Tony put it, gifted in the handsome department. Wanda thought of Greg as adorable more than anything else, with those bright eyes and white-blond curls that had grown out just long enough to be pulled back with tiny flower clips that matched his boutonniere.

During the ceremony, Wanda had caught Greg with a bewildered expression on his face, a look she recognized from many folks who had been abused in past relationships and still weren't certain they deserved to be happy. She decided to quote *Frozen 2*, impromptu to her wedding homily, instructing the couple to just "do the *next* right thing." Greg's face had cleared, and his radiant smile returned.

The wedding and reception choice of Greg's home away from home, the social hall of the library where he was the director of acquisitions, had been an "ark" thanks to those rides Rye and Lance had found. Much to eat and no alcohol—a library rule—so it didn't stand out that Greg and Wanda both were in recovery. Greg had also procured the space for free, leaving the budget for delicious food and fabulous live music. Wanda stuffed herself, then discovered she still had room to try small slices of all three wedding cakes. (Tony had claimed they couldn't decide, but Wanda knew that he just adored sweets.)

Before she had a chance to find a partner, Greg's parents found her to express their joy at the wedding.

"We noticed that you used the Lutheran service language for the ring exchange. That meant a lot," Greg's mother told her.

Her husband nodded in enthusiastic agreement. He was looking around, apparently hoping to corner someone who might have baseball scores, but he turned back to interrupt his wife's detailed recounting of the service with a question. "We drove past the high school and noticed that the sign said, 'Stoneridge High School,' one word. Aren't we in Stone Ridge, two words?"

That was an expected question from out-of-towners. Wanda smiled. "The town is Stone Ridge. A benefactor paid for that granite monstrosity, but he scribbled the information incorrectly. The stone mason refused to change it for free, and before the issue was resolved, the mason died. His family inherited the problem but were unwilling to change it, and the town was certainly not going to pay for it. And so Stoneridge is the school, one word. Thrifty and stubborn is not exactly the definition of New England, but it comes close."

He nodded thoughtfully as his wife drew him away to another guest. Wanda took the opportunity to cross the room to see Rye. Her friend looked like she had been crying, though her face was scrubbed clean.

"Hey," Wanda said, taking Rye by the elbow and steering her into a space between the coat racks and the wall where they couldn't be seen by guests trooping back and forth to the restrooms. "What's wrong?"

"Have you talked to my dad tonight?"

"No," Wanda replied, dryly. "He's been…occupied."

"Yes," Rye said. "With Kara."

Wanda faced few opportunities when gasping was the appropriate reaction, but this was one of them. In February, when Rye and Wanda had been studying a cold case, Rye had discovered she had an older half sister, Kara, as well as a step-uncle, Reuben. Rye's mother, Melanie, had never shared with Hardy the existence of these people.

In the last few months, Rye and Reuben had met a few times for coffee. Reuben had told her that Kara was raised by Melanie's aunt Nora in Colorado, but he didn't know what had become of Melanie after she disappeared when Rye was seven. Rye had been grateful that her uncle was genuine in his desire to get to know her, but Kara hadn't responded to emails Rye sent. Wanda knew that had hurt Rye deeply, although she tried to hide it.

And now here Kara was, Hardy's plus-one for the evening, with no warning. He apparently hadn't even bothered to introduce Kara to Rye; instead, she'd learned the woman's identity from Greg, who had heard from Tony, who was enthusiastically making the rounds. Tony was protective of Wanda and undoubtedly had set out to interrogate Hardy's date.

"What do you mean he brought Kara?" Wanda asked. Right behind "gasped" was "gobsmacked," a feeling she was sure she had never properly experienced until right now. "Why would he do that?"

"I have no idea, but you can bet I'm going to find out!" Any sign of tears had been replaced by fire Wanda recognized. Rye was marching into battle.

Wanda grabbed her by the arm and pulled her back. "Not right now you're not!"

"Why not? Aren't you curious?"

"I'm dying to know when he completely lost his marbles, but Greg and Tony are making a toast, and I will not tolerate any distractions. Got it?"

Rye glanced at the happy couple, then nodded. "I'm going to head home then. I can't be in the same room with my father right now and guarantee it won't end in bloodshed."

Wanda understood the sentiment. Only through pastoral restraint would she keep this summer from turning into five weddings and Hardy's funeral.

4

Rye didn't get a chance to ask Hardy about Kara. When she woke up around seven in her apartment, a converted barn behind the house she grew up in, and walked over to see if he was awake, she found a note saying he would be gone all day and to please feed the chickens and weed the garden. No mention of where he was going or any explanation of what he had been doing with Kara the night before.

Rye finished the chores her father usually did in twice the time he took and with a much worse attitude. When she was done, she took a shower and texted her friend Camila Santos. Camila, along with her twin, Ana, both taught at Stoneridge and had become good friends with Rye since she had moved back to town. The sisters were in the midst of planning Ana's wedding, so Rye hadn't seen them much. Today, though, she really needed breakfast therapy.

Sure! Come join me at 366 Hawthorne? came the reply almost immediately.

Rye gave the message a thumbs-up and finished twisting up her damp hair. She didn't immediately recognize the address, but it was close to the sheriff's office. Rye found it easily and then realized why the address had sounded familiar. It was Sheriff Ryan Phennen's building.

Rye loved the old colonial-style house reshaped into a triplex, with ivy cascading down one wall, a lush garden instead of a front lawn, and two stately old birch trees offering shade on this already hot morning. She followed the driveway to the back and took the stairs to the top floor, where Ryan had turned his small deck space into a vegetable garden with meticulously clean chairs and a table in the center.

She rang the bell. Her friend answered the door, a mug of coffee in her hand. Camila gave her a hug and then led Rye into the kitchen. Rye smelled bacon and spotted a huge pan of scrambled eggs on the stove. Ryan had his back to her, buttering toast.

She looked around the house Wanda had once referred to as "a shrine to modernity." Rye had been led to believe that Ryan's home was sterile, a white and chrome museum lacking warmth and personality.

It *was* clean, but Wanda was an indifferent housekeeper at best, and now that she lived with her nephew and two dogs, her home had become downright chaotic. Ryan had small pots of succulents lining the windowsills and a cornflower-blue cotton tablecloth spread out with a vase of daisies and a pitcher of orange juice in the center. The table was set for five, and although the plates were all white, Rye noticed that each seemed to be slightly different. Next to each place setting, there was a cloth napkin snugged neatly into a ring.

"Earth to Rye!" Camila said, poking her in the side.

Rye startled. "Yes?"

Camila looked amused. "Do you want some coffee?"

"Sure. Room for milk, please."

Signs of Camila were everywhere in the kitchen—neon-green running shoes by the door next to Ryan's black pair, a leather jacket hung on the coat hook, and her work computer plugged in on the counter.

The doorbell rang, but before Camila could open it, Ana burst through, followed closely by her fiancé, Tyler, Ryan's younger brother. Rye watched as the four greeted each other warmly with hugs all around, a twinge of jealousy in her gut.

Over the last few months, as she'd realized her feelings for both Camila and Ryan were more than friendship, she hadn't let herself daydream about what that meant. Three sets of sneakers by the door instead of two, an intimate knowledge of where the utensils and dishes could be found, an easiness with their families that Rye's father was so adept at facilitating but that she had never mastered.

So her two favorite people were dating. It didn't have to be a big deal. Rye held up her plate and allowed Ryan to scoop some eggs and toast onto it, feeling her mouth turn up when Camila poured her juice. It didn't matter that the idea of putting a bite into her mouth now made her feel ill. It would pass, surely.

Her feelings for them were complicated, and she had set a firm boundary after her last breakup: she would spend time on her own. She wouldn't rush into anything, and she definitely would not risk two of her closest friendships by suggesting more. Unfortunately, this did not preclude yearning.

She didn't want to spoil the light mood or the conversation about Ana and Tyler's upcoming wedding with whatever this feeling was that was causing her throat to close up, so when her phone rang, she answered it without a second thought.

"Hello?" she asked, stepping away from the table.

"Rye?" It was her father. "There's been a murder, and I need your help."

5

WANDA WAS IN THE MIDDLE OF *MIRACLE ON 34TH Street* for the church book club, the assignment being to read something at the "wrong" time of year and see how the impact would change. Figgy was draped over her lap, and Wink asleep by her side. She loved the summer schedule change for morning services at nine o'clock instead of ten. It meant that at twelve thirty on Sunday afternoon, Wanda could be decompressing after morning worship. She had to officiate at her second wedding of the weekend later today, so this was imperative downtime.

She looked out the window and wasn't altogether surprised to see Rye's car pull up. The wedding today was between Rye's childhood best friend/former boyfriend Andy and Crystal, whom he'd met right after he and Rye broke up a little over six months ago. If Wanda didn't know that Andy was the most risk-averse groom she'd ever encountered, she might not have agreed to perform a ceremony so soon.

He had fallen hard for Crystal, a pediatric surgeon, and Wanda had known where they were headed at one glance. They had the rare relationship that shone with certainty from the beginning. Andy might look tough, with his shaggy black hair and sleeves of tattoos, but he was a gentle person, a wonderful surrogate parent for his niece, Rachel, and generous with his grandmother, who had raised him. As Wanda had gotten to know Crystal, she'd appreciated the woman's ability to bring out Andy's innate playfulness without squashing his natural instincts as a caregiver.

Crystal brought joy into a household that had seen a lot of sorrow. She had even managed to find a way into friendship with Rye. Nevertheless, Wanda knew today would be hard for Rye. She and Crystal were on good terms, but it was still difficult to watch someone you'd cared for marry someone else.

Wanda expected Rye and Andy to continue rebuilding their friendship now that he brought Rachel over to learn a frankly incredible set of life skills with Hardy a few times a week. Hardy practically had a school running out of his house, and everyone was welcome.

Over the winter and spring, Rye had started to take over some of her father's lessons, especially in areas where she excelled—target shooting, long-distance running, and small construction projects. Hardy focused more of his energy on lessons in the garden and kitchen, as well as animal husbandry. He had purchased chickens a few months ago and had been keeping bees for years.

Today she was grateful Rye had a key, because it meant Wanda could wave her in through the front window without disturbing her cozy dog pile. She was already preparing a gentle, friendly conversation about transitions when she caught a glimpse of Rye's face.

"What happened? Are you okay?" She stood up, immediately sending both dogs off the couch and over to Rye for welcoming belly rubs.

Lance stumbled down the stairs as the dogs worked themselves into a barking frenzy, though at his presence and firm command, they immediately quieted. "Some of us work late, you know," he said through a yawn, stretching his arms above his head before pulling a scrunchie off his arm to wrap up his long hair into a bun.

"It's twelve thirty," Wanda pointed out as he pulled her into a quick hug and ambled off to the kitchen, the dogs following close behind. "And what happens 'late' at a funeral home?"

When the door to the kitchen swung shut, question unanswered, Wanda pulled Rye onto the couch. "Are you okay?" Her first thought was a stab of fear. Something had happened to Hardy—an accident, a heart attack…

"My dad got a call. A friend of his was killed last night."

Wanda was ashamed of the pure relief that flooded her body. He was okay. He was safe. Someone else was dead—someone Hardy cared about. It didn't matter. She could breathe again.

"He must be devastated," she finally managed. "Did you know the victim as well?"

Rye shook her head. "No, but you do. Jodi Franklin?"

Instant jolt. Her relief in learning that Hardy was safe had left her unprepared for knowing the victim of another violent crime. Jodi was a member of her church, although she missed Sundays more often than not. Wanda had seen her just last month at the funeral of another longtime member. Jodi had seemed as energetic as ever.

"I didn't realize Hardy knew Jodi" was all she could think to say.

"They were on the PTA together back in the day," Rye replied. "She left Stoneridge for Lincoln High when I was a freshman. I don't remember much, except that not many other kids really seemed to like her."

"Jodi certainly has…*had* a polarizing personality, but I always enjoyed her company. She…" Wanda trailed off. "She talked about *things*, you know? Paintings she loved, places she had visited. She never gossiped or gave 'life advice.'"

"Well somebody didn't like her, because Hardy says she was pushed down a flight of stairs. Broke her neck."

Trust Rye not to sugarcoat it. Wanda said a brief mental prayer before responding. "Does the sheriff's office have any suspects?"

"They think she tripped."

Wanda eyed Rye warily. "But you just said—"

"Dad thinks she was pushed. Her brother does, too. Apparently, she had been training for a twenty-mile hike in the Grand Canyon, and she was in the best shape of her life."

"Even people in great shape have accidents, Rye," Wanda pointed out.

"Sure. But do those same people have the brakes in their car cut a week before? Or a window in their classroom smashed with a rock? My dad told me that she had been facing harassment for a few months now, but none of it was brought to the police when it happened, and none of it is conclusive. So a sixty-year-old slipped or tripped and died. Case closed. My dad wants me…*us* to help him find out who killed her."

"Hardy is asking for help?" Surprise was not the right word for what Wanda was feeling. Total shock might be closer.

"Unheard of, I know, but Ryan says the department isn't going to investigate, and Jodi's brother is a private investigator. Apparently he's not going to drop it, and Hardy thinks we might be…how did he phrase it? A 'moderating force' for Daniel."

"I'm sorry," Wanda said in disbelief. "Your father thinks what now?"

"I know. It says a lot about what my dad knows about the brother. I guess he has a reputation for pushing limits."

Wanda cleared her throat. "And we're supposed to rein him in?" She didn't know whether to laugh or cry. The fact that Hardy trusted Wanda and Rye enough to bring them a case was gratifying, though. Her experience as a pastor and Rye's in school administration made them well-suited for "handling people," but this was a new one.

Grief-stricken, Wanda could do. Loud, abusive, aggressive? She could do that, too, but maybe she'd let Rye take the lead. After all, Wanda's sister was due in town in just a few days, and she would need to save her energy for whatever Mickey had in store.

"So?" Rye asked. "Are you in?"

Wanda could hear a crescendo of barking in the kitchen, which meant Lance had come back in with the dogs and must be making lunch. She thought about the nonstop wedding fever taking over her life for the next month on top of her usual duties at the church and the guests she would soon be hosting.

Despite all of it, she couldn't help the grin that slipped across her face. "I'm in."

6

WAS THERE ANYTHING WORSE THAN BEING AT AN EX'S wedding reception alone?

Rye looked around at the garden Andy's grandmother had labored over for years. Even in early June, lush rosebushes clustered around the gate and wildflowers attracted pollinators over by the tiny frog pond Andy had helped his grandmother build when he was a teenager. Gravel paths wound around raspberry bushes that weren't yet ripe, raised vegetable boxes filled with green shoots, and fragrant lilac and honeysuckle bushes. It was magnificent, and Rye wished she could relax and enjoy the night. But she was alone at the bone-dry reception of her ex-boyfriend who was also her childhood's best friend. She took a sip of ginger ale, wishing it was something stronger.

Andy and Crystal had been married three times this afternoon. A tender seven-minute ceremony took place in the lovely little chapel at Trinity for the families and a few friends. Andy's niece had been his best person, dressed in a moss-green slim-fit velvet sports jacket, tan slacks, and a bright gold bow tie. Crystal's cousin had been her attendant. Adeya was just sixteen and wore a kente cloth maxi skirt with matching headband to honor their Nigerian heritage. The wedding "party," consisting of these two, drew all the attire admiration away from the couple, in summer suit and pearl-colored sundress, to the introverted couple's delight. The younger two had been beaming with the honor during the ceremony but acted their ages for silly photos afterward.

An hour later, the four reconstructed vows, rings, and kisses in the memory care unit at Fair Havens Assisted Living, where Andy was a nurse, so that his dear ones could share the joy. The residents all had a very clear sense of what was happening and cried and laughed. They threw confetti and ate plenty of cake.

Finally, Wanda, the couple, best person, and the bridesmaid had ended the afternoon in the children's wing of the hospital where Crystal worked. There they had done introductions to the young patients' visiting parents and recreated the procession, the kiss, and the recessional. Crystal untied her bouquet and took it apart, so a couple of flowers landed in every room. A duplicate bouquet was produced by Andy for the nurses' station, where they toasted with sparkling cider.

It had been nice to have downtime between the first ceremony and the reception, but Rye found herself wishing she'd declined the invitation to dinner. It wasn't that she had to fake happiness for the couple. Andy and Crystal were such a good match that anyone who saw them would have thought they'd been together for a decade. It was just that she felt pity oozing from those who knew that she and Andy had dated, and she couldn't think of anything worse than people thinking she was envious of Crystal. Andy was great, and Rye hoped that at some point her friendship with the couple would feel easier, but she had no regrets about the end of her relationship with him.

Rye was just picking up her purse to sneak out when she ran into Andy's niece. It had taken Rye and Rachel time to lower their defenses, but they'd bonded over a mutual love of firearms training and shirking Hardy's lessons in the kitchen.

"Leaving already?" Rachel asked.

"I think I'm done for the night." Rye fiddled with the strap on the bag she had borrowed from her friend Ana. "I'm tired."

"Tired of watching Andy and Crystal moon over each other?" Rachel arched her eyebrow in an excellent imitation of Hardy Rye.

"No," Rye said, making a face. "I'm happy for them."

"Once more, with feeling."

Rye regretted binge-watching *Buffy the Vampire Slayer* with Rachel in the spring. The eighth grader now took any and all opportunities to quote the series' musical episode to her. "Don't you have any more ceremonial duties to fulfill?"

Rachel looked offended. She straightened her lapels. "I'm the best man—'person' to Grandmother—and according to Hollywood, my only jobs are drinking too much and trying to make out with bridesmaids. This reception has less booze than a school dance, and Crystal's cousin is way too old for me."

"Adeya is two years older."

"Almost gray hair! And you're weird." Rachel stuck her tongue out at Rye.

"That's true."

"At least I'm not weird and depressed," Rachel said, grabbing a cookie from the dessert table.

"So tell me, have you told Andy and Crystal that you want to be called Rafael, then? They are pro puberty blockers?"

Rachel grabbed Rye's arm and dragged her to the edge of the garden. "No, of course not!" she whispered fiercely. "And I'd appreciate it if you didn't announce it to the whole wedding reception!"

Rye held up her hands in surrender. "You don't get to call me out on my issues until you deal with some of your own."

"You know you aren't supposed to pressure me, right?" Rachel replied. "As a mentor, you're supposed to let me find my own path."

"I think you're confusing me with your therapist," Rye said. "I'm more like your kooky aunt who shows up unannounced wearing a bandanna and tries to get you to drink smoothies made with beet juice."

"That sounds nothing like you," Rachel scoffed. "And, by the way, where is *your* plus-one?"

"My mood has nothing to do with my love life."

"Or complete lack thereof."

"I went on a date last week, thank you very much!"

Rachel stood with her arms crossed, tapping her foot. The soft green jacket did look great. Rye couldn't wait until Rachel felt comfortable as Rafael, changing pronouns and wearing what she wanted all the time instead of accepting the tween girl clothes Andy bought because he wanted his niece to fit in.

"Fine, it was a friend of Claudia's, and it went terribly," Rye admitted.

"I thought you and the drama queen weren't speaking! Even I can tell she's a train wreck. She's just using you." Rachel's expression made it perfectly clear what she thought of Rye's recent ex-girlfriend. "Now she's throwing you dates?"

"It was just one bad date. She knows so many people."

"And you have ten friends, all of whom are exes, underaged, seniors, or related to you. I get that." Rachel pulled at her cuffs until the perfect edge of the crisp cream shirt showed. "But we've already established that your affections lie elsewhere. Why don't you just tell them how you feel and see what happens?"

Rye thought about how she'd felt standing in that sunny kitchen this morning. Had it really only been this morning? How it had felt like home, and also like her heart was being ripped out of her chest at the same time. "Listen, why don't you text some of your friends to come hang out with you now so I can go home and put on sweatpants?"

Rye almost missed the furtive glance Rachel snuck down at her outfit. "Yeah, I'm sure someone's around," Rachel said, brushing an invisible piece of lint from her sleeve. Rye had hoped Rachel had talked to some friends at school about her identity, but maybe not.

She bit her lip. "Or I can stay a little longer, and we can see how many things on the dessert table taste better dipped in the chocolate fountain."

Rachel's whole face lit up. "Can I just put a cup in there and drink it?"

Rye's stomach lurched. "Sure. Let me grab some Pepto and a barf bag, and I'll meet you there."

7

WANDA AND LANCE WALKED INTO THE HOUSE AT SIX thirty, and although it wasn't late, she felt completely spent from the three-in-one wedding. Of course, her phone started ringing as soon as she put the kettle on for tea.

"Lance, I need you to clean up the construction materials out front!" she called. Lance and Hardy had repaired an ancient ramp leading up to the porch in preparation for Rob Chamber's son Stephen's arrival in the morning. Rob was Wanda's sister's fiancé, and his son was arriving earlier than the rest of the wedding party. Stephen used a wheelchair most of the time. Hardy had left early, and Lance had "forgotten" to clean up the extra wood, bits of sandpaper, and debris that their work had left.

"Yeah, yeah!" was all she heard, but the front door slammed, and she had to smile as she answered her cell.

"Wanda speaking."

"Hi, Wanda! This is Ana."

Ana Santos and Tyler Phennen were getting married in a couple weeks in what was looking like it would be the opposite of the intimate weddings she'd attended today. Family and friends from Denver and Brazil were already pouring into town, and although Wanda had done a first premarital counseling session with Ana and Tyler last week, that had been just the beginning of the questions that were pouring in, mainly from Ana's mother via her daughter.

"I'm sorry to bother you on the weekend, but my mother wants me to find out what letters to put after your name on the program. Ph.D. or D.Min. or M.Div. or MTS, ThM…?"

"The closest thing I have to a weekend starts on Monday, so it's not a problem." This was true, and also a white lie. Wanda was ready to turn off her hearing aid and focus on moving the last of her office out of what would become Stephen's room for the duration of his visit. "And 'Rev. Wanda C. Duff' is what I prefer."

"What about Harvard? She found out you have an advanced degree from Harvard Divinity School, and even my father was impressed."

"I'm glad to hear it, but simple will do for me." Wanda kept her tone light. Ana's mother was running the wedding, but Wanda had a feeling that Ana's father's opinions on certain things were decisive. She was glad that her friend Father Paul from St. Joseph Roman Catholic Church was on hand to help with this service.

"If you're sure?"

"I am, and if you need me to email your parents, I can do that later," Wanda said gently. Ana was a very private person, and Wanda knew that this big wedding wasn't what she would have chosen for herself.

"Thanks, but she's coming over in a few minutes so we can finalize the programs together. I'll let her know."

There was a long pause. "Wanda, do you think…" Ana trailed off.

Wanda knew about patience when it came to weddings. She'd had brides who were angry at this level of control from a parent, but she suspected this was something else. She gave Ana time to work it out.

"My mother is so excited about the wedding. She has every detail planned in her mind. I know it's because with my brothers' weddings, she didn't get to do much, and we all know that if Camilla does get married, she won't allow my parents to have any say at all."

Wanda couldn't help herself. She laughed. "Yes, you two may look like twins, but that's where the similarities end."

"My parents have…well, not made peace with it, but they've accepted that they'll have no choice in wedding planning for her, if she gets married at all."

"That makes sense. But it also puts a lot of pressure on you and Tyler."

"It does." Ana went quiet again. She was a contemplative woman by nature, a fact that Wanda had grown to appreciate, surrounded as she was by as many outspoken friends. "I was willing at first, since I don't really care, but it doesn't feel like our wedding anymore."

Wanda was about to offer some very sage advice about how Ana and Tyler could talk about this with her parents when she heard Ana switch to Portuguese.

"My parents just arrived," Ana said after a minute. "Thanks again for your help with the program." She hung up, and Wanda had to bite back her pastoral speech on whose day this was. It would be better used with the needy parents. Six children and only one wedding to fill with all their dreams.

After checking to make sure that Lance was, in fact, on cleanup duty outside, Wanda went back into her office to make sure her desk, which Hardy had helped her move to the corner, was completely cleared and ready for a college student. She had a bed frame from the basement that Lance and Rye assembled one afternoon; fortunately it appeared to be at a decent height for someone moving into and out of a wheelchair. She knew Stephen used forearm crutches, but she wanted to be sure he was comfortable while he was here. To that end, she'd bought a new mattress and figured she could donate her own (very) old one after he went back to England.

She put on clean sheets and made sure she had fresh towels, then went and scrubbed the accessible shower that her predecessor had installed in the bathroom off the kitchen. Wanda would have preferred to be snuggled in the hammock out back with a good book, but cleaning sans hearing aids was a close second in terms of meditation. Events in crowds—and most of hers were weddings and funerals—always reminded her that her hearing was not nearly as good as it once had been.

In settings like that, where the sounds of scraping chairs, coughing, music, and other conversations all competed for her attention, she asked people to repeat themselves more than she used to. Sometimes she would just nod and smile, whether she'd heard a word of the conversation or not. One benefit to years of ministry was that she had a finely attuned sense for distress. She would never "fake" a conversation with someone who needed her, but small talk about the weather? Perfectly acceptable in her book.

When Lance tapped on her back, Wanda nearly jumped out of her skin, so deep was she in thought. She held up a soapy finger. She needed to wash and dry her hands before she could flip back on the outside world.

"What's up?" she asked.

"Apparently Hardy has called you so many times without a response that he decided to call me to make sure you were okay." Lance held out Wanda's cell phone, which she'd intentionally left charging in the living room. No more calls tonight, please!

She looked down. Eight missed calls. Really? What could be so urgent? She wasn't trying to be callous, but Jodi Franklin was already dead. Couldn't the investigation wait until tomorrow? The phone rang again in her hand, and she glanced up at Lance, who was grinning.

"I told him you were available," he said, one delicate eyebrow arched.

Wanda threw a dirty rag at him as he left laughing. She took a deep breath, then answered in her best impression of an Energizer bunny minister.

8

RYE FELT THOROUGHLY ILL FROM ALL THE CHOCOLATE she'd consumed by the time she arrived home. She was ready to put on something with a loose-fitting waistband and drink ginger tea on the couch until she could breathe easily again.

It was not to be. Her father was sitting on the porch with Kara and a man Rye had never seen before. Before opening her car door, she groaned loudly—apparently loudly enough that the three of them heard her, because Hardy shot her a disapproving look. She reluctantly got out of the car, trying not to rub her belly.

Even Wanda was here, stepping out of the house with a tray of mugs to pass around. Wanda smiled, though she looked wrung out from a long day. Rye climbed the steps slowly, wondering whether all that chocolate was about to make a reappearance. "I didn't realize we were expecting company tonight." She directed her comment at Hardy, but her eyes slid to her friend.

Wanda set down the tray and came to stand next to Rye. "Your dad called me—"

"A dozen times," Rye heard Hardy mutter under his breath.

"—and asked if I could come by," Wanda finished. "Hardy, don't you want to make some introductions? I think they're overdue."

Kara waved him off and addressed Rye. "I'm Kara, and I think I'm the one with some explaining to do."

Rye was glad there was a chair behind her. She sat down abruptly and, fortunately, she and everyone else chuckled.

Kara continued, smiling, "I asked Hardy not to share that I was in town until he and I had a chance to talk. I didn't realize the only time he was free would be during the wedding yesterday. I thought if he and I chatted on Saturday, you and I could spend some time together today, but then there was another wedding."

"I know I messed up," Hardy conceded somewhat grouchily, "but when she reached out to me, I wanted to have a chance to meet her to discuss some things about your mother. I should have included you. Both Kara and Wanda have made it very clear that I was wrong in every way."

"When Reuben told me about what happened in February, I wanted to reach out, but he said that you wanted to do so first," Kara said to Rye. "When I didn't hear from you, I eventually asked if Reuben had Hardy's number. I thought maybe you'd decided you didn't want to talk to me, and I wanted to respect that."

"She didn't respond to any of your emails because you had the wrong email address," Hardy added. "It's Kara *V.* Norris at Gmail, not Kara *U.* Norris."

"I feel terrible that you thought I was ignoring you all these months. I really thought you needed some time. Or that you didn't want to have anything to do with me."

Kara was picking at her nails, drawing Rye's attention to the dozen or so chunky silver rings Kara wore. On most people, it would be overwhelming, but on Kara it looked natural. Rye hid her own chapped hands in her pockets.

Rye knew when she was being managed, and right now Hardy and Kara—and even Wanda, with her anxious hovering—were trying to manage her. *Don't upset Rye; she'll blow up, or sulk, or run away.* It didn't help that she would have happily done any of those things at the moment. Instead she took a mug of hot water from the tray and stuck a ginger peach tea bag in it to steep. She crossed her legs, staring at the stranger on the porch. He sat across from her, twisting the brim of his baseball cap around in his hands.

"And who's this? Your husband?" Rye was proud of how calm her voice sounded.

"This is Daniel Franklin, Jodi's younger brother," Hardy said. "I invited him to come talk to us about the death of his sister."

Rye looked between Daniel and Hardy, to Kara, to Wanda, who was shaking her head. She'd been blindsided by her father twice this weekend, and every bone in her body screamed for her to retreat. Instead, she forced herself to lean back. "Is Kara helping with the case, too?"

"No." Kara shook her head. "I just showed up. I wanted to meet you, and your dad said it was okay for me to wait."

Rye studied the woman in front of her. Looking at her half sister was a little like time traveling to the near future. Her hair was the same shade as Rye's, and they shared the light brush of freckles across the nose. They stood almost of a height. The way Kara tossed her thick hair with just a hint of defensiveness as she returned

Rye's gaze made Rye feel like she was standing in front of a fun house mirror. A part of her wanted to raise one hand in the air to see if Kara would mimic it, but instead, she surprised everyone, including herself, by standing up and welcoming Kara with a hug.

Kara's grip was strong, and she smelled of vanilla and baby powder—very different from Rye's own preference for spicier scents—but even so, it felt familiar to hold her. When Rye started to pull away, Kara held her tight. "Our mother's dead. That's why she didn't come back to you," she whispered into Rye's ear.

Kara let her go, and Rye swayed slightly. Over the winter, when she had worked on her mother's cold case, she'd felt a shift, a need to know what happened in a way she never had before. A small part of her had even believed Melanie was still alive—maybe even alive and with this woman in front of her.

But no. Melanie was gone. It wasn't a new hurt, and Rye was no longer a seven-year-old waiting for her mother to pick her up at the bus stop. She was just another grown woman with a dead mother—grieving, but not tragic, not anymore. She had more now than many other women whose mothers were gone. She had a sister.

KARA STAYED LONG ENOUGH TO SHARE A CUP OF TEA with everyone gathered and then made her excuses, promising Rye she would call soon. Rye felt that after everything that had happened in the last few hours, she should be allowed to climb into bed and sleep for a week, or at least take a lava-hot shower and cry. But no, Daniel was waiting, and Rye was frankly too nosy to leave before she found out what he wanted from them. She settled back into her chair with a now-cool cup of tea and waited. Hardy and Wanda seemed to be trying to decide how close they could sit on the love seat before it got weird.

Daniel cleared his throat. His long, silver-glinting black hair was pulled into a braid that reached down his back. He wore scuffed cowboy boots with jeans and a white button-down shirt with the sleeves rolled up, reminding Rye of men she had known when she lived in Austin. If the pain he felt weren't written so clearly across his face, Rye would have passed him on the street and thought he was one of those superbly unbothered men who breezed through life without a care. He must be Wanda's age, but grief had aged him.

"Hardy, I know you said Wanda and Rye could help, but I'm a private detective, and with your connections at the sheriff's office, I can't imagine they can do more than the two of us," Daniel said.

It sounded like the men were picking up an argument begun earlier. "Daniel, you know you're too close to this." Hardy reached out and patted his friend on the arm. "Even for me, thinking about Jodi's death is—" He stopped to clear his throat. "It's awful. Wanda and Rye can help. They have an uncanny ability to appear innocent in their snooping, and it gets results."

Wanda stepped in, the pastor's hat clearly in place. "Hardy's right. You're so close to the victim that it will be difficult to think clearly. And as a PI, if you do something you shouldn't, you can be shut down by the police or risk your license." She held up a hand as Daniel started to protest. "I'm not saying you can't help. Of course you can. But let Rye and me share the weight. Ryan Phennen already thinks of us as the loose cannon brigade, and he'll ignore us until he can't help it. Trust us that we will ask you for all the help a private investigator can give."

"Can you tell us what you think happened?" Rye asked.

Daniel nodded. "Friday night, I talked to Jodi about whether she was coming to my concert in Peterborough. I had a wedding beforehand, so I couldn't drive her, and the weather was going to be so awful that I called her and told her she shouldn't come. Forecast and all, she told me she would be there. Saturday, she was a no-show, and I thought…I *knew* something was wrong. I thought maybe she'd been in an accident. I called her cell phone, and an officer answered. She told me to come to town."

"Jaz," Hardy murmured to Wanda and Rye. Jaz Malone was both a deputy and a good friend.

"I went to the morgue. Jodi was there." Daniel stopped and tried to compose himself. "I had just talked to her, and she was fine. But the officer said it was an accident, that she must have slipped on the stairs and fallen. She broke her neck and died instantly."

"But my dad said you think otherwise?" Rye prompted.

"Jodi had been receiving threats. Rocks thrown through her classroom window. Tires slashed. And last week somebody cut the brakes on her car." He held up his arm. There was an angry red wound on the back of it. "I was driving. Luckily the airbags went off, and the car we rear-ended was one of those SUVs masquerading as a tank. Her little Corolla was totaled, but nobody was hurt."

"Why didn't you report it?" Hardy asked. "Surely an officer came to the scene of the accident?"

"The other driver took off before we could even get a plate." Daniel was quiet for a moment. "There were skid marks to show someone had been there, but they were run-of-the-mill tires. Nothing I could track down. We had her car towed to a shop, and I know she called the insurance company to file a claim. I'll have to go over to the mechanic's and talk to them this week." He rubbed his eyes. Rye could tell that going through all of this was exhausting the man.

"The repair shop confirmed that the brakes were cut?" Hardy asked.

Daniel hesitated. "Well, no. But when I pumped them trying to stop, nothing happened. What other explanation could there be?"

"Worn brake pads, low brake fluid, seized caliper." Hardy ticked the possibilities off on his fingers.

Rye picked up where he left off, having spent endless hours with her father memorizing this list when she was fifteen. "Boiled brake fluid, a damaged brake line—"

Daniel held up his hands in surrender. "Fine! Maybe it was something like that, but Jodi had just gotten her car serviced. If they'd seen any signs of that, wouldn't they have repaired it?"

Rye shrugged. "Depends on the shop. Obviously a diligent mechanic would mention it and price out the repair, but if she just went in for a fluid top-up, they might not have noticed."

"What about the other things? The vandalism?" Daniel sounded frustrated.

"I don't know," Hardy replied. "I wish she'd gotten the authorities involved. If there were records of these incidents, they wouldn't be so quick to assume it was an accident. As it is, the stairs were wet, and she was wearing cheap flip-flops without tread. I know Jodi was in the best shape of her life, but we have to consider at least the possibility that it was an accident."

Daniel stood, his face clouded with anger. "I thought you said you would help me!"

"I told you I would help you find out the truth," Hardy said.

"It sounds like you've already decided," Daniel scoffed. He pulled on his hat and started down the stairs.

Rye stood up and followed him down to the driveway. She rested her hand lightly on his arm as he reached for the door handle. "After what I've seen the past year, I wouldn't put it past someone to cross the line from pranks to something worse. I'd like to help." Rye held out her phone, and after a moment, Daniel took it and typed his number in. "Let me know if you want to meet up and look through her things. Maybe there's something in her classroom or apartment that would give us a better idea of who was targeting her."

Wanda and Hardy stayed quiet, but Rye didn't miss the glance that passed between them. If they weren't on board, that was fine. Wanda had enough on her plate already with her sister coming to visit and a summer of weddings to officiate. Rye, on the other hand, needed a project, and she was not going to look a gift murder in the mouth.

9

It was not vintage Massachusetts June. A drenching drown-the-strawberries rain seemed to be replacing normal light showers. Last year, the sun had been absent for a month, and Wanda was seriously hoping it would not be repeated. She wondered when "climate change" would be renamed "climate chaos."

Wanda was in front of her computer, having dutifully finished the day's urgent personal items. Monday was a traditional clergy day off, and she had taken it gladly, especially after the two-wedding weekend and Sunday service. The downside of the practice was that she did not get Tuesday off when there was a Monday holiday. The upside was that church members remembered, expected, and respected the day she did have, for the most part.

Of course, the downside of lousy Junes was the popularity of outdoor weddings, far too often without indoor backup, while the upside was that most folks now used the ubiquitous officiants or ordained-for-a-day folks to officiate, meaning the job of hand-holding hysterical couples fell to someone else.

Another down-downside was that Tuesdays were unbelievably busy.

Wanda was still at home, working from the kitchen table since her office was no longer available. Pajama bottoms and bare feet below the Zoom-line and a soft knit cowl in lavender topped with handmade beads, tasteful makeup, brushed-to-a-shine hair, and long silver earrings that drew the eyes away from the hearing aids was her own day-off, top-only costume. Her associate conference minister, Rev Di, only had to tell her once after a committee meeting, "None of your comments are credited if you don't keep track of your screen equator."

Wanda's sister Mickey was not fooled, even from a continent away and five hours ahead. "Are you wearing *anything* on your butt and legs? Lance probably won't be shocked, but consider that Stephen will be there soon!"

Wanda could see Rob in the background behind Mickey, trying desperately not to laugh aloud. "I am sure Stephen will not be shocked by the pajamas of a fifty-year-old minister! He has a wheelchair, not a chastity belt."

Rob simply roared. "That's for sure! That boy has never let wheels slow him down with the ladies!"

Wanda laughed. "Sounds like I might have my hands full! Hopefully, Lance will keep him on the straight and narrow."

"My Lance? I doubt it. It's a miracle he made it through a whole school year with your laissez-faire attitude, Winnie."

Wanda cringed at the old nickname and her sister's evaluation of Lance's character. He truly had been the best thing to happen to Wanda, and she couldn't imagine what it would be like when he left for college. Secretly she hoped he would be one of those kids who opted to save money by living the first year at home—her home. She had never pressed him about why he and his mother had so much drama before Mickey moved to Europe with a young Italian scam artist last September. She was content with the fact that he'd seemed to blossom with her as much as she did with him.

Both of them had been living in a state of half dread and half anticipation at seeing Mickey in person, as well as meeting Rob and his son. Lance was only three years younger than Stephen, and Wanda knew that he was experiencing a lot of feelings about meeting his future stepbrother in person. However, even Lance—truly one of the most open high school juniors to ever grace this earth—had his limits when it came to discussing emotional upheaval with his Aunt Wanda.

"Lance has done beautifully this year, and I know he's excited to see all of you," Wanda replied, crossing her fingers at the white lie.

"I can't believe Stephen's flight got delayed a whole day," Mickey said. "Rob and I asked him if he wanted us to come get him so he could sleep at our place overnight, but he said he was fine at a hotel near the airport."

Wanda loved her sister, but she also knew that Mickey could be a lot, especially when plans were thrown into chaos. She didn't blame Stephen for wanting to avoid the nervous energy Wanda felt practically vibrating over Zoom. "Well, we're all ready for him here, whenever he arrives. The ramp has been installed, the office has been transformed into a fairly respectable monk's cell, and we've stocked up on all of Stephen's favorite foods…which incidentally align quite closely with some of Lance's favorites."

"Don't just feed the kids junk!" Mickey exclaimed.

Rob winked at her from his position safely over Mickey's shoulder. "I'm sure Wanda has taken all the recipes you sent her and has been making freezer meals and kale salads aplenty."

Wanda bit her lip and hummed noncommittally. She wasn't much of a cook, and her sister, who was both a chef and a health nut, knew it. Lance had inherited his mother's skills, though, and Wanda happily shared cooking duties with him. Between them, and supplemented by Hardy's frequent dinners, the "boys" would be well taken care of.

"Everything will be great, and when you and Rob arrive, we'll be here to greet you with bells on," Wanda said. She smiled warmly at her sister and Rob, saying another silent prayer of thanks that she was not trying to be gracious with handsome but sleazy Enzo. Hardy had helped Mickey escape to England, where she'd moved in with Wanda's ex-husband, Brian, and Brian's new husband. Rob and Mickey's plan was to have a religious wedding here in Stone Ridge, as well as some tourist time with Stephen. An application for a more permanent visa for Mickey, then legal marriage or civil partnership in the United Kingdom, would come next year.

Mickey had never intended to marry, but now that she was determined to do so, she was all over the visa complications. Wanda was pretty sure that Rob was the one who needed them blessed in a church, and that those vows would always be the real ones for him. She approved. Wanda was also stunned that he had her sister going to church regularly, if only to support his small but very good choir.

Wanda had insisted on premarital counseling with her friend Father Paul, including one session with Stephen and Lance. She was happy to do the ceremony for them, but an honest conversation about their marriage would be easier with someone other than Wanda.

She had spent a lifetime cleaning up Mickey's problems after her. Wanda had not felt close to her older sister since they were children, but taking care of Lance had opened Wanda up to the possibility of a new relationship. Rob certainly seemed to be a stabilizing influence on Mickey, and their phone conversations of late had a lot more laughter than strife. Maybe there was a chance this visit would bring them closer together.

As she closed the computer and glanced up, she realized that at some point Lance had come in. He stood just out of sight of his mother and soon-to-be stepdad. He was signing. Wanda waited. He kept on signing.

"You know I don't speak ASL!"

"But I'm learning, and I need someone to practice with! My class is starting a new session in a few weeks. I think you should join."

Wanda felt her skin grow warm. "I don't need it. My hearing aids are perfect, and—"

"Not perfect. I tripped over the coffee table and knocked everything off of it while you were in here, and there wasn't even an 'Are you alive?' yell from you."

"I was concentrating."

Lance pointed toward the door, where Wink sat patiently. "He was whining to go out when I came in here. He even barked. You didn't hear him."

It was true—Wanda hadn't heard the jingle of Wink's collar, hadn't heard Wink bark.

"I'll turn my hearing aids up," she replied. "I'll pay better attention."

"That's beside the point," Lance retorted. "You need a doorbell with flash lamps in multiple rooms and a louder jingle collar for the dogs. Your cell phone ringer is already so high it could wake the dead, and you still don't always catch it. And not learning to sign? You're cutting yourself off from a whole community."

Yes, her hearing seemed to have gotten worse. Yes, it made her feel old and angry, but that wasn't Lance's fault. She knew that. "I'm just not ready to go there."

He looked so disappointed. "Not even one class?"

She relented…and deflected. "I'll get a flashing alarm clock. I know my insomnia's been getting worse. I worry I'll miss the alarm."

"I got you something better." He held out a long, thin box. "It's a Shake N Wake! It's a wristband that vibrates." He looked so proud of himself.

"I…" There were a lot of things she wanted to say, things an able-bodied teenager couldn't really understand. He was just trying to help. "Thank you. I'll give it a try."

Lance bounded out of the room. Under his arm, she noticed her vintage copy of the *Interpreter's Dictionary of the Bible*, spine never broken. Wanda pushed herself up and opened the door for Wink to go out to the yard. She followed him, since the rain had let up for a few minutes. It smelled glorious out here. The rain was good for the growing things, at least.

Wanda watched the robins across the patio building their nest. They came back every year, and every year, Wanda loved to watch the eggs hatch and the babies grow. This year, though, she realized for the first time that, at this distance, their song was only silence for her.

10

Rye didn't miss much about living in Texas, but the school year wrapping up by the end of May? *That* she missed. This endless rain, combined with seven hundred teenagers who had been over any sense of urgency since mid-April, meant a lot of extra disciplinary meetings added to her calendar every day.

Just this morning, she had seen four students in danger of losing a full grade for repeated truancy from teachers who did not appreciate planning classes for empty seats, and three more in her office for fighting (two fighting and one enjoying being the cause of the fight). She'd had to reschedule a long list of phone calls to her lunch break and knew that she would be staying late to wrap up paperwork for the district that was already overdue.

At the knock on her door, she had to school her face into a neutral expression before calling, "Come in."

Claudia Ramirez stood in the doorway. "Is this a bad time?"

Rye had dated Claudia briefly in the fall until they'd realized they had too much incompatible baggage. Claudia had taken a leave of absence after her colleague and friend Jonathan was murdered, and Rye had known by then that Claudia wasn't over the death of her previous girlfriend, either. After the breakup, they'd tried to be friends, but it was mostly one-sided. Claudia needed something, and Rye needed to be needed.

Rye looked down at the piles spread across her desk and thought about the phone calls, then shook her head and waved the other woman into the seat across from her. "No, of course not."

Claudia dropped gracefully, pulling her feet up and tucking them under her long skirt. "It's about your murder," she said.

Rye looked at her blankly. "I'm…sorry. My what?"

"Your murder? Jodi Franklin?"

"Oh!" Rye said. "That murder."

"You have more than one?" Claudia looked bemused.

"I…uh—"

"Or maybe you're worried I had plans to finish you off." Claudia made a dramatic finger-across-the-throat gesture.

"I doubt most people come around announcing that sort of thing."

"Not if they want to get away with it," Claudia agreed.

Rye shifted in her seat. "What did you want to tell me about Jodi?"

"Before I came to Stoneridge, I taught music at Lincoln for two years. Even though our paths rarely crossed, no week went by without my hearing a student or parent complaining about her." Claudia shrugged. "She thought she was better than everyone, and once she got tenure, her rule of terror really began."

"I met her brother last night. He said she'd been receiving threats recently, and that some people had complained in the past about her classes being too difficult, but there are always going to be parents and students who don't like it when things don't go their way." She felt oddly protective of Jodi. Rye had been on the receiving end of more than one angry parent, both in her role as vice principal and in Austin, Texas, teaching English at a prestigious and very complaint-prone private high school. She didn't have a lot of patience for it.

"You're thinking of Deborah, right? Jodi's sister?"

"No. Definitely Daniel," Rye replied. "I met him last night."

Claudia sat up straight and pulled out her phone. She tapped a few things in, then handed it to Rye. There was a picture on screen of Jodi, much younger, and another woman who resembled Daniel—they could have been fraternal twins. "That's Jodi and Deborah."

"Daniel looks just like Deborah," Rye replied, handing the phone back. "Maybe they have a brother?"

"Not that I know of, but we certainly weren't close friends."

"Was she really as miserable as people say?" Rye asked.

Claudia seemed to deliberate. "She could be harsh. I think as she got older, she had less and less empathy for her students, but she did have a passion for teaching. You could ask Mike. He might know more."

"Nifterick?" Rye asked in surprise. As far as she knew, Mike's hobbies ran to maintaining his motorcycle, brewing beer, and Iron Man competitions. He was funny and friendly with students and teachers, as well as popular with parents. He sounded like Jodi's opposite.

"Jodi was a hard-core athlete," Claudia said. "She and Mike trained together a couple of days a week, or at least they used to when he worked at Lincoln. I don't know if they still did. It would be worth asking him."

"Thanks," Rye said. "It's not exactly a lead, but it's more than I had before."

"Oh, yeah!" Claudia smacked herself lightly on the forehead. "A lead—the whole reason I came in!"

Rye did not say out loud that she had been wondering about that.

"I overheard Noah Tesco and Wyatt Eames in the hallway." Claudia leaned in conspiratorially. "Wyatt lives in the same apartment complex as Jodi, and they were outside playing basketball at the actual time she died. This morning Wyatt was telling Noah that he saw a Suburban parked at the curb that night. He thought it was his sister's boyfriend, who had been failed by Jodi the year before and had to sit out athletics for a semester."

"That's a slim motive for murder."

"That's what Noah said."

"Daniel said he and Jodi rear-ended a Suburban a week or two ago, but the car drove off." She grabbed a pen and sticky note. "Do you have the boyfriend's name? Does he go here or to Lincoln?"

Claudia shook her head and stood as the bell rang. "They went into class before I heard anything else."

"Okay." Rye allowed the pen to drop from her fingers as Claudia strode out the door without a backward glance. "Thanks, I guess."

11

In the basement of St. John's Lutheran Church was a table with two carafes of coffee and a cooler with ice and soft drinks. Rolf Anderson was the pastor, but this was the one meeting held in his church that he did not attend. Introductions had already gotten around to Wanda.

"Hi, my name is Wanda, and I am an alcoholic. I have been sober for seven months."

"Hi, Wanda."

She gratefully received the seven-month medallion and listened as the circle went around. It was an open meeting. Usually she didn't say anything in open meetings, but she attended a couple times a week and had just started offering support to others. She went to a Twelve Step meeting Monday evenings that was only women, and there she would sometimes share.

Suddenly she found herself speaking up. "I think I used alcohol to cover my fear of appearing deaf. If I didn't answer someone at a party, they would think I was distracted. I still have a hard time understanding people who speak softly…even here."

Several people shared about ASL-interpreted meetings in person and online. That wouldn't help her, but she was glad they existed. At the end of the meeting, the leader pulled her aside and told Wanda that her concern was not really one to share at a meeting where folks were new to the program and often mumbled when telling their stories. He didn't think they should be discouraged from sharing at any volume. While Wanda agreed, she also felt pushed away. Seven months sober wasn't new, but it was new enough that she should be able to talk about hearing loss and alcohol. In fact, she was sure she'd used drinking to excuse forgetting what someone said when she probably hadn't heard it in the first place. Her minister self broke in, suggesting that the leader had probably had a bad day, and she should let it go. Or maybe it was her deaf self deferring…like always.

After the meeting, Wanda walked until she reached the halfway mark between St. John's and home, a pocket park with a nice bench. She liked the walk. It was an even hour each way, including her fifteen minutes on the bench. Sometimes she got more out of the walk than the group discussion. As she strolled, she was grateful for how good she felt physically; it was even better than the seven-month chip. She wouldn't allow a little rejection to change her mood.

Tonight there was someone on her bench, a man hunched over. Wanda's pastoral instincts kicked in, even though it was also dark and she felt a little nervous approaching him. She pulled her phone out and prepared herself to dial emergency services if necessary, then slowly approached. She made sure to stop far enough away not to appear threatening.

"Excuse me? Sir? Are you okay?"

Tyler Phennen sat up. "Wanda? What are you doing here?"

"Walking home from a meeting at St. John's." She sat down next to her friend. "You're sitting on my bench," she said with a smile. "Are you avoiding another busy evening with the Santos family?"

"They're a little overwhelming," Ana's fiancé said.

"Especially coming from a small family. My sister, Mickey, and Lance are all the family I have left."

Tyler was silent for a minute. "Is it okay to ask how your parents died?"

"Automobile crash. One car. Alcohol involved."

"I'm sorry."

"Thank you." Wanda had a feeling there was more to Tyler's mood than being overwhelmed by even Aline Santos's frantic need for wedding perfection. "So why are you really sitting out here under the moon, ready to howl?"

"Ana's pregnant."

"That's wonderful!" Wanda burst out. She covered her mouth, embarrassed at the slip. She knew better than to assume all pregnancies were happy news. "I'm sorry. Is it wonderful?"

"For me, yes!" He leaned back against the bench. "I can't ask Ana about it because she hasn't told me officially. But she hasn't been eating, and I've heard her throw up a few times recently. She's been napping every day, which is not like her at all."

"But you don't know for sure?" Wanda asked. "Some women respond that way to stressful situations, and this wedding has certainly taken a turn in that direction."

"I tried. I just feel like she's pushing me away."

Wanda thought about how many couples she had counseled through wedding challenges over the years.

The stress of parental input or money concerns often came between the couples. "What did you say when you talked to her about it?"

Tyler shook his head. "She says she's not stressed."

"But we both know that's not true. Maybe she's embarrassed to be capitulating to her mother when what Ana's family wants is very different from what you two had planned. She might even be feeling guilty for spoiling those ideas you came up with together. That can be difficult to admit."

"But I told her it was fine! I really don't mind if her mom plans a lot of the wedding. I know it's important to Aline." He sighed. "I guess I have been ducking enough events to give her reason to think I might be upset about that."

"You haven't asked her point-blank if she's pregnant, right?"

"No."

"Maybe she senses you're upset and worried, and she thinks it has to do with the wedding or her family. Maybe she is pregnant, maybe she isn't. Maybe she wants to keep it from her family until after the wedding. Maybe she hasn't even realized it herself," Wanda said. "But the fact of the matter is, unless you talk to her, you won't know."

"Romantic miscommunication is more attractive on the big screen than in my own house," Tyler agreed. "I'm just not sure how to bring it up."

"Use your own words. Just try to remember these three simple points: 'Ana, *you* are incredible, *I* would be happy to have a child, and *we* should get a test.'"

Tyler jumped up and pulled Wanda into a big hug. "Thank you," he said, drawing back and looking her in the eye. His big puppy energy was back, and Wanda couldn't be happier.

She might not hear everything, but she was glad she knew what she knew because of the work she did, and that she had a chance to give it away.

12

Finding time to chat with Mike Nifterick was not as easy as Rye had hoped. It almost seemed like he was avoiding her, although she knew the end of the school year was chaotic for everyone. He finally agreed to meet for an early morning run on the track. She was grateful for temporarily clear skies and the light breeze that kept her cool as she stretched while waiting for him. Rye couldn't mark the exact age when stretching before exercise had become more than a good suggestion. She was definitely there, though.

Mike looked like the kind of guy who would stand and shout at his team, but he was always out with them, running, encouraging. His classroom hours had been cut this year as belt tightening slowly reached physical education. Rye knew he covered for sub spots a lot more frequently now, and it was exhausting.

When Rye had first come back to town, she had gone out with Mike, Camila, and Ana a lot. They had run together, gotten beers, watched whatever game happened to be on TV on a free evening. Then Ana met Tyler, and most of her free time started going to him. When Rye briefly dated Claudia, Mike had stopped initiating plans with her. He'd never struck Rye as being homophobic, but he was clearly uncomfortable about something.

She waved at the figure in a hoodie jogging toward her before she realized that whoever it was did not have Mike's significantly broader frame. As the person came closer, she recognized Camila. Rye had been avoiding both Ryan and Camila since having brunch with them, and although she could almost guarantee that Ryan hadn't noticed, she was sure Camila had.

"Hey stranger," Camila said as she stopped in front of Rye. "Where have you been hiding?"

Rye stood. Her shorts were soaked from sitting on the track. "I've been investigating a case for my dad, and then Kara showed up this weekend."

Camila's questioning look turned into a full-on death stare. "Your long lost half-sister showed up, and you didn't immediately call me? Why not? Was it bad? Is she awful? What happened?" Camila loved a soap opera, and she clearly was not going to be denied.

"She looks a little like me," Rye replied. "She seems…nice?"

"Nice? That's it?"

"I'm—" Rye was interrupted by the sound of Mike calling her name from across the track. She gave him a wave and turned back to Camila. "I'm sorry. I have to talk to Mike for a few minutes before he has practice. Will you still be here?"

"I'm meeting Ana. Text me if you want to talk." Camila turned on her heel and started jogging back the way she came. Rye could tell her friend was upset, but she didn't know what to say. *I'm not sure how to talk to you right now because I have feelings for you and Ryan* seemed like a big swing.

Rye would have to worry about that later. She ran over to join Mike, who was already rounding the track for his first lap.

"Hey, Mike," she said, falling into step with him. His legs were longer, and his cardio conditioning was superior to hers, but Rye had been diligent about her workouts the last few months. Mike only had to slow his pace a little so they could talk and run. "I wanted to ask you something, but I know it might be a sensitive subject."

"It's about Jodi, right?" Mike didn't look over, but Rye could feel him tense beside her.

"How did you know?"

"It's not like it's a secret that you solved a couple of murders this year, Rye. Between the front-page news and working in the gossip mill that is high school, I probably know more about your cases than you do."

"They're not *my* cases," she replied, flustered. She and Wanda had asked not to have their names mentioned in the newspaper. Of course, one of the deaths had happened on school property. Another had been the father of a current student, while a third was the brother of another student. One murder took place at the church Rye could see from the track.

Maybe it shouldn't exactly be a shock that people knew she was involved.

"I knew you would want to ask me some questions. It's okay, really," Mike assured her. "Jodi was my friend, and I'm glad someone is looking into her death."

"I'm sorry for your loss," she said. "Were you two close?"

He held up a hand and waggled it back and forth in the universal "so-so" gesture. "We've been training together for a few years now. She gave me a run for my money, too. That's why I couldn't believe it when I heard that she'd tripped down the stairs."

"Accidents happen."

"Oh, I know, but I've seen Jodi running splits over icy terrain." He slowed to a stop and pulled out his phone.

After a minute of flipping through pictures, he handed it to Rye. She pressed play and watched Jodi absolutely fly around this very track. It was clear the ground was a sheet of ice, but when she reached the bleachers, she sprinted up, across, and down without breaking her stride. Rye watched Jodi's foot start to slide as she jumped off the bottom step. She caught herself with barely a wobble.

"You need to show this to the sheriff." She handed him the phone.

"You think?"

"Definitely! When did you take this? Recently?"

He nodded. "It was the end of April when we had that big snowstorm."

"I was imagining a woman who was physically fit for an older person," Rye said. "Jodi Franklin looks like a superhero. There's no way that woman could have slipped and fallen down the stairs without help."

She glanced up and saw that Mike's zero period class had started shuffling onto the field. "I better let you go." Rye went to collect her bag and water bottle, waving at the students as they passed. When she looked back at Mike, she was surprised by his dark expression. Maybe he was more distressed about Jodi's death than he wanted to show.

"Looking good out there, Ms. Rye," one of the girls called as she fell in with her friends to start warm-ups. "Are we going to start seeing you here more often?" She glanced suggestively at Mike.

Rye shook her head. "I don't think I could keep up with you all, and I definitely can't keep up with Coach Nifterick."

The girls looked at each other, then back at Rye, murmuring their agreement. Rye just laughed and headed home for a shower, glad she wasn't a student anymore and could handle the quick, dismissive assessment without breaking her stride.

13

Rye stepped out of the shower and pulled on her old flannel robe, a gift from her father when she started college that had proven impervious to the sands of time. It was ugly but soft, and one of the benefits to living alone was that she could walk around her house in an old, holey robe without a second thought.

Unfortunately Rye had gotten a little too cavalier about handing out keys to her apartment, and when she stepped out of the steamy bathroom, her father, Wanda, and Sheriff Ryan Phennen were sitting around her little dining table looking over some papers together.

"What on earth are you all doing here?" she demanded. "At seven a.m., no less."

"Wanda, you were supposed to poke your head in and warn her," Hardy said without looking up from what he was reading.

Her friend looked at her guiltily. "I'm sorry. I got here first, and I swear I texted you, but then I saw your phone was here on the charger, so I told myself I would wait until I heard the shower turn off, and then I would gently knock on the door to give you a heads-up."

"And?! What happened to that plan?" Rye felt her cheeks heat. She pulled her robe around her more securely.

Wanda made a face. "I assumed I would hear you banging around in there, and that would be my sign. When Lance gets ready in the morning, I can hear him even without putting my hearing aids in! I am so sorry."

"You don't need to be sorry!" Rye exclaimed, turning to Hardy and Ryan. "Both of you, meanwhile, have flawless hearing. You didn't think to call out a warning when you heard me get out of the shower?"

The men looked at each other. "Honestly, no," Ryan said. "I get dressed in the bathroom after my shower."

"Ew," both Wanda and Rye said simultaneously.

"It's so damp in there," Wanda said, making a face. "Do you just put your clothes on while you're still wet?"

"I use a towel first," Ryan replied.

"Same," Hardy agreed.

Rye needed to be at work in half an hour. She did not have time for this conversation. She went over to her dresser and pulled out a T-shirt dress and clean underwear, then disappeared back into the bathroom. When she came out a few minutes later, she was dressed, and her curls had at least been combed through with leave-in conditioner.

"So in addition to investigating my hygiene habits, what on earth are you all doing here, in my house, with no warning, on a workday?" Rye grabbed a smoothie out of the fridge.

"Trying to help you solve a murder," Wanda said brightly.

"It's not a murder," Ryan insisted.

"Then why are you here?" Wanda asked.

"To make sure the three of you don't go off half-cocked before I can prove that this case does not require any amateur sleuthing whatsoever."

Wanda smiled sweetly at him. "You're just mad that our amateur detecting skills have caught more murderers this year than your office."

Ryan growled. "No, I'm annoyed that my mentor approves of you and Rye putting yourselves in danger when it isn't necessary."

Hardy patted Ryan on the shoulder. "I'm honored that you think I could stop them."

Wanda snorted. "Neither of you needs to be here."

"*None* of you need to be here!" Rye said, pushing the button on the coffee maker. She took the opportunity to steal the muffin her father had been buttering and take a huge bite out of it. "This is mine now."

"I asked Ryan to bring over the witness statements after you told me about the hearsay evidence at school," Hardy said.

"Obviously I'm not going to do that," the sheriff replied, "because even though the chance of this being a homicide is very slim, I can't risk tampering with the evidence, even for you."

"But you did tell us that none of the statements mentioned a Suburban," Hardy said.

"And the names you texted me didn't match up with any of the statements either," Ryan noted, shuffling through some handwritten notes, which Rye could tell had either been transcribed by a pigeon or written up by Ryan's brother. Tyler had sprained his right wrist a few weeks ago and was still taking notes with his nondominant hand.

"The boys didn't give statements?" Rye asked.

"Jodi wasn't found right away," Ryan said. "According to this, a neighbor found her around nine p.m., but the time of death was about an hour earlier. No statements from a Tesco or Eames."

"Who did give statements, then?" Rye walked over to stand between Ryan and Wanda.

"The downstairs neighbor who found her and the woman who lives across from her apartment. No one else was home when uniforms knocked. No one they talked to saw or heard anything, but the upstairs neighbor, Martha Snider, was really upset. She must have known Jodi well. The fourth floor has an older and quieter group and they're pretty well acquainted."

"They might have been there but chose not to answer the door to law enforcement," Wanda interjected. "I have parishioners who live at the Cedars, including Martha, and it's not the kind of complex where police presence is appreciated."

Ryan nodded. "That's true, though calls from there have been minimal—not anything like the past. The new management has worked to upgrade the image. Then, about a year ago, the calls picked up again."

"Clearly Noah and Wyatt knew something," Rye replied. "Claudia said they were confident about when they saw the Suburban and what was happening around that time. Anyone coming out of Jodi's building right around the time of death could have been involved."

"Or seen something and chosen not to speak up," Hardy said. "They could be afraid that they'll be targeted if they do…or just shunned."

"That's true for the boys, too," Wanda agreed. "They probably don't want to be seen going to the sheriff's office about anything. Talk about popularity suicide! But when the news broke there was no public information about the time of death, so it took a few turns around the gossip mill before the timeline emerged."

"Too bad." The sheriff answered Wanda, but he was looking at Rye. "Even if Jodi Franklin's death was an accident, and even if the kids didn't make the connection right away, they obviously did at some point, and they need to report what they saw and heard."

Wanda laughed. "Do you remember being a teenager? Making the connection, having a sense of civic responsibility, and reporting to the police are way below, say, gossiping about a breakup."

Ryan grunted, acknowledging that she had a point.

"Can I talk to them first?" Rye asked.

"No!" Ryan exclaimed.

"Why not? Once they're forced to talk to you, they won't say anything helpful to me."

"Which is fine, because, again, you are not law enforcement," Ryan retorted. "In fact, aren't you going to be late to your real job?"

"Where I have permission to talk with students all day? Why yes, I am." Rye grabbed her keys and bag and started speed walking to the door.

Ryan jumped out of his seat, trying to grab all his papers as quickly as he could. He was practically running after her. "Don't you dare talk to them before I do, Rye!"

She stuck her tongue out at him as she reversed down the driveway, missing his cruiser by mere inches. Wanda stood in the doorway and waved as Ryan's lights started flashing.

"Oh, he's pulling out the big guns," she said to Hardy when he joined her. "Rye is not going to be happy about that."

Hardy just chuckled and handed her a muffin out of the basket he'd brought over. "Not our circus."

"Well, they *are* our monkeys," Wanda said, breaking off a piece to pop into her mouth.

"You could say that, and we could try to help…or we could drink the coffee Rye forgot she was making."

Wanda laughed and followed him back inside.

14

Rye did not have the benefit of flashers on her car, but she also didn't need parental approval to talk to her students. Ryan had to settle for beating her to the building, but once he was there, he was stewing in the front office while she called Noah Tesco and Wyatt Eames to her office.

Noah was either absent or running late. Rye knew he dropped off his younger sister at the elementary school before coming for first period and was often tardy. She'd gotten into several arguments with the district attendance liaison about it, knowing there was nothing the family could do about this situation and therefore nothing Rye could do. She was just happy Noah showed up at all, since he'd told her at the beginning of the year he was planning to drop out and get a job. She suspected his mother had a few choice words to say about that, so tardy was a win.

Wyatt, on the other hand, never missed breakfast. His parents owned a food truck, but they were open late and out early, so Wyatt had come to rely on the hot meals served at school. He was a goofy kid, stretched skinny by what must be a five-inch growth spurt and awkward with it. He had corkscrew curls and was the type of boy who wore crumbs on his shirt and couldn't care less. They scattered as he dropped into the chair across from Rye.

The smile vanished as Wyatt side-eyed the sheriff. "What's he doing here?"

"Observing," Ryan replied, just as Rye said, "leaving." He glared at her, but Rye just tapped her pen rhythmically on her desk and waited for him to step outside.

"Thanks for coming, Wyatt," Rye said when the door closed almost all the way behind him.

"Hey, you got me out of biology! I'm here as long as you need me." He lounged so far back in the chair, it almost tipped backward.

Rye hid a smile. "Noted. I just wanted to check in to make sure you're okay after what happened to that woman at your apartment complex the other day."

Wyatt's demeanor changed. He shifted in his seat, his backpack coming up into his lap protectively.

"I didn't see anything, Ms. Rye. I swear it."

"Of course you didn't. I'm sorry—I didn't mean to imply that. Part of my job is making sure that when students experience any trauma, you have the resources you need."

"It wasn't trauma," he replied.

"No?" Rye gently pushed the bowl of fun-sized candy bars toward him.

Wyatt grabbed a couple and proceeded to fill his mouth with nougaty goodness. "Not really. She was a mean b—" He swallowed. "Not a good neighbor. She had my cousin arrested last year, you know."

"I didn't know that."

"Yeah, no one at Lincoln liked her. I'm not surprised someone would kill her."

Rye nodded, taking her own piece of chocolate and slowly unwrapping it, keeping her eyes focused on the desk in front of her. "I thought it was an accident, but it makes sense what you're saying. If everyone hated her, anyone might have pushed her, right?" She stole a glance up at him.

He was busily searching through the bowl, and he nodded, more relaxed. "Yeah. probably."

"But you didn't see anyone leave her building? Not when you and Noah were playing basketball?"

He looked up at that. "Me? No. The basketball court is on the other side of the building. Definitely can't see the front door." He stuffed a handful of the candy bars in his backpack.

"What about Noah?"

"Oh, yeah. Noah. Ask Noah about it. He has a better memory than me. Can I get back to class now?"

"Sure," Rye said. "I'll buzz Mrs. Jones to let her know you're hurrying back to biology." She knew from experience that students tended to take every possible detour from her office back to class.

He did look a little sheepish. "Oh. Thanks, I guess."

"No problem. And Wyatt?"

"Yeah?"

"If you think of anything, like maybe about any cars you saw that night, or other people you know by sight, you'll let me know, right? Sheriff Phennen is a good friend of mine, and I know he can be understanding when witnesses remember something later, especially if he doesn't have to go to the trouble of calling them down to the station, getting their parents involved…"

Wyatt nodded vigorously. "Yeah, I get that. I'll let you know." He stumbled out the door, almost tripping over Ryan's long legs, which he'd stretched out in front of him as he waited.

"Hi…Wyatt, isn't it?" Ryan asked, his voice casual. "Wyatt Eames. Your folks run Dad Yolks, right?"

Wyatt mumbled something that sounded like acknowledgement. "Got to get to class." Apparently he'd discovered real love for biology after all.

Ryan let himself into her office, closing the door fully behind him. "Not bad."

Rye nodded. "He's going to text Noah now for sure, so we'll have to see what happens. Of the two of them, I would have expected to get more from Wyatt."

"Maybe whoever killed Jodi saw the boys outside her building," Ryan replied. "Sent a warning of some kind…"

"You do think someone killed her! I knew it."

"That's not the official line. The investigation isn't closed, but it might as well be. And honestly I have work I need to be doing at the station. I can't follow up on all of these leads myself, so I'll need to see if Tyler or Jaz might be willing to help you. If they have too much on their plates, you'll be on your own."

"At my house this morning, it didn't sound like you even suspected a murder, much less trusted me to look into it."

"In front of your father, who I assume still doesn't know you went to the police academy? Or Wanda, who needs to be taped up in bubble wrap to avoid being injured while investigating?" Ryan shook his head. "I do trust you, Rye. You're stupid about a lot of things, but not this." She shot him a look. He changed the subject.

"Camila called me this morning before I got to your place. You met Kara?"

"For like five minutes."

Ryan stared at her. It wasn't his interrogation glare, which Rye was easily able to withstand. It was more of an "I'm not mad—I'm just disappointed" look that made her feel guilty. She had been keeping the meeting with Kara to herself because Camila would make her talk about her feelings. Rye knew if she shared about meeting her half sister, she might let slip other things that she wasn't ready to talk about.

"Camila's one of your best friends."

"I know!"

"Then why are you ghosting her? She said she's texted you a bunch of times and heard nothing back." Ryan clasped his hands over his knee.

"I've just been busy—work, murder—you know, the usual."

"You haven't had a hard time texting her any of the times you poked your nose into my cases without approval," Ryan replied. "Do I need to ban you from this case, too? Would that be enough to reactivate your compassion?"

"Why are you hounding me about this?"

He stood up. "I just wish you'd talk to her. I think you could clear a lot up if you weren't being such a coward." He turned and left, closing the door behind him.

"You always have to get the last word, don't you?" Rye muttered. Not this time. She jumped up to follow him when her desk phone rang. It was Janet at the district office. Rye couldn't afford to play phone tag all day. She dropped back into her chair with a sigh and picked up the phone.

15

IT WOULD NOT MATTER IF SHE WAS INVOLVED IN A hundred weddings, six funerals, or the sanctuary ceiling caved in, the most important part of Wanda's work was visiting people in the hospital. Even if she drove an hour and a half each way, with only five minutes given by the intensive care staff to pray for and stroke the hand of an apparently unconscious person, it was worth it. Of course, in that situation, she hoped to have meaningful time with family and friends in the waiting room, but if it didn't happen, either because they weren't there or they were anti-religion, it didn't matter to her. The five minutes mattered.

Today she was at St. Joseph's, waiting to see a parishioner recovering from gastrointestinal surgery. It might be a while, but she knew the food was great here, so she had timed her visit to correspond with an early lunch. She was headed to the cafeteria and passing the nurses' station when she saw "Tesco" and a room number written on the nurses' whiteboard. There was only one Tesco family in town. It was probably one of the grandparents. Though Rye had texted Wanda earlier that Noah was a no-show at school, and she'd said her gut feeling about it wasn't good. She hadn't been able to reach either of his parents, though.

The teenager in the bed was absorbed in his cell phone, a not uncommon sight to Wanda. Noah's parents were regulars at Trinity, and even though Noah came with about as much enthusiasm as Wanda had for a root canal, he was still there almost every Sunday. Lately, though, she had seen more of the top of his head during her sermon, and she knew it was a phone distraction. Of course, she'd also seen his mother give him a smack if she noticed him doing it, but Noah was smart. He knew his father usually fell asleep about two minutes into the sermon, so he would sit on his father's far side and sneak the phone out after that, when his mother was distracted.

"Noah?" Wanda tried to get his attention. "Noah?"

"What?" He looked up with irritation, clearly expecting someone else. His face turned bright red, and he began apologizing immediately. "Reverend Wanda! I'm so sorry! I thought you were my aunt. She's been hovering since my parents left for work, and it's driving me up a wall!"

Wanda knew the aunt and could understand wanting a break from the woman's excessive criticisms. It was how she made conversation. "Nope. It's just me. I was headed to get lunch, and I saw your name at the nurses' station. I didn't mean to bother you. I can go." Wanda knew that Noah's upbringing would now demand he invite her to stay. Sure enough, he gestured to one of the two chairs.

"No, please stay."

Wanda hid a smile and sat down. "Can I ask what happened?"

"My…friend Abbie and I were hanging out by my building. She was waiting for her cousin to pick her up, and I was showing her some new tricks Wyatt and I learned from this guy on YouTube." He mimed holding up a basketball and spinning it on his finger. "I'm pretty good, but the ball slipped and went into the street." He paused for a moment, studying his hands. "Have you ever seen that Stephen King movie *Pet Sematary*?"

She shook her head. Straight horror was not one of the genres she enjoyed. "Not the book or the movie, I'm afraid."

"In it, there's a little boy, and he chases a kite into the street. A car hits and kills him."

Wanda could see genuine fear in his face. "Noah—"

"His father resurrects him, and the boy comes back…wrong." Noah clenched his hands. "The car that hit me, whoever was driving…it felt like they wanted to kill me. They didn't slow down, even though Abbie was yelling, and I was running to get out of the way. When the car hit me, I felt a bone in my leg just…break. And they kept on driving."

Wanda had been driven off the road a year earlier on another case, and she knew the fear Noah was talking about. That intentional malice directed at her had sent Wanda into therapy. "That must have been very frightening."

"That wasn't the worst of it," Noah said quietly. "I was laying there, and maybe I blacked out, and then I felt arms dragging me backward. It hurt so much going right over the curb."

"Why would anyone do that?" Wanda asked, appalled. Moving the victim of a hit-and-run?

"It was Abbie. She pulled me out of the street because the car was reversing. It was going to hit me again. On purpose." He looked so small laying there, and Wanda had never thought that about Noah Tesco before. He'd always been a charismatic, athletic kid with a big personality.

"She saved your life" a voice from behind Wanda said. She turned and saw a doctor standing in the doorway. "Although she didn't do that leg a lot of favors. Get some rest." The doctor looked meaningfully at Wanda and came into the room to examine the boy. Wanda started to gather her things when Noah's aunt bustled in. Zelda Tesco was an imposing woman, and Wanda knew she'd better make her escape, but Zelda blocked the door.

"Did you hear about poor Jodi?" was the first thing out of her mouth.

Wanda nodded. "It was a terrible accident. I heard she'd been training for a special vacation, and I know she was planning to retire next year."

Zelda nodded furiously. "None of us know how much time we have, Reverend Wanda!" She gestured to her nephew. "Just look at poor Noah! That maniac could have killed him! Driving those SUVs should be against the law. I'm always saying that, aren't I, Noah?"

"A Suburban is hardly a standard SUV," the doctor replied. "That's what did this, correct? A Suburban?"

Noah nodded, though Wanda could see hesitation in his face. "I didn't get a good look at it. No license plate. I couldn't identify it, even if I wanted to."

"Why wouldn't you want to?" Zelda retorted. "A maniac ran you down! You should be racking your brain for details!"

"He won't remember much while he's on painkillers, I expect," the doctor replied. She looked at Wanda. "If you aren't family, I'll have to ask you to leave."

"I understand." Wanda stood. "Noah, would you like me to say a prayer before I go?" He nodded, and she prayed quietly and briefly.

"Reverend Wanda," Noah said, "if you see Abbie, tell her I didn't see anything, okay? I don't even know for sure that it was a black car."

He was staring at her so intently that Wanda held his gaze for a long moment before she replied. "I'll tell anyone who asks that you didn't see a thing."

16

Rye was wrapping up for the day when Daniel texted her Jodi's address and asked if they could meet up to go through her things. She offered to pick up some dinner and agreed to meet him in an hour.

When she arrived at Cedars Apartments, she saw some students from Stoneridge hanging out on the concrete pad by the basketball hoop. They weren't playing, and, strangely, they weren't on their phones. Wyatt made eye contact with her and started to raise his hand, then looked away. The girls he was with glanced over before turning their backs on Rye.

No wave for the vice principal was not exactly a surprise. She didn't know any of them well. Their body language telegraphed the attitude of many of the students who ended up in Rye's office, but they must be adept at staying under the radar because she could only bring to mind one of their names—Sharon. Rye had never met anyone under the age of sixty named Sharon.

She didn't bother to go over, even though her gut said they were talking about Jodi or Noah or both. The four of them wouldn't tell her anything useful here on their home turf. Inside the door, she headed for the stairs, taking them two at a time but still trying to judge whether they were slick enough for a person to slip and fall and break their neck. Rye wondered why an athletic person with good reflexes wouldn't grab for one of the handrails.

Daniel opened the door at her knock, looking flustered. The room behind him appeared to have been turned upside down.

"Are you okay?" she asked, walking past him into the living room.

Daniel looked around, almost dazed. Today he wore sweatpants and an oversized sweater, and his long hair fell loose and wild. It was still pretty—dark hair streaked with pure silver. The look on his face aged him beyond Hardy, though she knew her father was older.

Hardy was the only person Rye knew who was both a friend of Jodi's and of her brother, Daniel, whose deadname was Deborah. Daniel had gone to the police academy. Hardy told Rye that he'd spoken to Daniel's class on several occasions, and that the two of them had become friends. Daniel was older than the average cadet, and because Hardy built up enough trust, Daniel asked him whether a transgender person would be welcome on the force.

Hardy had pushed for Daniel to complete training, but the anticipated public drama was too much for Daniel. He left two weeks before the end and decided to the take the PI route instead. When Rye had asked if Daniel and Jodi had other family to contact after her death, Hardy's best guess was no, since neither had ever spoken of parents or other siblings.

This evening, Rye could see that Daniel was distraught. She repeated herself. "Daniel? What happened here?"

"When the sheriff's deputy gave me the key, I came up, and the window had been left open. Papers had been blown everywhere."

"Do you need help cleaning up?"

"I was just looking for some letters I sent Jodi years ago. I can't find them anywhere." He grabbed a couch pillow as if to demonstrate searching and dropped it back in place when it revealed nothing but crumbs.

"Okay." Rye set a bag of Thai food on the table. "It's okay. We can look together."

"You don't understand—lots of people don't know about me. In those letters, I told Jodi everything. How I had felt growing up, why I made my choice when I did. My clients and even a lot of my friends—they just don't know."

"The letters have to be here somewhere, right?" Rye glanced around at the chaos. She could sense Daniel's fear, practically smell it on him. Yes, Hardy had accepted him, his sister did, maybe even a few of his friends, but she understood that privacy was safety in the current political climate.

"I've looked! They aren't!" Daniel threw himself down in Jodi's desk chair and began pulling out drawers and dumping them. She could see that along with the fear was grief, and that regardless of all that police training and detective work, he was struggling with the reality of his sister's death.

Rye knelt in front of him and gently took his hands in hers. "Daniel, I need you to look at me." His grip was tense, but after a minute he stopped trying to pull away and relaxed, shoulders slumped, tears streaming down his face.

She stayed there as he cried, remembering once, decades ago, finding her father doing the same thing a week after her mother had disappeared. Hardy had been taken off the case for obvious reasons, and Rye had come home from school one afternoon to find him dumping all of Melanie's clothes out of drawers. He had seemed frantic. Only seven years old, Rye was terrified.

When Hardy saw her, he tried to make excuses, tried to stuff Melanie's belongings back where they had been, until Rye had dropped her school bag by the door and walked over to him. He'd sat down on the bed and cried while she held his hand. It was the only time she could remember him losing control completely.

She wished he were here now. Jodi had been his friend, and maybe it would help Daniel to be with someone who had known her instead of with a stranger. Rye had seen this case as an opportunity to focus on something other than recent discoveries about her mother as an abuse victim and a teen mom. She also knew she was off-balance because Hardy was clearly in love with one of her closest friends, and the anticipation of what might happen between Hardy and Wanda was killing her.

The easiest people to be with these days were Lance and Rachel, and now that Stephen would be visiting, Rye knew Lance would be busy getting to know him and reconnecting with his mother. Rachel, a teenager with a father in jail and a mother deceased, was on the verge of her own transition. Rye wondered whether Daniel could help with that in spite of his own chaos. He might be willing to talk with Rachel, to explore whether at least it was time to share her new name. Rye hadn't been allowing herself to use "Rafael" even in her head because she was afraid she might slip up. She didn't want to risk outing Rachel if she wasn't ready.

Of course, this deep in his grief, Daniel might not be interested in taking a kid under his wing, but maybe the distraction would help.

Rye shook herself—search first, then suggest. And if searching Jodi's apartment meant straightening it up, that would be a good thing.

"Daniel, where should I start looking?"

He looked around vaguely, then pointed to the ornate rolltop. "I opened the desk and went through every pigeonhole and drawer. Those are my piles. I opened the kitchen cupboards, all the bedroom drawers."

"This place is a disaster. Is it really just from the wind?"

Daniel shook his head. "I never saw a dirty dish, a leaf off a house plant, or laundry on the floor anywhere Jodi lived, not even as a teenager." He waved his arm at the living room. "The police don't do it this way, especially when they know the family of the deceased is coming in. And unless a thief was in a huge rush looking for anything valuable, even a criminal wouldn't create this chaos. I think either Jodi came home and found this mess and rushed back out because she thought she knew who had done it, and that's why she fell, or someone did this after she died, hunting for something incriminating with very little time. Jodi kept notes and records of just about everything. Finding them could have been someone's motivation to push her."

"We need to call Ryan and ask what the apartment looked like the night she died. In any case, if there *was* something worth stealing, it's probably not still here."

Daniel actually laughed, though his eyes were red. "If that were true, I wouldn't be living an almost comfortable life on my detective income. Thieves, murderers, even spouses hunting for evidence of unfaithfulness ignore things right in front of them." He wiped his eyes. "Like me."

"You know, it's okay to be upset."

"I know." Daniel agreed. "But I need to put that aside. I have to do this for her first." He paused. "Before we clean up, we need to photograph everything."

They photographed, cleaned carefully, and looked methodically through everything as they put the apartment back in order. Under Jodi's undisturbed underwear and bras, Rye found what Daniel, at least, had been searching for. It was a thick white envelope with "2005 tax receipts" written carefully across the front, and if Rye hadn't already seen all of Jodi's tax folders she might not have opened it. Inside she found handwritten letters. After glancing at the signature on one, she immediately closed the envelope and took it to Daniel.

He hugged her, then went into the bedroom and closed the door. Rye could hear him crying again, so she made some tea and busied herself warming up the takeout dinner. When he returned, he sat with her and ate at the kitchen table.

Rye screwed up her courage. "I have a friend—they're thirteen, and they want to transition." Rye didn't want to share Rachel's story. It wasn't her place. She settled for saying, "Aside from me, they haven't told anyone yet. I was just wondering whether you'd be willing to talk to them?"

"Do they want to talk to someone?" Daniel asked.

"I think so."

Daniel looked down at his mug. "Can they keep a secret? I don't mind talking to them, but I'd lose most of my current clients if it became public knowledge."

"They're keeping their own," Rye replied. "And they've been through a lot. I trust them."

"You'll be there, too?"

"Considering they're a minor, I think it's a good idea."

Daniel nodded. "I agree. I'll look at my calendar tonight, and if they're amenable, we can set something up, okay?"

"That sounds great. Thank you." Rye was relieved. She picked up their cups and took them to the sink to wash them. As she dried her hands, she walked into the living room to see Daniel standing by Jodi's desk, looking out the window. She joined him. Even with the window closed, the sounds of basketball drifted up.

"If Jodi had been sitting here the night of her death, would she have been able to hear anything happening outside?" Rye asked.

"Maybe. At least anything happening on the courts."

Rye thought about what Wanda had told her after talking to Noah in the hospital. "What if she saw or heard something else?"

"Like what?"

The living room window looked out on cars parked along the street and the open courtyard. She could see Wyatt's father's food truck parked. There was a long line of customers waiting. "She could see everything from here. I don't believe she fell any more than I believe Noah Tesco only saw what he told Wanda."

"You think she left here that night to confront someone? A resident…or a visitor?" Daniel mused.

"You're the professional," Rye said, "but I think our pool of suspects just opened up."

17

Stephen finally arrived on Wednesday evening. Wanda and Lance met him at Logan Airport's Terminal E. He was dark haired but had a broad face just like his father, though his black-framed glasses added a youthful charm. Stephen had gone back and forth between crutches and a wheelchair his whole life. Lance told Wanda that for the last year or so, he'd favored the wheelchair and a cane. Disability was the first impression he made, but it didn't last long.

Even over Zoom, Stephen's personality was so infectiously cheerful that Wanda wasn't surprised to be nearly bowled over by the wattage of his smile in person. The young man's arms and chest were muscular, and he wore a black Cambridge United jersey signed by Liam Bennett. He was doing wheelie pop-ups for an audience of children when Wanda and Lance spotted him. A flight attendant strode by, and he gave her a wink, which she returned with a giggle.

Wanda looked at Lance, a kid who had honed his deception skills on the administrators of three private schools. He'd been online searching for news of his potential stepbrother when they pulled into the parking garage, but he switched to a wide-open welcome and strode forward on his long legs. "Hey, Stephen!"

"Lance!" The audience of children melted away to various parents. Stephen pushed himself to his feet and gave Lance a hug.

"You never mentioned being a powerchair football star! I've seen your name pop up in quite a few internet searches."

"I wish! I'm a bit busy with other pursuits at the moment." Stephen nodded at the retreating flight attendant, who had turned back to give him a little wave.

Wanda hurried over, dragging an enormous backpack and kicking a suitcase with wheels. Stephen got the suitcase and Lance the backpack.

"I can handle them both," said Stephen.

"I'll remember that, but right now we have Lance, who needs to be useful if we're going to make it to the parking garage before we move into a second hour!" Wanda led the way, surprisingly quick on her short legs. "I'm Wanda, Mickey's much more responsible sister."

"Does that mean we can't stop at McDonald's on the way home?" Stephen asked with a grin.

Wanda laughed. "I could swear Mickey said you prefer raw vegetables, free-range chicken, and tofu for your weight lifting diet."

"I do try to eat better, but when in Rome…" Stephen replied.

"Your wish is our command. McDonald's it is!" Wanda looked back at them. Lance's long legs and Stephen's wheels were no match for her race to the meter.

Wanda led the group with a determination that scattered several cars trying to find space at the curbside to pick up travelers. One had to brake hard and then was stuck in the outside lane, forced to circle the airport again. His verbal response was unprintable. Even Wanda heard it and barely controlled herself from flipping him the bird and shocking the young men following her.

She shoved the luggage into the trunk quickly and made it to the tollbooth under the hour mark, which meant paying nine dollars instead of twenty-three. She fought Boston traffic to the sounds of not one but two young men defying reticent stereotypes to chat all the way to Route 1, where conversation turned into serious scanning for burgers and fries. Easily found, speedily consumed.

When they arrived home, Wanda showed Stephen to his bedroom, then allowed Lance to give him the rest of the tour. It started in the kitchen, because apparently one two-thousand-calorie dinner wasn't enough to satiate them. Wanda wanted to sit with them, but she excused herself to bed. Lance and Stephen needed time to get to know each other on their own terms without an old lady hovering. She did steal both dogs to keep her company.

NEVER ENOUGH SLEEP, WANDA THOUGHT, AS SHE rolled into wakefulness. She glanced out the window. Of course there wasn't going to be a June day without rain, but this was ridiculous. The rain was pounding against the window, and the sky was dark.

This was the very first year that Wanda had tried a garden—a very small one—at the urging of Hardy, who maintained that homegrown vegetables were the best. The truth was that she did it more to please him than out of any desire to create green bean casseroles without the fried onions or eat an endless number of zucchinis. Her neighbor, Julia, whose yard backed up to hers, had told Wanda where to get a raised bed frame and showed her how to fill it with rocks, then soil that came in bags, to plant, and to cover the plantings. Wanda did not dare admit that she didn't know anything about actually buying dirt. They had fun, though, and Julia got behind in her own gardening because they laughed so much.

Hardy had needed to teach Wanda to cover the fragile sprouts during rains like this, and luckily she saw that Lance had texted her overnight that he had run out and taken care of it before the storm began in full force. When she'd woken to use the bathroom, she had heard them in the living room, and as she walked through now she could see that they'd had out the games *The Fox in the Forest* and *Rivals for Catan.*

When she entered the kitchen, Wanda had blinked to make sure she hadn't woken up in an alternate dimension, because there was cribbage set up with two cold teas beside it. In the dish rack, drying, she spotted evidence of plentiful snacking as well, so she didn't begrudge sticking their mugs in the dishwasher.

She knew that they had played online games rather than talk when their parents were trying to make them into long-distance friends, but it seemed some old-fashioned games also might have provided a way to talk with their hands busy. They were certainly sleeping now, and she hoped they would get good rest before the arrival of Lance's mother and Stephen's father in a few days. That was when the preparations for the wedding began in full "Mickey" force. The office door was ajar. She could see that her terrier, Wink, was now curled up in bed with Stephen. Traitor.

Wanda made herself some oatmeal and sat down to check her email. Usually she didn't start work until after her coffee, but she'd brought her computer to the kitchen yesterday, and it was staring at her, urging her to get ahead on some of her tasks. She had a bulletin to do, and she needed to prepare for the trustees meeting. She also had promised to arrange a meeting with Ana, Tyler, Ryan, and Ana's parents, and that needed to be taken care of today. The Santos family was heritage Roman Catholic, and though the wedding would be at Trinity, Wanda was going to include Father Paul. She checked her watch. Still a bit early to call him, but she would set a reminder for herself to do it at nine, when she knew he would be back from his daily swim after early Mass.

She yawned and deleted a bunch of junk mail, delaying her actual duties as long as possible. One email caught her eye, though. It was from Noah Tesco.

> Rev. Wanda, I hope it's okay that I asked my aunt for your email address.

Wanda rolled her eyes. Noah had been in her youth group for four years, and she emailed them on a regular basis.

> Abbie texted and said someone set a fire by the basketball court. Nobody was hurt, but it spread pretty quickly. A couple of cars had their windows broken too. Nothing stolen, just a rock left inside each on. Maybe it doesn't have anything to do with what happened to me but be careful.

Wanda sat back in her chair, studying the message. She had been a minister long enough that she'd had youth groups who communicated by phone, flyer, and email. The last few years had been by text. She'd had to learn to use WhatsApp and create a group with the teens and their parents to send information. No one ever called her anymore, and she could count on one hand the number of actual emails she'd received from kids in the past five years.

Wanda hit "forward" and sent the email on to the sheriff's office, blind copying Rye and Hardy. If Noah had gone to the trouble of sending this, he was scared—for himself, and also for her. She'd learned enough in the last year to know to trust not only her own gut but those around her. If Noah was shaken, she was, too. She answered Noah over email, too, and thanked him for "information that was very important," suggesting that he could share anything else he saw or heard about at any time.

18

RYE HAD BECOME AN EXPERT IN AVOIDANCE OVER THE last week. Instead of having dinner with her dad, Wanda, Lance, and Stephen, she had worked late. Hardy had been tempting her with some of her favorite meals, but she wasn't ready to forgive him for springing Kara on her. Her avoidance of Ryan and Camila, on the other hand, was only compounding the problems she already had, but every text she typed out sounded wrong.

Unfortunately Rye had forgotten that she'd invited Ana and Tyler over for drinks a month ago, and when they showed up on her doorstep, she was wearing ratty sweats and ignoring an episode of *Is It Cake?* while chipping her nail polish off. Now she scratched the label off a bottle of overpriced IPA under the intense scrutiny of the bride while her fiancé chattered.

"And that's why we decided to have a band instead of a DJ at our wedding!" Tyler announced, wrapping up an overlong story about a concert he and Ana had been to in April. He shot his fiancée what Rye could only assume was his not-so-subtle "your turn" look.

"That sounds great," Rye replied. "I'm sure it's going to be wonderful."

"Tell that to my mother," Ana murmured under her breath.

"When will your family arrive?" Ana and Camila were born in Salvador, Brazil, but aside from visits every other summer, they'd spent their childhood in Denver. They had four brothers whose families still lived in Colorado.

"My parents are already here," Ana said. "That's why Camila is staying with Ryan. They took over her apartment for the five weeks they're in town." The look she gave Rye was significant. "Wasn't it nice of him to offer?"

Rye did her best to pretend this wasn't significantly important news to her. If she were honest with herself, finding out that Camila and Ryan were living together had hit her hard. Since February, Rye had been struggling with her feelings for both of them, but her fear of losing either or both of them as friends had been overwhelming, so she had remained silent. "Oh? I thought it was strange that she hadn't mentioned the move. It probably slipped her mind in all the chaos of your parents arriving."

"Probably so," Ana agreed. "Like how you forgot to mention meeting Kara."

"Because of the murder," Rye replied, her gaze meeting Ana's.

"What murder?" Tyler asked, startled.

"Jodi Franklin," Rye said. "Isn't that one of your cases?"

He shook his head. "That was ruled an accidental death. Jaz is the lead on it. I've just been doing paperwork." He looked at Rye suspiciously. "Does that mean you and Wanda are getting involved? Because between wedding planning and my regular caseload, I do not want to be on civilian investigation alert!"

"No need," Rye replied. "Jodi's younger brother is a private detective. Daniel has some questions, and I've been helping him out. Jodi was a friend of my dad's, and I know this is important to him."

"Now I'm definitely worried." He pulled out his phone. "I'm telling Ryan."

"He already knows." Rye failed to keep the smug smile off her face. "He—" She paused. If Ryan hadn't told Tyler that he considered the Franklin case to be a possible murder, there must be a reason. "He told me to be careful."

"Hey, Ty, can you go out to the car and grab that piece of cake we brought for Rye?" Ana asked. She gave him a meaningful look. The real interrogation was about to begin.

"Of course. I might go see if Hardy's at home, too," he said. "We haven't had a chance to catch up for a while."

The women watched him leave, and when the door had shut, Ana turned to Rye. "What's going on?" she asked. "Why is my sister moping around?"

"Well, you did mention that your mom is in town." Rye knew that although Camila had told her parents years ago that she was polyamorous, her conservative mother more than hoped it would turn out to be "just a phase."

"You might be able to talk your way around the point with everyone else, but it's not happening tonight."

This was not a kitchen table conversation. Rye stood up and grabbed one of the afghans from the back of the couch, wrapping herself in it like a shield. "I know she's upset because I didn't tell her about Kara."

Ana walked over and curled up on the other end of the couch, watching Rye intently. "And?"

"And I don't think I did anything else, but…"

"Why haven't you been answering her texts?"

Rye shrugged and stared down at her lap, winding her fingers through the holes in the crocheted throw. "I guess it threw me off when I went to brunch and she hadn't said anything about…about living with Ryan. I thought they were just friends. I didn't know it had gotten more serious."

Although Camila typically dated women, Rye knew that, like herself, Camila resonated with the "love the wine, not the label" analogy made popular by *Schitt's Creek*. Camila and Ryan had been good friends for a while. It made sense that it might turn into something more.

"Have you asked her about what's going on?" Ana asked.

"No. I want them to be happy," she replied. It was true. More than anything, Rye had a desire to see her friends happy—not just Camila and Ryan, but Ana and Tyler, Wanda, Lance, Andy and his family, and even her dad when she wasn't mad at him. In the last two years, she had made more connections than she could count, and when good things happened to those people, it filled a part of her that had been empty for a long time.

"Well, Camila isn't happy now," Ana said, breaking the silence that had stretched between them. "It's because of you, and you need to fix it."

19

After her talk with Ana the night before, Rye had forced herself to text all the people she had been ignoring. Now she was paying the ultimate price—too many plans.

After the last bell rang, she stuffed her laptop into her bag and headed to Locals for a little snack with Wanda, Lance, and Stephen. She looked forward to meeting Stephen, but after that, she had promised Camila she would hit the gym with her, then make it home for her weekly dinner with her father, who'd developed a habit of inviting other people to join them for meals without giving Rye a heads-up first. She was preemptively exhausted.

She slapped on a big smile, though, as she neared the table in the back, giving Wanda a hug and Stephen a firm handshake. Lance was engrossed in the menu, so Rye settled for a gentle shove to get him to shift over so she could sit down.

"Rye, it's nice to meet you," Stephen said, his accent catching her off guard. He and Rob were of Scots heritage but had lived in London for years. Stephen's accent had the soft blending that children often got when they moved from place to place and wanted to fit in.

"It's good to meet you, too. I'm sorry it's taken a few days. Between work and helping my dad with a case, I've been swamped."

Rye noticed Wanda shaking her head vigorously a moment too late. "What case?" Lance asked, suddenly all ears.

"It's nothing," Wanda replied. "Just a little inquiry. Hardy is helping a friend."

"Another murder?" Stephen asked, clearly as intrigued as Lance.

"Spill," Lance demanded, his menu forgotten.

Rye could see that Wanda most definitely did not want her to provide any more details. She shrugged helplessly at her friend, indicating with a look that, by all means, she should redirect the boys' attention elsewhere if she thought she could.

"Stephen, why don't you tell Rye about your studies?" Wanda said, clearly desperate. In a calmer state, Rye knew her friend would recognize that the topic of school would never outbid murder.

"I'm studying psychology, with a focus on avoiding the subject," Stephen replied with a grin. "I'm taking notes right now." He took a sip of his water, watching Rye intently.

Thankfully, the waiter arrived, and Rye was spared for a few moments while they all ordered. She needed something light, but Lance and Stephen were eating enough to satisfy her entire daily caloric intake. Rye sighed. She missed those days when her digestive system wouldn't rebel against a huge helping of all things deep-fried.

Rye glanced at Wanda apologetically, but Wanda looked resigned. "There's no losing the scent now, so you might as well tell them."

Rye gave them a recap of what she'd learned about Jodi Franklin's life and death. Wanda was captivated once Rye showed them the Senior Olympics training video that Mike had sent her.

"And her younger brother is a PI?" Lance asked.

"He is," Rye admitted, "but he's way too close to the case to see things clearly."

"We wouldn't know anything about that," Wanda murmured, sipping her iced tea.

"Noah Tesco's accident is looking less like an accident every time you talk to him," Rye replied. "And there was the fire and vandalism, not to mention Jodi's apartment getting searched…trashed, really."

Wanda nodded. "Noah was in bad shape. I think I should talk to him again after he gets out of the hospital if his parents will let us."

"I'll check with Ryan, too. I know he can't tell us much, but maybe he can at least give us a hint to point us in the right direction."

"If the sheriff knew something, wouldn't he arrest the person responsible?" Stephen asked. "From what I've heard"—he glanced at Lance—"as much as Sheriff Phennen has enjoyed help from both of you in the past, it *is* his job to apprehend suspects."

"You're probably right, Stephen," agreed Wanda. "If Ryan and his team had a lead, they would be following up. That being said, in the past Ryan has sometimes let things slide for a while in hopes that a lead will pan out. And he has complained about our assistance but used everything we have found."

"Protecting the kids should be our first priority," Rye added.

"Wouldn't finding the murderer take care of that?" Lance asked.

"I agree," Stephen said. "Without knowing who did it, how could you possibly help them?"

Rye looked at Wanda and was met with a blank stare. "I'm not sure," Rye admitted, "but if Jodi died because she knew something about an ongoing crime, then that 'murderer' has a lot at stake to prevent someone else from putting pieces together. If she died just because someone really doesn't like her, then things should be quieting down. Of course, if we didn't have jobs, maybe we could camp out in the neighborhood, keep an eye out for the Suburban, or watch for any other sketchy behavior."

"At Cedars Apartments?" Lance laughed. "Word is that you'd have your hands full there."

"And we really don't want to find ourselves involved in any other crimes," Wanda pointed out.

"Speak for yourself," Lance replied. "I promised Stephen we might get to help on a case while he's here, and one has fallen into our laps. I'm done with school tomorrow. He and I can do some recon."

"No," Rye said.

"Absolutely not," Wanda added. "Your parents are going to be here, and there is no way, as your legal guardian, I am allowing you to go looking for a murderer."

"I'm an adult," Stephen pointed out. "I can go."

"And I can drive my future stepbrother, since my car isn't equipped for him to drive it," Lance said.

Rye was about to object again when the food arrived. It took several trips for all of it to be delivered. As the waiter turned away, Rye stopped him. "Excuse me—I think you brought us someone else's drink." There was a beer on the table, and she was well aware that none of them had ordered it.

"Oh, it's from that guy," the waiter said, pointing to the bar where Daniel Franklin sat, nursing a drink and a bowl of pretzels. He gave them a little wave.

Rye glanced at Wanda, who shrugged. "Better invite him over."

Rye waved to Daniel, and he stood and walked over, squeezing in a chair next to Wanda. Wanda introduced him to Lance and Stephen, who perked up when they heard his name.

"We're willing to do some recon at the Cedars," Lance told him, hurriedly outlining a plan he and Stephen had devised.

"That would be a huge help," Daniel said. "I can't be there twenty-four seven, and I just have this feeling that Jodi's death has stirred up something."

"So you want my seventeen-year-old nephew to take the job?" Wanda asked.

"I'm twenty," Stephen reminded her, as though his age were some unlocked gate to adulthood that she should recognize.

"Even worse!" Wanda exclaimed. "You're old enough that I can't stop you but young enough to have an underdeveloped prefrontal cortex."

"Neither of you are equipped for this job," Rye said. "It's tedious and dangerous, and one of you is underage."

"Don't forget to hold my wheelchair against us," Stephen replied.

Rye looked him over. He clearly worked out, and his upper body was heavily muscled. She couldn't see his legs, but she was guessing he hadn't skimped there, either.

"Aside from the fact that getting in and out of Lance's car is probably a slowish process, and Lance would have already gotten himself killed sprinting ahead of you, I don't think the wheelchair is the issue. The problem is that you two don't seem to understand that this isn't a game. This person potentially killed a woman and has tried to kill a teenager to protect secrets."

"Ugh," Wanda groaned. "I just realized what Ryan probably feels like when he talks to us."

Rye made a face. "Thanks for that. Now I feel like I should let them put themselves in danger just to get the sanctimonious stink off me."

"Absolutely not," Wanda said.

"What if Hardy comes with us?" Lance asked suddenly. "He has the training. Neither of us would dare to cross him, and we could move the case forward while you two are busy being responsible adults."

Rye hadn't expected that argument, and now she was frantically racking her brain for a reason why it wouldn't work.

Daniel looked up with a smile. "I just texted him, and he's in! I have an extra key to the apartment. I'll get it to him."

Lance and Stephen high-fived, then went back to devouring the food in front of them. Rye had lost her appetite. From Wanda's face, she could tell Hardy was about to get an earful. Rye felt her phone buzz and pulled it out to check her text. She glanced up at Daniel, who just nodded at her to keep reading.

She typed back quickly.

What kind of lead?

> The repair shop I told you about. Want to check it out with me?

Rye glanced at the time. If they left right now, she could still catch Camila for a short workout.

> I don't want the kids coming on this one—how can we make our escape?

Daniel glanced up and smiled warmly at Wanda while dropping a twenty on the table. "I hope you don't mind, but I need to steal Rye away."

"Where are you going?" Lance asked, immediately suspicious.

"She's obviously forgotten, but I promised I'd follow her to a car appointment in case they can't finish her repairs tonight and she needs a ride home," he said smoothly, standing up. "It's been wonderful to meet you all, though, and I look forward to hearing anything that comes up from the stakeout."

"Rye?" Lance rose slightly to interrupt their leaving. "When you're at the auto shop, can you ask how much it would cost to adapt a car for hand controls?"

Rye looked at Wanda, who shrugged. "I'll see what they say."

Wanda touched Rye's arm. "Mickey and Rob are coming in on Friday. Let's talk before then, okay? And, while they're here...Listen to me!" It was the preacher voice. Everyone fell silent. "While they are here, there will be no investigation by the two of you or by me. Rye and Daniel and maybe Hardy can sleuth to their hearts' content, but we are sidelined!"

"Sounds good." Rye grinned at Stephen and Lance, who were speaking softly to each other. She knew there was no way Wanda could hear them, but Rye had caught the phrases *snack run* and *pee bottle*. "Good luck with those two," she said. "You're about to have your hands full."

20

Silence descended on the table as Rye and Daniel left. Wanda forced a smiled. "Stephen, do you watch much TV?"

"Mostly crime dramas," he said with a grin. "But the drama you all live has it beat."

"It's not a drama most of the time. It will not be at your dad and Mickey's wedding. I promise you on my ordination vows—"

Lance interrupted. "That's tempting fate!"

"It will be elegant for her, faithful for your dad, and fun for everyone else."

Lance gagged dramatically. "This is my mother's wedding you're talking about? Michelle Bates? Are we thinking of the same woman? The one who thinks spending Christmas in Las Vegas is 'a dream come true?'"

They both collapsed into laughter thinking about the Mickey they both knew so well, while Stephen stared on, baffled. "You don't think Michelle will enjoy an elegant church wedding?"

"Stephen, you have met the reformed version of my sister. Your father is a wizard—no, a saint—who has performed a miracle. But you should know that life with Mickey will always come with the unexpected," Wanda replied. Lance snorted. "Although she will insist through it all that she prefers everything to go exactly to plan."

"Yeah, her plan," Lance said, "that she hasn't shared with anyone else!"

"You two are the only attendants, correct?"

"As far as we know," Lance replied.

Wanda had a sudden thought. "Who will subdue the dogs during the ceremony?"

Wink and Figaro would be walking down the aisle with Rob and Stephen, wearing collars covered with flowers. Not the rings. Wanda had refused. She had no idea how the boys had talked their parents into agreeing to this chaos-waiting-to-happen, but Lance, who worked part-time at Fairchild's Funeral Home, had promised the dogs would be as clean and sparkling as a hearse.

"Hardy!" Lance exclaimed, and Wanda realized it was the only good answer.

"Sure—" she started to reply, then realized that, in fact, the man was standing behind her, one hand lightly resting on her shoulder. "What are you doing here?"

"Daniel called and said the boys needed a chapero—*partner* for some surveillance down at the Cedars Apartments?"

"I did not agree to tonight!" Wanda looked panicked. "We need a plan…"

"We aren't doing anything dangerous," Lance said. "We're just watching."

"I'll keep an eye on them! Don't you trust me?" Hardy joked, but one look at Wanda wiped the smile off his face. "I'll make sure they stay in the car and out of sight. This is not my first rodeo."

"Hardy, there's something going on over there," Wanda said. "That email I sent you—you didn't see Noah in the hospital, but if the same person is behind that attack and Jodi's death, they aren't afraid to protect themselves."

"I spent my career handling trouble at those apartments and others like them," Hardy replied. "I know there's more to this than we're seeing, which is why I want to check it out."

"And you think it's okay to involve *our* young people in this surveillance?" Wanda's voice was low.

"What if I take them up to Jodi's apartment? We can watch from the two windows that give a view of back and side. No one will know we're there." He looked at the boys. "We'll talk in whispers, and we will be bored, probably tired. It will be work, not fun."

Deep breath. Very tight smile. She took a bite of her salad and chewed slowly, her eyes going between the three of them.

"Hardy, I am holding you one hundred percent responsible for anything that happens, and *nothing* better happen. It had better be the most boring night of your lives." She held up her hand to forestall further comments. "Stephen, do not mention that you are legally an adult one more time, or I will lock you in my office. Lance, do not remind me that you have been in dangerous situations before. That is not the compelling case you think it is. Against my better judgement, I'll let you go, but if you are not home by eleven o'clock, so help me—"

"We'll text you every hour," Hardy promised.

"Every thirty minutes," she replied, staring him down. "With photographic proof that you are in the apartment, not outside chatting with strangers or following suspicious vehicles."

"I think we're more likely to see something if we stay later than eleven—" Lance started to say.

Hardy hauled him out of his chair. "Don't push your luck, my boy. She will take you home right now."

"But—" Lance saw Wanda's face and closed his mouth. "Yup. Eleven. We'll come home." In a softer voice, just to have it on record, he added, "Then you'll trust us to go back, right?"

"I heard that!" his aunt said, and Lance smiled guiltily. He pushed his seat in so that Stephen could move past him. They followed Hardy out the door, and Wanda watched them go, a pit in her stomach.

She stared at her glass. Iced tea, when her nerves craved something stronger. She needed to get out of here, go to the church, and get some work done. Anything that would take her mind off her desire to stake out the stakeout. She calculated that it had been years since she had felt anger and fear in equal parts bubble up like this. That must mean something about love.

21

D ANIEL AND R YE PARKED HIS CAR A BLOCK FROM Gayle's Auto Service and walked up to the building. A few cars sat in the small parking lot surrounded by stacks of tires. One person was working in the bay, but they didn't glance up as the two walked past into the shop.

A young woman sat at the counter filling out paperwork. The patch on her coveralls said "Samantha." She looked up as the bell dinged. "We're closed."

"We're not here for a repair," Daniel said. "Are you Sam Gayle?"

"Depends on who's asking," she replied, putting down her pen.

"I'm Daniel Franklin. I just wanted to ask you a few questions about one of your customers." He flashed his PI license, and Sam looked at it, then back at him.

"You're not the cops. I don't have to talk to you."

"You don't, but why wouldn't you want to?" Daniel asked.

"Who is she, your femme fatale?" Sam replied with a glance at Rye.

Rye was caught off guard by the reference. It didn't fit the image of this young woman with grease-stained hands. "Not exactly," she said. "One of your customers was killed."

"So?" Sam asked. "As far as I know, the police didn't storm the place looking for a body in a trunk, so I don't see how that's my problem."

"It's not," Rye said. "But the fact that her brakes were tampered with is." On the drive to the shop, Ryan hadn't exactly confirmed that, but he had hinted broadly.

Sam straightened, calling through the door into the garage. "Charlie! Get in here."

A woman not much older than Sam walked in, wiping her hands on a dirty towel. She was broad-shouldered, and her hair was cut close to her skull.

"I've got plans tonight. I'm not staying late to work on any more cars," Charlie said bluntly.

"These folks said we let a customer drive off with damaged brakes."

"Where's the car?" Charlie asked. "I'll take a look."

"It's impounded," Daniel replied.

Charlie shrugged and dropped the towel in an overflowing laundry basket by the door. "I've never had any complaints before. If you show me the car, I can see what's going on, but otherwise I don't know what to tell you."

"Maybe you could tell me why my sister was driving around with damaged brakes after getting her car repaired here," Daniel replied, his temper clearly rising.

"Isn't it a conflict of interest for you to be investigating a case involving a family member?" Sam asked.

"Isn't it strange that my sister failed you senior year, leading to BU withdrawing their scholarship offer, landing you here instead?" Daniel replied.

Charlie's face darkened. "Jodi Franklin? She's your sister? You're better off now that she's dead."

Rye was not prepared for Daniel to take a swing at Charlie. He missed, but only because she dodged quickly to one side and landed a punch at his kidney. Daniel howled. Rye was wading in, used to breaking up fights between amped-up students, when she felt someone grab her hair and yank her backward.

"Don't touch my cousin," Sam said, using the advantage of her position to push Rye aside. Rye tripped over a chair and fell, stars exploding behind her eyes as her head connected with concrete.

Sam grabbed Daniel, and Rye couldn't tell if she was trying to separate the two fighters or hold him steady for her cousin to hit him. Charlie threw one good punch that sent Daniel stumbling back, taking Sam with him. He staggered up, throwing the smaller woman off of him, and went at Charlie again.

Rye could see that Daniel had fury and grief on his side, but Charlie was clearly the better fighter, and she maneuvered him up against the door between the shop and the bay, landing more hits than were blocked. Rye was struggling to push herself to her feet when Charlie surprised Daniel, dropping low under a hit that should have laid her out. Instead her fist went through the glass behind Daniel, shattering the window.

For a moment, the room was silent. Daniel had pieces of glass glittering on his head and shoulders. Rye could feel a few pieces sticking to her own face as she stood, head throbbing.

"Charlie!" Sam raced to her cousin's side. Charlie was frozen, staring down at her bloody hand.

Daniel grabbed a folded towel from the counter and thrust it at Sam. "Try to stop the bleeding!"

Rye already had the phone out to call 911. "Ambulance is six minutes out," she announced, turning to check on Charlie. "Wait!" She pushed Sam aside and gently took Charlie's hand in her own. "If we wrap it now, we could push glass in further and risk hitting an artery."

"She's bleeding so much," Sam insisted. "We have to do something."

"I know." Rye pulled out one of the biggest pieces of glass and dropped it to the floor. Charlie screamed in pain.

"Stop! You're hurting her!" Sam exclaimed.

"I know, but if she wants to keep the hand, I have to get it all out." Rye ignored Charlie's whimpers as she removed as many of the pieces as she could find. "Go to my car. In the trunk I have a first aid kit with a pair of tweezers. If we can get the glass out quickly, that will help."

Sam grabbed Rye's keys and ran out to the car. Daniel stood beside the women, holding a trash can so Rye could drop pieces of glass into it. When Sam came in, she had the tweezers.

Rye concentrated on looking for any pieces she'd missed. "Sink?"

Sam led them out to the garage bay, and Rye turned on the water, waiting for it to warm as close to body temperature as possible before helping Charlie put her hand under it. The younger woman's body spasmed, but she didn't pull away, and Rye was able to check her hand and wrist for any pieces she had missed. None of the cuts were as deep as Rye had feared. She led Charlie out into the sunlight to double-check her work as the ambulance pulled in.

She gratefully passed Charlie off to an EMT and sat gingerly on one of the waiting room chairs while Daniel got checked out. His wrist was swelling, either sprained or broken, and a black eye bloomed on his face. Sam had a bloody nose but otherwise seemed fine.

Rye concentrated on using a tiny mirror Sam had handed her to remove glass from her face while she waited for one of the med techs to check her for a concussion. Sam helped, silently pulling pieces out of Rye's thick hair.

"I'm sorry Charlie said that to your friend," Sam said softly, dropping a piece of glass into the trash can Daniel had left for them. "Thank you for helping her anyway."

Rye glanced up, not sure how to respond, when a squad car rolled up.

"Are you kidding me?" she heard Tyler say as he and Jaz Malone stepped into the shop.

"What did you do?" Jaz asked Rye, looking around.

"Me? I didn't start this!"

Tyler gestured to the camera mounted in the corner, aimed at the cash register. "We'll get the video and see what happened." He looked her over. "Want me to call your dad?"

"No. My car's outside," Rye replied.

"You need to go to the station to make a statement," Tyler argued. "He can bring you some clean clothes, at least."

"I have gym clothes in my car," Rye said. She stood up and immediately regretted the decision, her hand flying to the egg forming on the back of her head.

Jaz waved the other EMT over. "We've got another patient for you. Do you have room in the ambulance?"

"I don't need a doctor," Sam declared.

"Oh, I know," Jaz said. "You're riding with Officer Phennen back to the station." She eyed Rye. "I'm going with this crew to make sure they all get back there after they finish getting stitched up."

"Would you mind following us in my car?" Rye asked. After Jaz took possession of her keys, Rye closed her eyes. Her head was pounding. She might not have a concussion, but all she wanted to do was take a bottle of ibuprofen and sleep.

Of course that wasn't going to happen. An emergency room nurse did give Rye a couple of Advil that would probably cost her seven hundred dollars out of pocket, as well as an ice pack that would require payment in blood diamonds, before confirming that Rye did not have a concussion and allowing Jaz to chaperone her to the station.

"I don't know how you get yourself into these things," Jaz said as she finished recording everything Rye told her. "Can't you find a less dangerous hobby, like skydiving or swimming with sharks?"

"Those sound expensive," Rye replied, closing her eyes against the glare of the fluorescent lights. "Why pay for the rush when I can get my butt kicked for free?"

"You know," Jaz said, leaning back in her chair, "I've been taking my car there for years. It's the only women-run mechanic shop I've ever found, and I've always had a good experience. I think Sam's mother owns the place."

"Oh, yeah?" Rye asked, her eyes half closed as she signed her name.

"I remember Madeline Gayle telling me that she had custody of her niece and a couple of nephews as well."

"Charlie?"

"I think so."

"Do all of the kids work at the garage?"

"I think they're still at Stoneridge," Jaz mused. "I'll ask her when she comes to pick up Sam."

Rye groaned. "If Madeline Gayle is a parent, I'll probably be hearing about this at work, too."

"Isn't tomorrow the last day of school?" Jaz asked. "Surely no one's going to bother to show up and throw a hissy fit on the last day of school."

"You may be brilliant at your job, Jaz Malone," Rye said, standing up to go, "but you don't know parents. Hell hath no fury like a mama bear."

22

WANDA OUTLINED AN ENTIRE SERMON WHILE WAITING for Lance and Stephen to get home. It was for Pentecost Sunday, and she was liberal with language about tongues of fire. Then she read it over, prayed a little harder, and followed a vein about listening to many tongues even if you don't fully understand them—like the slang of people under the age of twenty-five, or sheriffs who are supposed to be retired and not leading seventeen-year-olds into dangerous situations.

She forced herself to ease off that train of thought and focus on what the text actually said about communicating love between people who don't speak the same language. That reminded her to email a friend who had connections with an immigrant support group; Wanda had been meaning to reach out to see if she could offer the group space at the church for its meetings. That led her down a rabbit hole of other emails she hadn't answered, and by the time she heard a car pull in, she could call her sermon basically done.

Wanda looked up as Lance bounded in. The two sleeping dogs were awake in an instant and bouncing all over him. They hadn't needed to go out, but now they would.

"Making hot chocolate," he said, and went to the kitchen. Wanda could hear the trunk slam and then the car door. She assumed Hardy and Stephen had made the wheelchair switch. She could hear them speaking in low tones as they came up the ramp. Figgy snuck past them and out the door, but before Wanda could so much as stand, Hardy had given a sharp whistle and the dog was back inside, panting mischievously. Hardy slipped him a Milk-Bone, and then one to Wink, before coming into the living room.

Lance returned with a tray and four mugs. He put the tray down and helped himself to the one with the most marshmallows floating on top before folding into his favorite chair. Hardy handed Stephen a mug, then Wanda, taking the final one for himself. He looked around for non–dog-inhabited cushioned furniture and failed. He shoved Figaro over to make a little room.

"It's nice to see you're all in one piece," Wanda said, taking a sip of her cocoa.

"As I promised they would be." Hardy arched an eyebrow at the passive-aggressive tone she'd taken.

"Hmm," was all Wanda said.

"We parked two blocks away, then went to Jodi's apartment," Stephen said. "There wasn't really anyone outside when we arrived, but Lance wore a baseball hat to hide his hair, since it's the most distinctive thing about him."

Lance waved an LA Dodgers cap and pulled it over his auburn bun. Wanda had to admit he did look a lot different with even that small change. She noticed that all three of them were dressed differently than usual, with the younger two in Adidas sweats and T-shirts that she knew were popular, at least among the boys in her youth group. Hardy was dressed in navy scrubs he must have gotten from Andy, who was about the same size as him, and he wasn't using the cane he sometimes brought when his leg was bothering him. He'd shaved, and his own hair was tamed for the moment.

"You all look suitably undercover," Wanda said, trying to hide a grin. She still wasn't happy they had taken the risk, but it was also difficult now that they were safely home not to think it was a bit adorable.

"We kept the lights off and took turns keeping notes about what was happening outside," Stephen said.

"I saw a couple of kids from school playing basketball," Lance added. "You know, Wyatt and those guys. Noah was out there, too, sitting in a lawn chair. He looked pretty good, even with his leg in a cast."

Stephen flipped through the spiral notebook. "A bunch of men came out to smoke. A few of them talked to the guys playing basketball."

Wanda and Hardy exchanged a look. "All men?" Wanda asked.

"But who's to say that isn't the norm," Stephen pointed out. "Those could be the same people who are always out."

"In which case, they would be the people who either know about illegal activity happening on the property or are perpetrating it," Hardy said.

"Did you get any pictures?" Wanda asked. "Rye might be able to identify some of the other kids playing ball."

Hardy held up his phone. "I've already sent them to her."

"Anything out the other window?"

"No food truck tonight, just folks walking dogs."

"Did you report to Ryan?" Wanda asked.

"I didn't exactly mention this to him," Hardy said, trying to appear nonchalant. "If anything comes of it, though, he'll be the first to know."

"Someone sounds like he's been spending too much time in the Prudence Rye school of excuses," Wanda replied. She waved at Lance, who was trying a little too hard to blend in with the furniture. "You still have one more day of school tomorrow, so get to bed."

Lance stood up and stretched. "One weird thing happened. A car pulled near the basketball court. It idled for about half an hour. People were coming and going, talking to whoever was in the car."

"Drugs?" Wanda asked.

"I'll admit it is suspicious," Hardy said, "but at complexes like that, it could be any number of things. Could be a bookie. It could be a teenager listening to music and chatting with his friends."

"Not the Suburban everyone's been talking about?"

"No, this was an Outback, if you can believe it."

"I cannot," Wanda said solemnly. "Unless you're about to tell me the trunk opened up and it was full of golden retriever puppies."

"No such luck." Hardy put his mug down on the tray. He shook hands with Stephen. "It was nice to spend the time with you, Stephen. I hope I get to see more of you while you're visiting…even tomorrow night, if that seems necessary."

Stephen took the opportunity to escape into his own room when he spotted the look on Wanda's face.

She gathered the dogs and their leashes for a quick walk. Hardy took Figgy's lead and snapped it on, then followed her and Wink out the door and onto the usual path they took the pups on when Hardy stayed after dinner for coffee or tea.

"The bottom line is, there are some shady things happening at the Cedars," Hardy said. "I dealt with it when I was sheriff, and I'm sure Ryan is dealing with it now. Maybe Jodi was harassing some of these guys, but murder seems like a big leap for the people we saw out there tonight."

"Unless it was a warning gone wrong," she said, enjoying, for the first time this month, a warm breeze.

"These things do happen," Hardy allowed.

"I still don't like involving Lance and Stephen." Wanda slowed to let Wink sniff a tree.

"I know."

"And I'm still mad at you for agreeing to take them."

"I know that, too," Hardy said. He was standing close to her, close enough she could have leaned forward and kissed him, but she didn't.

He did.

Wanda was caught off guard, frozen as she felt his lips brush hers. As she started to lean in, Hardy pulled away, clearly embarrassed.

"I'm sorry, Wanda." He took a step back and rubbed at his neck. "I shouldn't have done that."

She grabbed his shirt and pulled him back toward her until their lips were a breath apart. "Yes, you damn well should have," she said, and kissed him deeply, pushing him back against the tree.

She would have stayed there all night if the dogs hadn't started winding around them, nearly sending Wanda sprawling back ungracefully on her behind as they tangled up their leashes. She laughed as they broke apart, absolutely delighted and dizzy. "You should always do that. But I'm still angry," she reminded him before she brushed her lips against his once more.

23

By the time Rye got to Stoneridge, sporting a face pink and tender from the few tiny bits of flying glass she'd had to remove, she had a message from Principal Gerard Mendoza that they would be having a meeting with one Mrs. Madeline Gayle at 8:30 a.m. She was the guardian of three students currently enrolled at Stoneridge High, and she was not happy.

"What kind of example are you setting for the students at this school when you're arrested for brawling and destruction of property?" Madeline Gayle came in hot.

"First of all, I was not arrested, and your daughter and niece attacked us. We were just asking questions." Rye knew Daniel was to blame for the pugilistic escalation, but she bet this woman did not know much of anything.

Madeline waved her hand dismissively. "There's no sound recording, but Charlie says you were harassing her and my daughter! Of course she had to defend herself!"

"Mrs. Gayle, I'm sorry to contradict you, but that's not what happened."

"Samantha graduated from Lincoln with a near perfect GPA. She was so close to being salutatorian, did you know that? She was planning to go to Boston University, but she decided she wanted to continue the family business," Madeline replied. "She is not the kind of person to get into a common street brawl."

"Two of your nephews have been involved in just that sort of fight in the last month," Rye pointed out. "Are they the sort of people who would do that sort of thing?"

"My sister dumped her children with me two years ago," Madeline replied, looking disdainful. "I had to move into her apartment just to have room for all of us. Luckily Sam had graduated by then and was living above the shop. I would not want her living where we are now. The Cedars are…well, they're a step below where she and I lived when it was just the two of us. Charlie has a two-year Automotive Technology Associate Degree and joined Sam in the business and the apartment. They're best friends, and they watch out for each other, I'll tell you that. But I provide for the three boys myself, and I do my best to keep them in line."

"I'm sure you do," Gerard replied smoothly. "You took on a huge responsibility out of the goodness of your heart. I'm sure your sister and her children are grateful."

"Ha! You'd think so, but no! I've never even heard a thank-you from her—not one! And her children! Trying to keep the boys in line is a never-ending battle. Not Charlie—she's a good girl, and a very hard worker, which is a good thing because she's not exactly pretty. But her brothers, Logan, Jack, and Caden—the three of them are a constant headache."

Rye wondered if this is how Lance's mother, Mickey, came off when he'd gotten into trouble at his old school. Rye knew Lance was a great kid, but also smart enough to cause plenty of trouble when he was unhappy. It sounded like Madeline Gayle's family hadn't had an easy time of things. Maybe the kids were acting out because of it.

For now, she needed to suck it up and placate, or this woman would escalate to the school board. She knew the type—somehow both overprotective and incredibly critical of their children, while always trying to take anyone in authority out at the knees, especially if a remediation plan was suggested.

"I made it clear that I don't want to press charges against Sam and Charlie," she said. "I believe it was just a misunderstanding, and I'm sure I can convince my friend to drop any charges he's considering." She let that hang in the air, watching as Madeline Gayle processed her choices.

The woman finally relented. "Fine. But if insurance doesn't cover that window repair, I'll be back." She stood up and left without even a goodbye.

"Rye," Gerard began, massaging his temples. "Can we just get through today? Last day is supposed to be a principal's moment of happiness."

She checked her watch and grabbed the bottle of Tylenol. "Your guess is as good as mine."

GERARD HAD JUST LEFT WHEN THERE WAS ANOTHER knock at the door. Rye wanted to cry out of sheer frustration, but instead she called out, "Come in!"

Camila stood in the doorway, her face a thundercloud.

"Oh no! I forgot we were going to work out yesterday!" Rye jumped up. "I'm so sorry. Daniel asked me to check out a lead on the case, and I thought it would take twenty minutes and then I would come meet you, but then things sort of spiraled."

"I can see that," Camila said, her voice deceptively calm. "Luckily for you, Ryan's in bigger trouble for not mentioning to me that something happened that landed you in the hospital."

"That's not an excuse. I should have called as soon as they released me to go give my statement."

Camila jumped as there was another knock at the door. She stepped forward and opened it. Rachel stood there holding a pink detention slip. She walked in and threw herself into one of the chairs next to Rye's desk, dropping her backpack with a resounding thud.

"Mrs. Jones hates me," she announced, slapping the paper on Rye's desk. "I'm pretty sure she's transphobic because whenever I dress masc, she gets on my case."

Rye studied Rachel's clothes. Track pants, a hoodie, sneakers. She would consider this a genderless norm for the majority of students at the school. Then she saw that Camila was pointing to the back of the sweatshirt.

"Rachel, what does the back of your hoodie say?"

Rachel slouched down. "I have free speech, you know."

"But you don't have a right to wear a shirt to school that threatens violence," Camila chided her, "and I think you know that."

"Are you wearing a school-appropriate shirt under your hoodie?" Rye asked.

Rachel sighed dramatically. "Yes."

Rye held out her hand. "You can come get your sweatshirt at the end of the day, or—"

There was another knock on the door. Claudia opened it without waiting for a response, glanced around, then turned her attention back to Rye. "You might want to go see what happened to your car, babe."

"Babe?" Camila muttered. She and Rachel exchanged a look.

Rye ground her teeth. "What about my car?" It was the last day of school. It was supposed to be a cake walk.

"Unless you drove it here with a cracked windshield and four missing tires?" Claudia was slurping on a green juice. "And someone painted 'Die b-word' on the side of it."

Camila already had her phone out. As she stepped out into the main office, Rye could hear her talking to dispatch.

"Was it just my car, or…?"

"I think so," Claudia said. "I wasn't looking too closely, to be honest. I was just shooing some kids inside and I noticed it."

Rye's cell phone rang. She dug into her pocket and pulled it out. "Andy?"

"Why is Rachel texting me in the middle of the last day of school saying she has detention? Who is even going to be supervising detention on the last day of school, Rye?"

"Aren't you on your honeymoon?" Rye shot a glare at Rachel, who shrugged and tilted back in her chair.

"Yes, we're in Vermont enjoying a beautiful Airbnb, and I don't want my grandmother to have to deal with this while I'm gone," Andy replied. "I need you to be on it."

Through the window, Rye could see the sheriff's car pulling up. "Andy, I am on it. You and Crystal just enjoy yourselves. Don't worry about a thing—it was a misunderstanding." She hung up and turned to Rachel. "Sweatshirt, now." Rye held out her hand, and Rachel deposited the offending garment into it. On the back, it read "Protect trans kids…or else." There were a bunch of pictures of semiautomatic weapons silkscreened on it. "Go back to class. I will call Mrs. Jones and let her know you don't have detention but that 'appropriate action' will be taken."

She watched as Rachel grabbed her bag and slunk out of the room. Rye made a quick call asking Janet Jones to stop handing out detentions on the last day of school when no teacher would be on duty. By the time she hung up, Ryan Phennan was talking with Claudia and Camila in the main office. She wondered if it would be possible to ninja roll across her desk and lock them all out, but after the bruises she'd gotten yesterday, it didn't seem like a great idea.

"Hey Rye, let's go look at your car before the tow truck gets here," Ryan said, sticking his head into the room. "I don't have all day."

"Like I do?" Rye muttered under her breath, but she followed him out and into the faculty lot, where, sure enough, her car was in much worse shape than when she'd parked it that morning.

"They took all four tires without anyone noticing?" Ryan whistled. "That's impressive in broad daylight."

"I'm pretty sure I know who's responsible." Rye studied the side of her car. She recognized the graffiti tag from the fence next to the repair shop. When she'd pointed it out to Daniel, he said he'd seen it all over the Cedars complex, too. She wondered if Madeline Gayle's nephews had come up with this idea on their own or if their aunt had talked them into it.

"You got proof?"

"Of course not," Rye said with a sigh. "But I might be able to get some. In the meantime, please send it to Gayle's Garage."

His eyebrows nearly reached the top of his head, but then he shrugged. "You could have become an undercover officer. Instead, you take real risks."

24

FRIDAY, IT RAINED. IT WAS WINDY. ON BOTH SIDES OF the pond, flights were delayed, but Wanda's hundredth check of the status informed her that her sister's flight had taken off on time. Wanda needed to get some sleep. She hoped her sister could, because although Mickey was an intrepid traveler, she was also a real grouch when she didn't get enough shut-eye.

Stephen hadn't been able to tell Wanda what kind of traveler Rob was, because he apparently didn't fly much. Stephen had gone with his dad on short flights and train rides around Europe, but never anything longer than two hours. Wanda hoped Rob was prepared for the version of Mickey who emerged at international airports.

This morning the three of them had enjoyed a quiet breakfast and taken the dogs to the park to get some energy out after Rob texted to confirm that he and Mickey didn't need to be picked up from the airport. On the one hand, Wanda hated driving to Logan. On the other, she had been looking forward to having time to talk to Rob before Lance met him in person. Yes, she was feeling protective; someone had to, and it sure wasn't going to be Mickey.

As it was, catching the bus and then renting a car would take forever, so Wanda didn't expect her guests before three, giving her plenty of time to do a last-minute vacuum and then sit with Wink and Figgy to polish her sermon. Lance and Stephen had been tasked with putting away all the board games and video game accoutrements that had been left out in the living room over the last few days. After that, they had disappeared into Stephen's room with their computers.

Lance only appeared to make a couple of ham sandwiches and grab a party-sized bag of chips, so Wanda took the pups out for their noonsies and stopped at Harvey's to pick up croissants to go with the chicken salad she had in the fridge. She didn't know how hungry Mickey and Rob would be when they arrived, but she figured having something she could pull out and throw together in five minutes would be good. No one needed to know that Hardy had brought over the chicken salad before she even woke up, with a bow and a bag of candy hearts. The conversation hearts dated back to Valentine's Day, but she sucked on "Be Mine," "Kiss Me," "I'm Yours," and "Let's Get Busy" all morning.

She also pulled some cookies Hardy had made a few weeks earlier out of the freezer, amazed that Lance hadn't discovered them yet. She threw together an arugula salad and put it in the fridge, then went back to noodling on the sermon. It was not as logical as it had seemed the night before, which was always her justification for writing at the last minute, but she loved the much-needed snuggle time with the dogs, who had been ignoring her the past week in favor of Lance and Stephen's company.

Wanda felt herself tapping her pen against Wink's back as it got closer to three. He stood up in a huff and went to scratch on Stephen's door. As soon as it opened, Figgy made a leap off the sofa and went to join the rest of the boys. Wanda loved having a full house, but she could really use some feminine energy in here today.

She hadn't told anyone about the kiss. When she'd gone to the church office to check the mail and pick up messages, she had considered telling Lisa, her friend and the church secretary, but the phone had been ringing off the hook, and there was never a chance. Tony and Greg were still on their honeymoon, and there was no way she was interrupting that. She knew she would have to tell Rye at some point. That point was not today.

She'd just gotten up to make a cup of tea and locate her cell phone when she heard a car in the driveway. Wanda set the electric kettle to keep warm and hurried back to the front door. Mickey made an entrance like the threadbare runner was a red carpet. She flung her arms out, sending water droplets flying everywhere. Somehow she still managed to make it look glamorous.

Wanda spoiled the effect by grabbing Mickey in a bear hug, which, given their size difference, was much like a teddy bear embracing a springtime-skinny grizzly. Then she stepped back to let Rob in. He was all smiles, even with his armload of luggage. He immediately deposited everything and headed out for a second trip. Wanda grinned to see Mickey look after her fiancé with a sweet backward glance.

She held out a hand for Mickey's coat and hung it up near the radiator so it might have time to dry out a bit before she and Rob headed to the Airbnb. Her sister did not look like she'd been traveling for fifteen hours. Her skin was glowing, her light brown hair fell in picture-perfect waves despite the deluge outside. Mickey somehow managed to make joggers and a half-zip sweatshirt look chic. Wanda knew if she wore the same outfit, it would look like she was taking a sick day.

Rob stomped in, pulling the door shut loudly behind him. As if on cue, there was an explosion of dogs and young men from the downstairs bedroom. Lance and Figgy bounded into the hall, while Stephen rolled out with Wink on his lap.

"My boy!" Rob roared, coming in for a big hug. Stephen pushed himself up and gave his father a squeeze. Rob's hair was close cropped and a very light white-blond with strawberry undertones, and his cheeks were bright red from the cold. As he swept Wanda up for a hug, he reminded her of the Scottish father in the animated movie *Brave*. His energy would fit right in with her passel of teenage boys and dogs.

Wanda watched Lance give his mother a hug and a kiss on each cheek, and she felt her heart constrict. They weren't "her" boys, at least not in the long run. She was just borrowing them and the chaotic joy they brought into her life.

Wanda wiped a tear away and hoped no one noticed as they shuffled out of damp clothes and shoes and into the kitchen, where she kept busy pouring tea. Apparently Lance had made scones in the "night kitchen," as he called it, to add to lunch, and soon, everyone was settled around her kitchen table catching up together.

25

Usually the day after the last day of school, when staff were in the building cleaning out their classrooms and getting ready for the summer vacation, summer job, or summer school, there was an air of celebration. If that was the case today, Rye wasn't feeling it.

Yesterday had been interminable, and a failure to boot. None of Madeline Gayle's nephews had been on campus when Rye went looking for them. She had a sneaking suspicion she knew why. Without being able to talk to the boys, she couldn't confirm any alibis for Ryan except to say that they had all been in first period, but by fourth all three were marked absent. It seemed like quite the coincidence, considering what time her car had been vandalized, but without hard proof—spray paint on the hands or clothes, cans found in a locker or backpack, or any witnesses—Rye was left with an expensive car repair.

When would someone target something cheaper to replace than her only way to get around town? Did these teenagers think vice principals made the kind of money that could afford new tires and body work on a regular basis? Well, they could not—or at least Rye could not—and after calling her father and Wanda for a ride home with no success, Rye had decided to try Kara, who turned out to be on the road for work and not far from Stone Ridge.

Rye's half sister had shown up in a gorgeous blue Audi convertible. Although the roof was up to keep out the rain, it was still the nicest ride Rye had been in for a long time. Kara had insisted on taking her out to eat, and they had spent a few hours getting to know each other.

Rye was surprised by how much fun she had with Kara. Her half sister had a sharp wit and a no-nonsense approach to life that Rye felt instantly comfortable with. They even spoke about their mother without either of them crying, which seemed like a monumental accomplishment.

By the time Kara dropped her off at home, Rye felt more relaxed than she had in a month, and she was fairly certain that wasn't the cocktails and comfort food talking. It had just been nice to feel like she could say whatever was on her mind without judgment. Even though they were related by blood, Rye knew that neither she nor Kara was convinced yet that they would have a long-term relationship, and somehow that made sharing easier. Rye talked about her breakups, the investigations she'd carried out this year, and the problems she was having with her friends.

Kara listened and laughed and sympathized and then helped to take Rye's mind off of things by telling her about the farm she had grown up on in Colorado. Apparently Kara had learned to raise bees, to milk cows, and to collect manure and sell it to homesteaders.

She reminded Rye in some ways of Hardy, raised to be independent and thrifty.

Of course Kara also told her about how she'd won her car in a card game against her ex's uncle, which reminded Rye of some of her friends back in Texas. They had been women with lives much riskier and glitzier than Rye's, and although she wasn't cut out for that, it energized Rye to hear a big sister's wild stories.

She went to bed happy and woke up hungover to the unwelcome task of riding the bike her father had bought her in high school to that same high school. It was brutally hot, and the humidity clocked in at about a hundred fifty percent. By the time she got to work, she was drenched in sweat. She snuck into the gym and showered for a second time, but having to put on the spare clothes that lived in her desk didn't make her feel much fresher.

She wished she'd taken time for coffee and breakfast before she'd left for school, but there had been no opportunity, and now she was trying to sign off on grades, finish paperwork, and answer emails from the district in between calls to the repair shop for an estimate on damages (unanswered) and the bank to see if she might qualify for a loan (call on Monday for those services) while her stomach growled. She didn't have the money this month to order lunch, and she had also forgotten to pack something the night before when she was footloose and fancy free, so her midday snack had to be a beef jerky stick from the vending machine and an iced tea she made using a stray tea bag and cold water with shards of ice from the staff room.

By the time she biked home, Rye was so hungry, she felt as if she might faint. She dropped the bicycle by her front door and went to unlock it when she realized the knob was turning on its own. Rachel stood inside the door, drinking a Coke. She looked like she had been crying.

"Hey, kiddo," Rye said, trying to hide how massively disappointing it was not to be able to walk straight into her kitchen and start drinking chocolate milk from the carton. "Did my dad let you in?"

Rachel nodded, following Rye into the living area. "I told my great grandma today that I want her to call me Rafael, and she asked me to leave."

Rye turned and opened her arms. Rafael fell into them sobbing.

RYE FIXED THEM SCRAMBLED EGGS AND TOAST AND had them eat before anything else. They needed fuel to face Rafael's call to Andy.

"I'll be right here, okay?" Rye asked. Rafael had seemed a little calmer while they were eating, but now their eyes were full of tears, and Rye could see that the idea of Andy's rejection was so real that Rafael was shutting down. "I need his permission to let you stay with me. Do you want me to be the one to call him?"

Rafael nodded and slipped over to the couch to curl up in a little ball, eyes squeezed shut.

Rye grabbed her phone from the charger and dialed her old friend. Andy answered on the first ring. "Is Rachel with you?" He sounded panicked.

Rye left the call on speaker and came to sit on the couch. "Yes," she replied carefully, holding up a note she had scribbled on the back of a receipt. *Can I call you Rafael?* Rafael nodded hesitantly. *They or he?* Small voice, "He."

"Yes, Rafael is here, and he told me that your grandma asked him to leave."

"Gran called me," Andy said. "I don't really understand what's going on. I'm not sure she does either, but she was upset. Can I talk to Rachel?"

"*Rafael* is sitting beside me, Andy." Rye looked at Rafael and held out the phone. At first Rafael shook his head, but Rye didn't budge. She couldn't have this conversation for her young friend. There would be so many more, and they wouldn't all be with the Andys of the world.

"Uncle Andy?" Rafael finally managed.

"Why haven't you been answering your phone? I've been worried sick!"

Rafael bit his lip. Rye reached out and took his free hand and gave it a squeeze. "I told Gran this afternoon that I don't want to be called Rachel anymore. I'm Rafael."

"Okay…?" Andy's tone was questioning. "Can you tell me more?"

Rafael began to cry again. He handed Rye back the phone, his hand shaking. Rye opened up her arms, and Rafael sank into her body.

"Give us a minute," Rye said. "We're just catching our breath over here."

"I love you. I'll call you whatever you want," Andy said. "I just want to know that you're safe."

Rafael wiped his eyes. "Gran doesn't want me in the house anymore. Where am I going to go?"

"First of all," Andy replied, "I am your legal guardian, not her, and you will live wherever Crystal and I live."

Silently Rye breathed a sigh of relief that she wasn't going to have to ask Wanda to excommunicate Andy. "You can stay here for now," Rye added. "Until everything is sorted out."

"What are your pronouns?" Andy asked.

"He/him," Rafael replied quietly. "For now."

"How long have you felt this way?"

Rafael let out a watery laugh. "My whole life? I don't ever remember feeling like a girl, but when your dad is a drug dealer and you spend half the time living out of his car, you don't get a lot of time to explore your gender." He paused and took the phone off speaker and put it to his ear. Rafael stood up, and as the bathroom door closed, Rye heard him say, "This is the first time I felt safe enough to—"

Rye stood up and started washing the dishes so she wouldn't be tempted to listen to their private call. When she was done cleaning up, she pulled out a cookie from the box that her father kept stocked for her in the freezer and poured a glass of milk. She got out her computer and sent a message to Daniel about moving up his conversation with Rafael to as soon as possible. She highlighted the details.

Then she messaged Camila and gave her an update, because she missed her friend. Ten minutes later, Camila showed up at the door in her pajamas with snacks. The three of them ate junk food, and watched Elliott Page interviews, and talked through what kind of clothes were missing from Rafael's wardrobe until Rye couldn't keep her eyes open anymore.

26

WANDA'S PHONE RANG. SHE HUNTED—HUNTED IN THE Lance and Stephen mess, hunted in the sermon mess, hunted in the wedding mess. She was so grateful that she had put it on a ten-ring-before-voicemail format, because finding the phone was an ongoing challenge.

The phone kept her in touch with the world. In the comfort of her own home, she could put it on vibrate, remove her hearing aids, keep it in her pocket, and not continue to worry about how much and how frequently her hearing was failing her...and what it would mean when the latest update would not be enough.

Those who loved her and lived with her adapted. Lance knew one shout unanswered meant he needed to go find her. Wink came to her and nudged with his wet little Jack Russell nose to beg for an "out." It only took Figgy a week to realize that barking was useless. He ran to her whenever he wanted something or was just checking in on where his silly humans were. Wanda often wondered why a teenage boy and two dogs were better at accommodating her disability than many highly educated adults.

Ah! There was the phone, ringing at top volume and vibrating like a barroom rodeo bull under a pile of young male wedding clothes. Lance and Stephen had either changed in the living room or dumped the dress wear on their way out with friends.

Wanda tried to not breathe like she had just jumped off the stationary bike. "Hello?"

"It's Bellona. I am just calling to let you know that Lara and I won't need you to officiate at our wedding. A dear friend has just been fixed up to do it by American Marriage Ministries' Free Online Ordination. You won't have to drive to the Cape."

Pray before saying anything. Pray. Breathe. Wanda had steam coming out her ears. Bellona Pond was the mother of one of Lance's best friends and the widow of the victim of the first murder that Wanda and Rye had solved last year. Bellona and her sweet fiancée, Lara, were both Trinity Church members. And now, apparently, Bellona did not need Wanda to officiate. She should be relieved, but Bellona was exacting and had spent endless hours in Wanda's office trying to make the ceremony perfect. She'd sent back to Wanda no fewer than six drafts.

"Aren't you going to say 'thank you'?" Bellona demanded.

Deep breath. "I was just a little startled."

"You aren't getting any younger, so isn't it great you won't have to drive to the Cape?"

Deep breath. Figgy started growling. Wink woke up and sniffed for danger. Wanda knew she must be giving off some truly strong fight-or-flight pheromones. "Does your friend have any experience, or is this her first time?"

"It will be her first time, but she's good at everything." Bellona left it unsaid that the same was not true for Wanda.

"Does she need any advice on shaping a service or running a rehearsal? She could call." *Turn the other cheek…heck, get some power back!*

"Of course not! There are rehearsals and weddings in lots of movies. It isn't exactly rocket science. And your last draft of the ceremony is just perfect for her to use. If she likes it and wants to do other weddings, I can always just give her the earlier five variations."

You thieving, scheming little… She did not say it out loud. But at this point Wink was in her lap, and Figgy was licking her other hand. Wanda had never, ever thought of herself as saintly. This might be her one chance. "Well, Bellona, you must have many details to arrange, so I won't take up any more of your time. I hope you and the family have the most beautiful day!" Her only satisfaction was hanging up before Bellona had a chance to respond.

Wanda addressed the two pups. "Hey boys, let's go for a good walk! I bet you two would like to go pee on some trees." She shut off the ringtone on her phone and jammed it into her pocket. Then she removed her hearing aids and placed them carefully in a satin bag on a lanyard on the rare chance she saw someone who proved to be as good company as the dogs. Unlikely in the extreme.

Tomorrow, she might admit that Bellona's betrayal simplified her summer, but today…

27

THE NEXT MORNING WAS SUNDAY, AND RYE, CAMILA, and Rafael slept in. Rye had found sleeping bags, and the three of them had sprawled out, finally falling asleep to streamed episodes of *The Price Is Right*. At ten, Lance and Stephen knocked on the door to let them know that brunch was ready.

"Hardy says if you want bacon, you have two minutes," Lance told Rye as she stared groggily at them.

"There's bacon?" Rafael popped up from a dead sleep. He was up and out of bed, headed for the bathroom before Lance could confirm.

Lance pulled Rye aside. "Just a heads-up—my mom and Rob are coming over as soon as Wanda can pull herself away from post-church duties." He checked his phone. "The service is over, but they anticipate it will be twenty minutes at least. Your dad is staggering the bacon and sausages so that the old folks will get some hot food, too."

"Pancakes?" Camila asked, popping up behind Rye.

"Blueberry muffins, fruit salad, and Hardy's homemade strawberry yogurt," Lance replied.

Camila pawed through Rye's drawer and came up with basketball shorts and a rec league T-shirt Rye never wore. She tossed them to Rafael before heading into the bathroom herself.

Rye took the opportunity to tell Lance that his friend Rachel was now officially going by "Rafael." He was unfazed. Rye wouldn't have been surprised if Rafael had talked to him about it. The two of them spent a lot of time at what Rye called "Hardy Rye's School for Wayward Youth."

Rye heard Rafael's laugh drift back to her and felt something release in her chest. No matter what happened at school or out in the world, Rafael would always find love here.

"You coming?" Rye asked Camila. "Hungry?"

"Starving, but I was supposed to meet Ana and my mom for a dress fitting. Mama went to Saturday Mass so she could get this appointment."

"When?"

"Five minutes ago," Camila replied.

"And I'm guessing you aren't supposed to be dressed for a slumber party." Rye gestured to Camila's ratty sweats and T-shirt.

"Absolutely not. My mother will kill me!"

Rye pulled open her closet door. "What fits you? I just got everything dry-cleaned, since I won't need work clothes until August. I have some sundresses in there— what do you want?"

"Oh, I could kiss you!" Camila rushed past her and started flipping through the hangers. "Could you text Ana and tell her I'll be about fifteen minutes late?"

Blushing, Rye took Camila's phone to send Ana a quick message.

The reply came back in English instead of the Portuguese the rest of the thread was in.

"You're in trouble," Rye said, handing her back the phone as Camila stripped down and pulled a teal sleeveless dress over her head. Camila rarely wore anything but black and gray, but clearly that wasn't because she couldn't.

"I know! My parents are never late—I think they've lost touch with their Brazilian roots," Camila said with a laugh. She looked herself over as she combed out her hair. "I look good!"

"You should keep the dress," Rye replied. "It looks incredible." She grabbed a pair of mauve sandals from her closet. "These are too big for me—they might pinch a bit, but I think they'll be okay."

Camila slid them on as Rye scrounged for a protein bar. She knew Camila never went without breakfast, and she could only imagine that wedding dress fittings would require stamina. "I'm sorry you can't stay for brunch," she said, handing over the bar.

"It's killing me, but the wedding is so close, and my mother isn't going to let Ana and Tyler plan one minute themselves! She has been back and forth between here and Denver four times since they got engaged!"

"I thought they just wanted a little ceremony?"

Camila raised her eyebrows. "You think that matters? Nothing either of them says matters to her because the whole family is going to be there."

"Your brothers and their families. Who else?"

"Everyone! If they're related to us, they will be here. If they're friends of my parents, they'll be here. If they lived in our old neighborhood, they'll be here. No one misses a wedding."

"Wow." Rye was properly cowed. Having been brought up as an only child by a person without living relations, her idea of a big wedding was the seventy people Greg and Tony had hosted a few weeks before.

Camila shoved her phone charger and the snacks they hadn't finished into her bag. "She even has second cousins here. She told me that's the reason she allowed Ana and I to move so far away." Camila rolled her eyes. "Anyway, I'm out of here. Call me later if you need anything." She dropped a kiss on Rye's cheek and slammed the door behind her. A moment later, it popped back open, scaring Rye half to death. "Do you want to come meet my mom?"

"Right…now?"

"Yes. We're going to get ramen after we're done with the dresses."

"I don't want to interrupt family time—" Rye started to say.

Camila waved her off. "Put on that cute navy romper and your gold slides. We can fix your hair on the way."

Rye thanked her past self for having French braided her hair before bed so it wouldn't be a total nightmare. She was changed and in Camila's car before she had time to think about what she was doing.

Ana was waiting outside of the bridal shop when Camila and Rye pulled up. She looked anxious—not at all the self-confident woman Rye was used to seeing. Camila jumped out of the car, and Ana immediately burst into rapid-fire Portuguese. Rye followed along behind, wishing she had stayed at brunch instead of walking into the lion's den.

The shop was well-lit, and several women sat around chatting when the three of them entered. A striking woman with gorgeous black wavy hair rose with the grace of a queen. Camila immediately went to her and gave her a hug. The woman waved her off as she caught sight of Rye standing beside Ana.

"Who have you brought with you this morning?" She held out a hand to Rye.

"This is our friend, Prudence Rye." Camila opened to mouth the say more, but her mother interrupted.

"Prudence?" The woman looked her up and down, and Rye wished she'd had time to put on some makeup to cover the bruises from her fight earlier in the week. "From the stories I've heard, the name doesn't suit you."

"Oh," Rye replied, nonplussed. "Well, people call me Rye."

"Oh, no—I won't be doing that."

"Mamãe!" Camila blushed furiously. "You're being rude!"

"What's rude? It's a strange name!"

"You haven't even introduced yourself, and you're already making my friend uncomfortable." Camila switched back to Portuguese to continue, but her mother waved her arguments away.

"I'm Alina Santos, Ana and Camila's mother," she said calmly. "These are my sons' wives"—she gestured to the women around her—"and this is my cousin."

A woman Rye recognized emerged from behind the curtain. "The girls are ready, Aline!" Madeline Gayle's smile dropped from her face as she locked eyes with Rye. "What is she doing here?"

Sam and Charlie followed Madeline out, each dressed in a yellow bridesmaid's dress that did not flatter Sam's skin tone or Charlie's shape.

"You know each other?" Aline asked, one perfectly plucked eyebrow raised.

"She attacked the girls!" Madeline replied hotly. Apparently the mother who had come to Rye's office was not about to be outmaneuvered here, surrounded by family.

"Your fight was with my second cousins?" Camila hissed. "You didn't tell me that!"

"I didn't know they were related to you until this second," Rye whispered back.

"I think you should ask your friend to leave," Aline said coolly. "This is Ana's day, and all of this drama is just a distraction."

"If she leaves, I leave," Camila said.

"No," Rye replied instantly. "Absolutely not. Your mother is right—this is a special time, and I know you don't want to miss it. I'm happy to go."

"At least your friend has better manners than you do, minha filha," Aline said. "You are already late, and now you are being disrespectful. Go and change into your dress so we can get it fitted."

Rye took one look at her friend's face and knew Camila was about to shout the house down over this. She put a restraining hand on Camila's arm. "I haven't spent enough time with my dad this week."

"See, Camila, even she has respect for her father!" Aline interjected.

"Mamãe!" Ana took her mother's hand and led her away from the group.

"I swear to God!" Camila muttered under her breath. "I am never getting married!"

"Hey, you want Ana to have fun, right?" Rye asked.

"Of course, she deserves a beautiful day, but my mother's going to spoil it!"

"You don't get to decide that for Ana," Rye said softly. "All you can do is be your wonderful self, and your sister will relax, knowing you're here to support her."

Camila looked like she was going to argue, then deflated. "Fine. I'll try for Ana. But tonight you're telling me the whole story about what happened with my cousins. Deal?"

"Deal."

28

Rye made a quick escape out into the rainstorm that had been threatening all morning. It was going to be a long walk home. She pulled out her phone and texted.

> Daniel, could you pick me up at Harvey's Bakery downtown? I think Rafael could use your help this morning.

> I have another lead.

> I'll go with you, but please, I need your help with this first.

> Fine. Get me an orange cranberry scone.

Rye ran to the bakery and ducked inside the relative warmth. By the time she'd picked up two lattes, Daniel's scone, and a ginger muffin, he was at the curb.

"I don't know if this is a good idea," he said, accepting his coffee and pastry as she got into his car.

"You took the scone," Rye told him. "You're doing it."

"I've never talked to a kid about this before. My story is not pretty."

"Rafael's mother is dead. His father is in jail awaiting trial for international drug trafficking and murder. His great-grandmother just threw him out. Is your story worse than that?"

"Different."

"Rafael is young, but he's also connected to a lot of teens online who are going through similar situations. I want him to talk to you and see that there are a lot of paths to explore," Rye explained. "I'm not trying to be all silver linings, but I do want him to know that he has support and love."

"I just don't want to mess it up," Daniel replied.

"I know." Rye picked at the lid of her to-go cup. "None of us do. Just let Rafael take the lead and ask questions. You can be honest. You can say 'I don't know.' You can tell him where you've found information for yourself."

Daniel took a bite of his scone and chewed. "You know, you're actually pretty smart."

"At work, I have personally said every possible wrong thing to a teenager." Rye was silent for a moment. "And I couldn't save all of them, Daniel. But I refuse to stop trying."

"They couldn't pay me enough to care as much as you do, and for peanuts," Daniel said as he pulled into Hardy's driveway.

Rye shrugged and called Andy. "Just wanted to let you know that Daniel and I are going to chat with Rafael for a little while. Is that still okay with you?"

"You'll be there the whole time, right?" Andy asked.

"Yup."

"And Hardy knows this guy, too? Trusts him?"

"Yes."

"Then it's okay with me. Just so you know, Crystal and I are headed home early. Tell Rafael that we'll see him tonight."

RAFAEL WAS IN THE KITCHEN WASHING UP. "RYE, YOU missed the good stuff, but I put a plate in the fridge for you."

"Thanks." Rye pushed Daniel forward. "Rafael, this is my friend Daniel. I told you about him last night?"

"Yeah." Rafael wiped his hands on a dish towel and held one out to shake. "Hey."

Daniel shook it. "Hey."

"Do either of you want something to drink? Tea? Coffee? Water?" Rye asked.

Daniel held up his Harvey's cup. "I'm still good, thanks."

"I'm fine," Rafael said.

The room was quiet enough that Rye could hear the kitchen clock ticking. After ten seconds, she had to break the silence. "So, Rafael, Daniel transitioned…how many years ago?"

"About fifteen," he replied.

"But you're old!" Rafael blurted out. "Why would you wait so long?"

He shrugged. "It was…I'm not going to say 'not an option' when I was young, but it would have been dangerous for me. My parents were strict and very conservative. It just…didn't feel like a choice for me."

"My gran kicked me out when I told her yesterday."

Daniel nodded. "I'm glad you could come here."

"Rye helped me tell my uncle, and he was pretty cool about it."

"That's great. You live with him as well?"

"Yeah. My dad's in prison. My mom died a few years ago, so Andy took me in." Rafael shrugged. "He's a good guy."

Daniel sat down at the kitchen table and pulled out the rest of his scone. He picked a little bite off and popped it in his mouth. After a minute, Rafael sat, too. "Did you always know you wanted to transition?"

"You mean when I was your age?" Daniel asked.

"I've known forever—as long as I can remember," Rafael said. "My mom might have understood, but she was…I don't know. I was six when she died. She was always sick."

Rye had met Rafael's mother once. Alicia was Andy's younger stepsister. A few years after Andy's own mother died, his father had gotten remarried. Andy had already been living with his grandmother because his father traveled every week for work.

After Alicia was born, Andy reached out to try to get to know her. Rye remembered that it had been tough going, but he'd established enough of a connection with Alicia to be named Rafael's guardian in her will. Once Eric had been arrested last year, Andy was able to take custody.

"This is going to sound weird," Daniel said, "but the good thing about having a dead parent who never knew the true you is that you can tell them now and imagine the best possible response."

"That is weird," Rafael agreed.

"I told my parents when I stopped using 'Deborah' and started going by 'Daniel,' and they were thrilled. My mother was so happy that I'd picked a good Christian name, and when I reminded her that it means 'God is my judge,'—my only judge—she cried."

"But they were…dead?" Rafael confirmed.

"I made sure they were buried twelve feet deep, just to be on the safe side."

"Would you do that?" Rafael asked, turning to Rye. "Talk to your mother like that?"

"I don't know," she said. "I'm not sure I could believe she was listening, you know?"

"Not really," Rafael replied. "I talk to my mom every night before I fall asleep."

"So why am I weird, then?" Daniel asked indignantly.

"Because I try to listen for my mother's voice," Rafael said. "I don't know exactly what she would say, but I'm not trying to make it up."

"Well, your mother sounds nicer than mine. So I'll stick to putting words in her mouth."

"What do you think your mom would say?" Rye asked Rafael. "If you told her?"

Immediately Rafael lit up. "She would definitely want me to dress better. Uncle Andy has the worst taste."

"He always has," Rye agreed. "Although I think Crystal might be a good influence on him."

"Yeah, she's cool," Rafael said. "Last night, she called me and said she would take me shopping. It was like ten minutes after Rye called Andy. She said we can even drive to Boston if there are stores there I want to try!"

Daniel smiled. "That's great."

"Can I ask you another question?"

"Shoot."

"Why didn't you cut your hair?"

Daniel wrapped his long braid around his hand and smiled. "My parents—not my adopted parents, but my biological mother and father—grew up in residential schools in Canada. My mother was seventeen when I was born, and she was forced to give me up for adoption. The people who raised me were missionaries, and they tried to 'scrub the Indian out of me'—their words, not mine. My hair was always cut to here." Daniel held a hand up to just under his chin. "My sister, Jodi, was adopted from a white family, and she was encouraged to wear her hair long. She had ringlets that my parents adored. When she was eight, she chopped her hair off herself because she knew I wanted to grow mine out and wasn't allowed to. Anytime a curl grew after that, she would cut it off."

"That's awesome," Rafael breathed.

"She was beaten with a belt every time," Daniel replied softly. "She didn't care. She was the toughest person I knew."

He began to cry, covering his face. Rafael stood up and walked around the table. He sat down next to Daniel, squeezing his hand. Rye pulled a chair around and sat beside Rafael, putting an arm around him. She didn't want to take this moment from her young friend, but Rye also knew what a burden it was to carry around the pain of the adults who were supposed to care for you. Daniel was allowed his grief and Rafael his empathy. Rye had the strength to be Rafael's support, if and when he needed her.

"I'm sorry," Daniel said, trying to wipe away his tears. "Rye asked me to come help you, and now I'm falling apart."

"So?" Rafael replied. "You're allowed to be sad."

Rye stood and handed Daniel a box of tissues. He blew his nose a few times, then excused himself to go wash his face in the bathroom.

"Do you think he'll come back?" Rafael asked.

"From the bathroom?"

"No! If I wanted to talk to him some more?"

Rye shrugged. "Ask him."

"I will. I was going to ask you...do you think you could help me find someone to cut my hair? I have a couple of pictures of what I want."

Rye held out her arms and enveloped Rafael in a hug. "I would love to. Thank you for asking."

Rafael wiggled out of the hug and shrugged in that uniquely adolescent way. "Cool," he replied before heading out to the hall to catch Daniel. He was talking with Hardy, who had just come in. Hardy high-fived the young man, and it was just right.

Rye grinned as she fished a long-awaited breakfast out of the fridge. "Cool."

29

"I just want to try them on!" fumed Mickey, slamming her cell phone down on the table, a holdover from when that gesture meant something.

"What's that?" Wanda asked vaguely, worn out from Sunday morning.

"Wedding gowns! I'm looking for a consignment or secondhand shop for my dress. Everything I find online thinks I want a cheap dress made…like a couple hundred dollars and sent to me in six weeks. But I want a divorce-dumped thousand-dollar dress for a hundred."

Rob looked up from his copy of the Sunday *New York Times*, which he'd bought on the way to the parsonage. Deciding that the discussion on dresses did not need his attention, he returned to an article complaining about the Tony Award choice for best musical.

"You don't have a dress already?" Wanda asked in surprise. When Mickey went to her high school prom, she'd had their mother buy her a custom-made dress months earlier. This lapse seemed out of character. Wanda had expected her fifty-year-old, gorgeous, never-before-married sister to have flown over with a two-thousand-dollar gown in a padded garment bag secreted in the overhead compartment. Men often rented a tux or suit, so she didn't expect Rob to be prepared, but he'd brought his "good-luck" suit, which he had worn when he met Michelle and again the evening he proposed.

"No! I looked in London, and I couldn't find anything that wasn't dumpy. The styles there, especially for my age, are so conservative." Mickey flexed her well-toned arms. "And I certainly don't work out every day to hide under layers of lace."

Wanda was a little glad that her sister had not returned from England a saint. She was still the star of self-promotion. Wanda sighed. As a clergywoman, she was expected to be a wedding "fixer." She knew which emergency stain remover to use on which fabric and where to get a high heel fixed in thirty minutes. She had four saved videos about turning grocery store cakes into wedding cakes. She had the perfect recommendation for a bride without a dress. Once and Again, an amazing consignment shop in Newmarket, New Hampshire, was a bit of a drive from Stone Ridge, but, given Mickey's almost nonexistent lead time, an appointment with its lovely proprietor would be worth it.

"Maybe I should take Lance out to get a suit, too," Mickey said.

"Well, if you're economizing on clothing, he has a bespoke suit for his job at the funeral home. It's black, but with the right shirt—maybe no tie—it could be dressed down to look more summery. He could match the flowers?"

Mickey tapped her manicured nails on the table. "Rob is wearing a charcoal gray suit with a white shirt. Maybe they could get matching ties."

"What about Stephen?" Wanda asked. "He'll be beside his father, right? Should he and Lance coordinate at all?"

"Oh, he won't be in a suit," Mickey said, hardly glancing up from where she was studying gowns.

"Why not?" Wanda hoped the answer didn't have anything to do with Stephen's wheelchair.

"Huh?" Mickey looked up. "Why not…what?"

"Why isn't Stephen in the wedding?"

Mickey stared at her. "Of course Stephen is in the wedding! What are you talking about? Stephen is the one who introduced Rob and me! He's going to be reading a beautiful piece he wrote when we got engaged, as well as coming in with his father as best man."

"But he doesn't need a suit?"

"He's wearing a kilt," Mickey replied. She patted Rob's hand, but he was deeply involved in the Sunday *Times* crossword puzzle. "It's a lovely tradition, but sometimes it can be a bit revealing when he's in his chair."

"I promise to be sure he has appropriate underclothes for our wedding," Rob said without glancing up. "I doubt he wants any elderly aunts getting a flash!"

Wanda bit her tongue, then smiled. "So what about food? Cake? Did you book a photographer?"

"Of course I booked a photographer," Mickey said, straightening up.

"Great! Check that off the list!" Wanda was relieved that at least one thing was already done.

"And I was put in charge of catering," Rob spoke up. "There's a very nice place in town—Wing-Time? I've set that all up."

The look on Mickey's face was priceless. Wanda wished she had a camera as she saw Rob's lips twitch.

"Robert Chambers! You didn't!"

He couldn't contain himself. He burst out laughing. "Of course not! We agreed on that lovely tapas restaurant Lance told us about, remember? We have a tasting tomorrow evening, and then we'll sign the contract if we like what they have."

"With your short time frame, you're lucky to have found such a great option," Wanda added. "Most places are booked months ahead of time for the wedding season."

Rob winked. "I may have called Lance for recommendations the day after she said 'yes.'" He stood up and gave Mickey a kiss on the cheek. She beamed up at him. "I'm going to find the boys and see if we can figure out the cake. I spoke to someone at Harvey's, and they said they had no problem creating a cupcake display for us."

"Are you going to want any Scots customs?" Wanda asked.

"No 'Ye Banks and Braes.' No theme from *Braveheart*. Yes, handfasting. Yes, Luckenbooth rings. Yes, Scottish blessing," Rob replied, ticking items off on his fingers.

"Luckenbooth ring is…a dance?"

"Oh, no. It's our wedding rings. I know you've seen them—two hearts intertwined with a crown. Then there's our favorite blessing." Rob drew himself up and declared, "May the blessing of light be on you, light outside and light within. May the blessed sunlight shine down on you like a great fire, so that strangers and friends alike may come and warm themselves with it. And may you two be a beacon of light for everyone around you, like a candle set by the window of a house, bidding the wanderer take shelter from the storm. And may the blessing of the rain be on you; may it wash your Spirit fair and clean, leaving a shining pool where the blue of Heaven shines. May the blessing of the earth be on you, soft under your feet as you walk along the roads, soft under you as you lie on it when you are tired at the end of the day. May the Lord bless you and bless you kindly."

Rob smiled and reached out to squeeze Mickey's hand. She was wiping a tear from her eye. Wanda tried and failed to remember her sister ever reacting to a partner this way, and in that moment the hard, protective shell around her heart made of difficult sibling memories cracked, and she just wanted to enjoy the sister standing here now.

She hated to break the mood, but if these two wanted a beautiful wedding, there was work to be done. "Let me call our local florist. I work with her all the time, and hopefully she can squeeze us in this afternoon, since we can't go dress shopping until tomorrow. Does that sound good to you, Mickey?"

"Yes," her sister agreed, snapping the computer closed and tucking her tenderness away. "And then we need to figure out what you're going to wear, Winnie."

"I'm sure I have something."

"If you're going to be in all of my photos, I will be picking, thank you very much!" Mickey stood up. "I need to fix my face, and then we'll go."

By Monday afternoon, Lance and Stephen were already over wedding planning. They assured Mickey, Wanda, and Rob that they would be available by phone, but there was no way they were shadowing every wedding detail.

Wanda, on the other hand, had more than her fair share to handle, and the presence of antsy boys underfoot was not making that easier. "You can either take half of my list, or you can call Luke Fairchild and ask if Stephen can come with you to work this week," Wanda finally told Lance after shooing them out of the refrigerator for the fifth time. "Someone needs to help pay for all the food you two are devouring!"

"Want to come with me?" Lance asked Stephen. "I have to work for a few hours today at Fairchild Funeral Home. Luke's embalming someone today and said I could watch."

"Really?" Stephen looked impressed. "You've done that before, then?"

"A few times, yeah. Luke has a no-tolerance policy on graveyard humor when we prepare a body for viewing, though."

"Of course, man. I would never! "

"Do you have time to take the dogs out first?" Wanda asked. "I have to go pick up Mickey and Rob."

"Of course," Lance said. "Oh, and do you have a suit?" he asked Stephen. "I could ask Luke if you can help with a service we have later this week, if you want to make a little money?"

"That would be great!" Stephen nodded. "I have the clothes I brought for the rehearsal dinner. Do you think that would work? I'd be a great greeter, and I could direct people to hang coats and the WC."

"It's the 'restroom' here. And please make sure the clothes are clean on Friday," Wanda warned as she headed out the door. "Mickey will lose her mind if anything goes wrong."

30

When Camila texted Rye to invite her over for a late dinner and movie on Thursday, Rye showed up with three falafel pitas and a six-pack of hard cider. Ryan was pulling a pan of brownies out of the oven when she arrived, and Camila was still showering.

Ryan handed Rye a pint glass, and she popped open a drink and helped herself to the cheese and crackers laid out on the table.

"Haven't seen you in a while," Ryan said as he grabbed himself a plate and sat down at the kitchen table.

"End of school has been busy," Rye replied through a mouthful.

"And you've been looking into Jodi Franklin's death." It wasn't a question.

"You said it was okay."

"I know, and I haven't changed my mind. Usually you and Wanda end up at the station a lot more often, though."

"Are you feeling left out of the loop?" Rye asked with a surprised chuckle.

"Yeah, a little bit," he replied. "Not a single disturbance of the peace? No fights—wait, you did get into it with—"

"I promise you we didn't go to the shop looking for trouble. Daniel thought they might have some information about Jodi's car. I know she didn't report that her brakes went out, but she'd been in for repairs a few days before it happened. We were going to ask them if they'd mentioned a problem to her, but one of them came out swinging."

"You're positive you didn't provoke anyone?"

"I let Daniel take the lead, although, if anything, he's more short-tempered than I am!" Rye shook her head. "But there is something going on at the Cedars. I feel certain of it at this point, but I can't put my finger on what."

"No evidence?"

"None," Rye replied as Camila came in from the living room dressed in black shorts and a threadbare Weezer T-shirt.

"Ooh, cheese," Camila said, cutting herself a healthy slice of gouda and popping it into her mouth. "And did you bring goodies from the Hummus Shuffle?" She helped herself to a sandwich and plopped down next to Rye. "You're the best."

As Ryan grabbed himself a sandwich, a smile crossed his face. "No cucumbers?" he asked, looking at his wrapper. "You remembered."

"And fries," Rye said, pulling out a damp bag. "Although they were probably better hot." Camila stood up and dumped the bag into the air fryer and turned it on.

Ryan shook his head. "You're supposed to preheat it first."

"It's French fries. Potatoes can handle it," Camila retorted. "So how's the case going?"

"Not well," Rye replied.

"I talked to the kid who broke his leg, Noah. He was a vault," Ryan said, leaning back in his chair.

"Noah Tesco?" Camila asked. "That's funny. He's usually pretty chatty in class."

"He talked to Wanda," Rye mused. "But she said he was scared. She got the impression he didn't want to be left alone in his hospital room, and he definitely didn't want anyone thinking he knew any details about what had happened to him. Wanda did say the car that hit him was a black Suburban, if that helps." Rye took a big bite of her sandwich.

Ryan's phone rang. He wiped his fingers, then dug into his pocket. After glancing at the screen, he retreated to the living room. Camila and Rye glanced at each other before hopping up to go listen at the door. Ryan waved them off, but they stayed where they were, watching as his face shifted.

"Who's at the scene?" He glanced up and shook his head. "If Tyler and Jaz get there before me, have them take over and start canvassing. I don't want anyone to leave."

He hung up and headed into his bedroom. He returned a minute later, having gotten his gun and badge from his safe. "Listen," he said as he strapped his belt on. "I could pretend you aren't going to call Hardy to find out what he heard on the police scanner as soon as I leave, but I'd rather you hear it from me. There's been a shooting. Two victims. One of them is Wyatt Eames. He's on the way to the hospital. The other victim hasn't been identified."

Camila grabbed Rye's hand, and they made their way to the couch. "Is Wyatt...alive?" Rye asked.

"He's being rushed in. I don't have any more information yet. I'm sorry." He dropped a kiss on each of their heads. "I hope this goes without saying, Rye, but—"

"Don't worry. I'm not going to show up to your crime scene." She wrapped her arm around Camila. They watched as he headed out the door.

"This has something to do with Jodi's death," Camila said after a long moment.

"What if my talking to Wyatt made him a target?" Rye asked. "Noah and Wyatt were both there the night Jodi died."

Rye's phone dinged, and she stood up to retrieve it from the table.

Can you come pick me up?

The text was from Claudia.

Rye had gotten a few messages like this since they'd broken up. Claudia would never drink and drive, but she also never arranged a ride or designated one ahead of time. It made Rye felt a lot like a Lyft driver in a town without any cabs.

Where are you?

The Cedars.

Rye showed the phone to Camila. "I have to go."

"I thought you told her after last time that she needed to find someone else to take advantage of."

"You and I both know Claudia's friends won't be in any condition to drive either."

"Still," Camila said, clearly frustrated. "You shouldn't go."

"And feel responsible if she kills someone?"

Camila stood up. "I'm coming with you. If she gets a ride, it comes with a lecture."

"Fine with me." Rye grabbed a small paper bag off the table and tossed it to Camila.

She looked inside. "Salted chocolate chunk cookies from Hardy?" She clutched the bag to her chest. "I'm eating two."

"I ate one on the way here," Rye admitted as she slipped her shoes on.

"I wonder what Claudia's doing at the Cedars."

"I've picked her up from there a few times lately. She said a friend moved into one of the units in April."

"If I'm seen by any students in my pajamas, I'm blaming you," Camila grumbled, grabbing her keys.

"I can wait for you to change."

"I have a bra on," Camila said, a cookie halfway to her mouth. "As long as we don't run into Ryan's investigation, I think we're fine."

As Camila pulled into the entrance of the Cedars, Rye realized she had failed to ask Claudia a few crucial questions. The drama teacher was sitting on the curb with about forty other residents, and police cars were everywhere. The ambulances were gone, so the entire apartment complex was lit up with blue and red lights in eerie silence. Yellow tape marked off a swath of the grass. Ryan was talking with a few of the uniformed officers—probably the first responders, given that he couldn't have arrived more than five minutes before the two of them.

"Maybe he won't notice us?" Camila said as an officer came up to their car to wave them off.

When the officer saw Rye, she signaled for them to roll down the window. "Hey, ladies!" Lieutenant Olivia Chen acknowledged them. "Need you to head out. This area is closed."

"We're picking someone up." Rye pointed to the thin woman sitting with her head resting on her knees toward the end of the line. "Has she given her statement yet?"

"No. And I'm guessing it'll be a while." Olivia shook her head. "They already took eyewitnesses down to the station." She gestured to everyone who was waiting on the curb. "These are residents and guests who were home when the shooting took place."

"I already went door to door to see if anyone had enough sense to stay inside after hearing gunshots, but I only found your…friend." Olivia leaned on the windowsill and lowered her voice. "She's pretty wasted."

"That's why we came. She texted for a ride home."

Olivia glanced over at Ryan. "If you want, I can ask the big guy if he'd mind if we bumped her up."

"Oh no! You don't have to do that—" Rye started to say, but Olivia already had her walkie out.

Ryan excused himself and walked over to the car, where he thanked Olivia and told her to get back to processing statements. The look he turned on them was not nearly as genial. "I asked for *one thing*," he whispered furiously. "Did you follow me here, or did Hardy tell you where to come?"

"Neither," Camila said. "Rye's burnout ex texted her right after you left asking for a ride."

Ryan glanced over his shoulder and spotted Claudia. "Rye, what is she doing here?"

"How would I know? If this town had a taxi service, I wouldn't be on call."

Ryan glanced between Rye and Claudia and sighed. "I'll let you take her if you're willing to drop her at the station. She can sleep it off there overnight."

"Can we have cuffs?" Camila asked. "In case she gives us any trouble?"

Ryan glared at her, then called to one of his officers to bring Claudia over. On the way, she stopped and gagged, and Camila looked like she was ready to change her mind about allowing her in the car, but Rye reached into her pocket and pulled out a couple of plastic grocery bags.

"Don't worry. This isn't my first rodeo." She pushed her car door open and grabbed Claudia by the arm. "In you go," Rye said, using her shoulder to lever Claudia into the back seat. Rye slid in after her. "Just in case," she told Camila, "I'm going to be on puke patrol back here." Camila nodded and followed Olivia's directions to get back out without impeding the investigation.

Claudia perked up after they'd driven about a mile. She sat up and rolled down the window to let in the warm summer night air. "I didn't know you and Camila were a thing now? Last I heard, she was with the sheriff," Claudia said in a stage whisper. "It's about time."

"We're giving you a ride, not the chance to shoot off your mouth," Camila replied.

There had been a time when Rye would have said that Camila and Claudia were, if not friends, at least friendly acquaintances, but something had happened during the short time when Rye and Claudia had been together to change 'friendly' to 'frigid.'

"Did I interrupt date night?" Claudia asked. Her posture was erect. Rye could have sworn they'd picked up a completely intoxicated woman, but she was starting to suspect she had been played by the high school drama teacher.

"Are you even drunk?" she asked.

Claudia waved her hand back and forth to indicate so-so. "I had a couple of drinks tonight."

"You seem fine now," Camila said through gritted teeth.

"Yeah, well, maybe I am, maybe I'm not, but either way, I wasn't getting out of there anytime soon without a ride from the sheriff's favorite girl." Claudia started to light a cigarette. Rye batted it out of her hand, and the lighter flew out the window. "I'd think you might have some sympathy for me. My date witnessed the shooting, and they took her to the station."

"Luckily you'll be reunited in no time," Camila said, her tone acerbic.

"What are you talking about?"

"We only got permission to pick you up if we took you to the drunk tank. You get to spend the night in jail." Camila sounded immensely pleased to be delivering this news.

"What?" Claudia sat up. "No!"

"Oh, yes," Rye said.

"You don't understand. I can't go to the station right now. They'll take all my stuff!"

"That's generally how it works," Rye replied. "Are you carrying?"

Claudia hesitated a beat too long. "No."

Rye turned to face her ex. "You're lying."

"I am not." Claudia looked out the window. "Just take me home."

"How is it that your friend saw the shooting but you didn't?" Rye asked.

"She went down to her car to get something. I was talking to some guys, and when she didn't come back after about ten minutes, I texted her. She told me what happened."

Camila snorted. "You didn't hear anything? The rest of the complex was outside, but you weren't?"

"I told you," Claudia replied. "I was talking to some people."

"We were told you were found alone," Rye said. "So which was it? Were you talking, or were you alone?"

Claudia glared at Rye. "They went outside to see what was going on."

"You just said—" Camila started to say, but Rye shook her head at her in the rearview. There was no need to let Claudia know that her alibi was full of holes.

"You know what?" Rye replied instead. "I don't care what you were doing or who you were doing it with. I just want to dump you at the station and go back to enjoying my night."

"I bet you do," Claudia said lasciviously. Camila slammed on her brakes. Claudia slammed into the seat in front of her.

"Probably should have put on a seatbelt" was all Camila said as she pulled into the brightly lit parking lot of the sheriff's department.

Claudia opened her door before Camila had come to a stop, but she wasn't completely sober, and she tripped as Rye slid out after her and grabbed her by the arm. Rye wasted no time in hauling the protesting woman up the stairs and into the building. The front desk officer took one look at them and restrained the struggling Claudia. "I've got it from here."

"Thanks," Rye replied. As she walked back to the car, her phone started ringing. It was Wanda. "Hey, Wanda. What's up?" She listened in silence. "Yeah, I heard about it." Rye slid into her seat. "Who told you that?" Camila gave her a questioning glance, but Rye held up a finger to ask her to wait. "Okay. Okay. Yeah. Thanks for letting me know. Okay. Bye." She hung up and looked at Camila. "That was Wanda. Noah Tesco called her. He's at the hospital waiting for Wyatt to get out of surgery. She just wanted to let me know that the doctors told Wyatt's parents that the wound wasn't life-threatening. He's going to be okay."

Tears had been threatening to spill over. Rye put her head down and let them go. She felt Camila's hand on her back, rubbing gentle circles, and after a few minutes the sobs slowed to hiccupping. Rye looked up and saw that Camila was crying, too. She dug some napkins out of the center console and offered them, then used one to blow her nose. She took another shuddering breath and reached for Camila's hand. "He's going to be okay."

Rye felt her phone buzz again. She sat back and answered. "Hey Lance, what's up?"

BY THE TIME CAMILA PULLED INTO THE PARKING LOT of the funeral home, Rye already had a good idea of what Stephen and Lance had been getting into all week. Apparently they had told Wanda, Mickey, and Rob that they were working extra hours for Luke when in fact they'd been hanging out at the Cedars, trying to score more information about the investigation. Lance had told her that they'd been chatting up the kids who lived there, playing some basketball—trying to look like they belonged in the hope of seeing something fishy.

"Apparently, tonight, before the shooting, things went sideways," Rye was telling Camila as they parked next to Lance's Corolla.

"Thank God they were out of there before it happened," Camila replied.

Rye felt as shaken as Camila sounded. It could have just as easily been Stephen or Lance in surgery for a gunshot wound right now. Instead they were coming down the steps on their own two feet. Granted, both of their faces were purpling with bruises, and Stephen had a bloody nose.

Rye got out of the car and stared down the two of them. "What the hell were you thinking?"

"We just wanted to help," Lance replied. "Wanda's been so busy with my mom—"

"What about Hardy? Or Daniel? Or me? I don't remember you calling to ask if I had anything you could help with." Rye was furious, but she knew from experience that she needed to keep her temper in check with teenagers if she wanted even a chance to get through to them. "Do you know there was a shooting at the Cedars an hour ago? One of your classmates is in the hospital, and another man is dead."

"What?" Stephen's face drained of all color.

"Who?" Lance asked.

"Wyatt," Rye replied. "It sounds like he's going to make it, but there will be a long recovery."

"Not to mention the trauma," Camila added.

"How many people have to be killed before you two realize this isn't a game?" Rye asked.

"We don't think that—" Lance started to say, but Rye held up her hand to silence him.

"You need to go home and tell Wanda what you've been doing. She has a right to know." Rye sighed. "I just hope your mom doesn't blame Wanda for this. If she does, I doubt you'll be finishing your senior year at Stoneridge."

It was clear this had not occurred to Lance. He started to cry, and Stephen wrapped an arm around him. "It's not Wanda's fault," Stephen said. "She didn't know anything about it."

"No, but she's the one who's been involved in other investigations," Rye pointed out. "She's the one your parents will think approved this."

"And it's not like you can hide all this," Camila said, gesturing to their faces.

Lance looked at Rye plaintively. "What are we going to do?"

For once, Rye didn't have an answer.

31

From Wanda's perspective, her sister's short visit passed in a whirlwind. There was so much joy between them that Wanda felt as though she had entered another dimension where she and Mickey had always been the closest of friends.

Wanda's pre-wedding meetings—one with Mickey and Rob and one with the boys—went well. She and Rob came back from talking to Father Paul on the same page. Rob was grateful for his childhood Roman Catholic faith and had been comfortable in the Scottish Episcopal church he joined years later. Having Father Paul say that God was in every church seemed to settle any nerves he had about the name over the door. Mickey and Rob both scrutinized every line of the ceremony Wanda had written and then approved it enthusiastically.

Mickey's bouquet was five long-stemmed roses, and the boutonnieres were white roses. Pink roses with baby's breath would sit on the tables. Rob and Mickey gave Wanda a locket with a rose engraved on it and a photo inside of Wanda and Mickey when they were much, much younger. The locket was Rob's family heirloom, although he couldn't remember which of his great aunts had gifted it to him as a boy. They both assured Wanda that it wasn't Michelle's style and that it would look beautiful over her robe. It was rose gold, Wanda's favorite. She tried to hide her tears but failed miserably.

Mickey found a shell-pink gown. She said Rob would laugh if she wore white. She also surprised both herself and Wanda by finding a beautiful veil at 'Once and Again' that she wanted Lance to lift up at the ceremony. Lance and Stephen had started to laugh when they were told, before realizing that Rob had tears in his eyes at the tenderness of that bit of ritual.

Mickey had a darker complexion than Wanda but had nevertheless scheduled a tanning appointment for Thursday to rid herself of her "European pallor." The women did haircuts and nails on Friday morning. Mickey's nail color matched the shell pink of her dress, and Wanda found a wedding-themed shade called "Please Say Ecru" that made her chuckle. It went perfectly with her navy dress, which had purple and magenta ribbons sewn into the low neckline and the skirt hem. The dress needed altering and was not due to be finished until Saturday morning. Mickey had bought her a backup dress in deeper pink that would make her look like a bridesmaid and was wrong in just about every way. Wanda kept the tags on and prayed that any seamstress would want to be known for making deadlines. "Didn't get the dress in time for the wedding" was the kind of online comment that could take out a small business—not that Wanda would post such a thing, but her sister certainly would.

And then there was the rehearsal. By Friday night, Wanda was almost as excited as Mickey and Rob. However, when Mickey walked in, Wanda was shocked into bluntness. "What happened to your hair?" This morning, they had left the salon, both happy with their new cuts. Mickey's hair had not been so…pink.

"You don't like it?" She had obviously returned to the salon in a rash decision to split dye her hair. One side of her light brown hair was untouched, while the other half faded from a light pink to a bright pink.

"I was just caught off guard. It won't show under your beautiful veil, but it will look stunning at the reception."

In the era before Rob, Mickey would have become hysterical. "I just wanted something different. I know my hair is great, but I wanted something…fun. I never got the big wedding when I was young, you know?"

Talk about letting her hair down. "You look beautiful. Do you think I could get mine done before tomorrow morning? Maybe in blue?"

"No," Mickey and Hardy replied. Rob wisely stayed silent.

Stephen, who had been wheeling around as the rehearsal photographer, was serious about his job. The camera never left his face, and he must have captured at least a hundred photos of his soon-to-be stepmother's new hue.

When Tony arrived a few minutes later, looking relaxed from his honeymoon, he burst out joyfully, "This must be Michelle! Your hair is magnificent!"

And the regular old Mickey smiled in acknowledgement, no longer a self-reflective saint but the belle of the ball she always had been. Wanda rolled her eyes. He was a charmer, and, of course, they had only spoken on the phone to plan the music. Greg and Hardy were helping with setting up for the following day, but Mickey had not invited others to the rehearsal. Wanda knew that her sister always wanted things to be perfect before they were public. Wanda had also cautioned against a rehearsal dinner and a mini-reception.

"I've got good news and bad news," Tony said after he and Greg were introduced all around.

Mickey's face turned sharp as a fox's. "What's the bad news?"

"There are leaks in the air supply lines of the organ, and no one can come to fix it till Monday."

"But we were going to have the violin for three verses and then the piano come in for the processional, so does it matter?" Mickey was still being reasonable. Wanda silently applauded her sister.

Tony shrugged. "I was going to play 'Highland Wedding' as the recessional."

Stephen rolled over. He dropped the camera, displaying a very black eye. "I'll rent bagpipes—that's how it should be played."

But no one was thinking about the pros or multiple cons of bagpipes when they saw his swollen face. Mickey turned pinker than her hair.

"Stephen! What happened?" Mickey gasped. "Do you have your heart set on—" Wanda was on the brink of interrupting something that could not be unsaid, like 'spoiling my wedding,' when Mickey finished, "—scaring me to death?"

Lance stood up slowly and turned to them. His bruises were not as distinctive, but one cheek was swollen, and there was a scratch above his left eye that had surely come from a long fingernail. "Some guys jumped us. It was stupid."

"Where? What happened?" Wanda's heart was in her throat.

Lance glanced at Stephen. "We were just talking to some girls, and this guy took offense. I'm sorry about the bruises. We've been watching YouTube videos to see how we can cover them with makeup for tomorrow."

There was something they weren't telling her—that, Wanda was certain of. "Where were you?" she asked again. Neither of them answered, and Wanda took a step closer to her nephew. "Where, Lance?"

"We went back to the Cedars—"

Rob whirled on Hardy. "You took these boys back there *last night*? I read the newspaper. They could have been killed!"

"He didn't have anything to do with it!" Stephen interjected. "We've been hanging out there all week, and nothing's happened."

"You *what*?" Hardy replied, his tone furious.

Mickey turned on Wanda. "You *knew*, didn't you? And you not only didn't stop it, but you also didn't tell me!"

"I swear I didn't know. I never would have allowed it!" She could tell Mickey didn't believe her.

"You get into these investigations, and it's one thing to put yourself in danger when you're Lance's guardian, but to let him do something so reckless—"

"Mom! Aunt Wanda had nothing to do with this!" Lance interrupted. "She hasn't even been investigating! She's super strict about me getting involved in anything!"

Wanda felt like her world was collapsing. What if Mickey took Lance away? What if she no longer trusted that he was safe here? What if he wasn't? "Lance, how could you do this?" Wanda could see her tone of wounded disappointment hit her nephew harder than anything else.

"It was my idea," Stephen said. "Lance didn't even want to come, but I asked him to take me."

"That's not true, Stephen," Lance interjected. "It was my idea—"

"You could have been killed," Rob said again.

"I'm sorry," Lance replied, more quietly this time. "I messed up."

Hardy looked nearly as distraught as Wanda felt. "I never should have let Daniel talk me into bringing you two along."

"None of us are innocent of doing something stupid for a good cause." Rob put his hand on his son's shoulder. "But you can't do this sort of thing. I know you're out of school, Stephen, and Lance, you will be soon enough, but part of growing up is recognizing when the risk outweighs the reward."

"I know, Dad," Stephen said. "I really am sorry." He turned to Mickey and held out his hand. She took it, tears glittering on her cheeks. "And I'm sorry this is going to mess up your pictures. I hope we haven't spoiled the wedding."

Mickey shook her head. "I don't care about the photos." She looked at Lance. "I know I haven't always been the best mother. And I know you've had to grow up a lot faster than you should, but you boys are the most precious things in the world to us. Please, act like it."

"I'm sorry, Mom," Lance murmured, burying his face in her shoulder. He reached out an arm and pulled Wanda in, too. "I'm sorry, Aunt Wanda."

Wanda and Mickey's eyes met for a moment, and Wanda saw a flicker of hurt in her sister's eyes. It was true that Lance had lived with her for less than a year, but it felt like so much longer. To Mickey, though, the closeness between them, when she and her son were not nearly so connected, was still a shock. Wanda gently extricated herself from the group.

Mickey wiped her eyes. "I think we all need a bit of normalcy. Can we get on with the rehearsal now?" She looked tired, but Wanda nodded in agreement.

Tony had made himself scarce during the drama. Now he reappeared, phone in hand. "I've called in a favor, and we will have bigger music tomorrow. For the moment, I'll just play on the piano so you get your timing."

Wanda picked up where Tony left off. "Let's find our places for the ceremony." She looked around. "And remember, you will be here tomorrow at one, except for Lance and Stephen, who will be here at noon. My friend and office admin, Lisa, is a makeup wizard, and she should be able to do a masterful job at hiding the evidence of last night's…encounter." She looked at each of them solemnly. "Do not be late."

"WHEW," SAID WANDA TO TONY AFTER HER FAMILY had left the building. "I hope the old adage, 'tough rehearsal, beautiful wedding' is in our favor."

Tony laughed. "And on the off chance my organ guy doesn't come through, I know just the bagpiper who will be brilliant. Plus, he's handsome, and he knows how to soften when he's inside the building and lift the volume when he's out the door. He's already providing the car for the couple, anyway."

"Luke Fairchild? You're kidding! He truly is a man of many mysteries!" Wanda replied.

Tony laughed. "Believe me, he does not self-promote." His phone buzzed, and he looked at his text, a silly smile on his face. "My new husband has dinner ready for us." He gave Wanda a kiss on the cheek. "I'll see you tomorrow."

Hardy had stayed behind to give Wanda a ride to dinner, and he waved to Tony as the younger man left.

"How are you holding up after all of that?" he asked.

"Not great. You read about the shooting?" Wanda felt tears rise up. "It could have been them. I should have been keeping better tabs—I knew they were curious! If anything had happened to them, it would have been my fault."

"No," Hardy replied firmly. "It would not…but it would have felt like it."

"I thought I knew what love was," Wanda said softly. "But I don't think I did until Lance moved in with me. If anything happened to him, or if Mickey took him back to London…I don't know if I could bear it."

Hardy held out his arms, and she dropped her head on his chest, allowing the tears to come. After a minute, he said, "Having children is allowing someone to pull the heart from your body and allow it free rein to do the stupidest, most dangerous things."

"And he's not even mine."

Hardy pulled back so he could look Wanda in the eyes. "Of course he is. Maybe in a few years, someone will come along, and you'll have to step aside to let them love him as fiercely as you do, but for now? Mickey is his mother. You're his rock."

She kissed him then, and neither one heard the side door open and close, or the soft footsteps crossing in front of the pews, stopping, more steps, more steps, stopping. In the darkness, the soft sound of a timer began.

32

And then there was the wedding.

The rehearsal dinner had gone well. It was expanded to include relatives who came to town for the ceremony. On Mickey's side, there was an aunt from California and three college girlfriends from New Mexico. On Rob's, there was a sister from Aberdeen and an aunt from Glasgow, as well as an appearance from a golf buddy who had succeeded in keeping his plan to attend a secret.

The big win for Lance on Saturday was that ten of his new friends came to his mother's wedding. Wanda guessed he hadn't realized he had so many good friends after only nine months in town. Lance's best friends, Leslie and Nicole, had organized it with Wanda.

The biggest surprise, though, was when Wanda's second ex-husband, Brian, and his husband walked in. They had taken care of Mickey after she had been ripped off by the man of her foolish dreams in Italy. Brian poked his head in the church office, and Wanda greeted him with a kiss so enthusiastic, Lisa almost smeared powder in Stephen's eyes. Unlike Wanda's first ex-husband, who had left her for a younger, slimmer redhead, Brian had the decency to meet his auburn-haired hubby a few months after coming out. Brian and Wanda's divorce had been amicable; and if Wanda had been lonely for Brian's boisterous energy for a long time after he left, it wasn't because her heart was broken.

The weather even cooperated. The wedding party was on time and lined up without the usual amount of pandemonium. Nothing could go wrong, Wanda thought, raising her shoulders and dropping them to release the tension. Tony and Nicole processed in from the right, followed by Wanda from the other side. Tony began to play, and Rob walked in on floor level from the left with Stephen in his kilt with his chair. Nicole sang the first two verses of Robert Burns's poem:

> *O my Luve is like a red, red rose*
> *That's newly sprung in June;*
> *O my Luve is like the melody*
> *That's sweetly played in tune.*
>
> *So fair art thou, my bonnie lass,*
> *So deep in luve am I;*
> *And I will luve thee still, my dear,*
> *Till a' the seas gang dry.*

As Tony continued an instrumental solo, Lance and Michelle came down the aisle. Lance lifted his mother's veil and kissed her check, and it seemed like just about everyone was crying, Wanda in particular.

Nicole sang:

> *Till a' the seas gang dry, my dear,*
> *And the rocks melt wi' the sun;*

I will love thee still, my dear,
 While the sands o' life shall run.

Wanda began her opening words, first shakily and then with more strength.

"With deep affection for Michelle Bates and Robert Chambers, we gather here today to witness and bless the vows that unite them in marriage. To this moment, they bring the fullness of their hearts as a treasure to share with each other. They bring dreams that bind them together. They bring that particular personality and spirit which is uniquely their own, and out of which will grow the reality of their life together. We rejoice with them at this outward symbol of an inward union of heart and mind and invite you to celebrate it in the presence of God."

It was seven minutes after one when the first stink bomb went off. Then a second one, and a third. The stink was immediate, but so was the fear of what else might come next.

"Will everyone please make your way out of the sanctuary?" Wanda called, trying not to inhale. She reached out a hand to Mickey. "Let's get you out of here."

Mickey was in tears. Rob took her other hand, and they hurried out of the sanctuary and into the fresh air. Wanda's eyes were streaming. She pulled some tissues out of the pocket of her robe to dab at them.

Wanda could already hear a siren in the distance. She glanced over and saw Hardy was on his phone. She continued moving guests out to the parking lot, away from the building, just in case.

She felt a wave of relief when she recognized Jaz and Tyler in the first car on the scene. A second car with two other uniformed officers arrived right behind them, and within half an hour the small building had been cleared of further threats, if not of the odor.

"Can you believe it?" Lance came up to his mother, who was inconsolable over the ruined ceremony. "Your wedding is news! Some of my friends caught the whole thing on video and uploaded it to TikTok." Wanda looked horrified, but her sister's expression lifted. Mickey truly did love to be the center of attention. "Don't worry," Lance assured her. "I checked them out, and you look stunning."

Mickey straightened her shoulders and accepted the tissue Wanda offered. "I can't imagine who would do such a vicious thing to us."

"Don't worry about any of that right now," Wanda replied. "You are the bride with courage, not daunted by pranks. Lisa will fix your makeup, and I can Febreze your dress. You're going to be a star."

Mickey's emotional pendulum swung to I-dare-you-to-mess-with-my-wedding as she and Wanda went into the hall to freshen up. Glasses of water were being passed around to guests by the ever-resourceful Greg, while Tony and a crew of volunteers got the Clavinova plugged in and tested. Lance and Stephen helped guests set up some chairs for those who needed them.

As Mickey and Lance got in place, Rob leaned over to Wanda. "You and Lance really know how to help her rebound, don't you?"

"She's always stronger when she sees herself as the underdog. Take pride and take warning!" Wanda replied softly. "Also, despite last night's chaos-at-the-Cedars headlines, this is a town with minimal news. You may find yourself in the paper."

Rob straightened his tie as his betrothed started down the aisle again. The trees were still holding on to some of their spring blossoms, and in the breeze, a few fell around Mickey and Lance. Rob had tears in his eyes as she took his hands for a second time.

Wanda began again, from the top, and this time there were no interruptions. Stephen didn't drop the rings. Nicole sang Richard Gillard's "Won't You Let Me Be Your Servant?" Wanda's words were eloquent, accompanied by a sniffle-less flow of tears. Rob and Mickey's kiss was long and wonderful. Practically the whole crowd joined Wanda in pronouncing them, and after a hearty round of applause, the music of the bagpipes began to play sweetly. Luke Fairchild serenaded them out with "The Highland Wedding." An Italian, he did not offend by wearing a kilt, but he had miraculously found a tie in Rob's family tartan.

Afterward wedding pictures were taken. And, yes, a photographer from the newspaper had come. Mickey had a beautiful shot to go with the headline, "The Bride Says Yes!" But Wanda's favorite photo was of Stephen, who stood with his brace and one elbow crutch and slowly escorted his elderly Great-Aunt Cariad from her chair into the social hall for the reception, where Taste and Tell Bistro had outdone themselves.

For dessert, there was the chocolate fountain Andy had lent the couple from his own wedding. Then there were the cupcakes from Harvey's! They were magnificent to see as well as eat. The cupcakes had been placed on tiers decorated with multicolored roses. Wanda hadn't known Harvey's created displays. Usually they brought the cake and left it for the wedding planner to finish. This was spectacular and must have broken the budget.

As she was admiring it, Luke sidled over and in a low voice expressed his hope that Mickey would not be upset that he and his wife, Irie, had jazzed up the dessert table.

Wanda gave him a hug. "I think she's in love…Rob should be jealous of the cupcakes!" Wanda said, pointing at her sister, whose face was the picture of delight.

"We shouldn't tell her the roses were left over from a funeral, then?" Luke asked, grinning.

Wanda laughed. "No, no, and *no*! I think the stink bomb was quite enough to stretch my sister's equilibrium!"

She excused herself to go talk to Ryan, Tyler, and Jaz, who stood in the back waiting for her attention. She brought them a plate loaded with cupcakes, which Tyler happily took off her hands.

Wanda led the three of them inside the sanctuary, where even fans and open windows hadn't dispelled the odor. She pointed out where everyone had been standing when the stink bombs had gone off. As they arrived at the lectern, Wanda noticed something she definitely hadn't seen before the ceremony. On the legal pad she used to write prayer requests on Sundays, someone had scribbled, "Forget about Franklin, or next time it won't be a stink bomb!"

Wanda reached out to brush the spot where she had written so many heartfelt pleas for grace, but Jaz gently caught her wrist and pulled her hand back. Tyler bagged the notebook with gloves. "Whoever did this, they were here. Today."

"You didn't notice any strangers? Anyone who didn't seem like part of the crowd?" Jaz asked, taking notes.

Wanda shook her head. "I didn't know all of the guests, but Mickey and Rob seemed to. I hate to ask them—I don't want to scare my sister—but maybe Lance and Stephen would know."

"If they don't," Ryan said, "we'll have to talk to Mickey and Rob."

"Do you think that note will be enough for a handwriting analysis?" Wanda asked.

"Maybe. We can also hope whoever wrote this left fingerprints." Ryan already had his phone out. "Meanwhile, I'm calling in backup"—he held up a hand as Wanda started to protest—"because this is a legitimate threat. I don't want to ruin your sister's wedding, so I'll make sure they come dressed as guests, but I want eyes here." His tone brooked no argument.

Wanda nodded. She would feel better if she could be certain nothing else would ruin Mickey and Rob's special day. A part of her wished she'd never seen the note. It was going to be hard to fake a good mood without any worry-numbing drinks once she got back out there. "Do you need anything else from me?"

"We found the devices already, and we're checking for fingerprints. If I find anything else, I'll text you."

Wanda looked down at the beautiful navy dress that had indeed arrived early in the morning. "I don't have anywhere to keep my phone right now."

"I'll text Hardy, then," Ryan replied.

Wanda studied his face, looking for a hint that he was teasing, but he just stared back.

"Or don't you think you'll be dancing with him most of the night?" he asked.

"Did he say something to you—"

"I didn't become sheriff based on good looks alone," Ryan replied smugly.

"Although I doubt they hurt," Tyler added as he strode past.

"And it certainly wasn't your charm," Wanda muttered.

"I heard that," Ryan said. "Oh, and I don't need my former boss poking his nose into this, got it?" He arched his eyebrows at her. "No one can hear about the note."

"Scout's honor," Wanda said, holding up three fingers. No need to tell Ryan that she'd only made it a week in Girl Scouts before getting booted for being "a bad influence on the other girls."

33

RYE'S PHONE RANG, AND AS SHE REACHED FOR IT, SHE fell off the couch where she'd passed out after brunch. She hadn't been sleeping well recently, and she knew she needed a nap before Mickey's wedding.

"Where are you?" Her father's voice came through the receiver. "It's six o'clock! Wanda has been looking for you everywhere. I can't cover anymore."

Rye sat up and stared at the clock in disbelief. She had slept right through the wedding and at least an hour of the reception. There was no way Wanda hadn't noticed, and Rye didn't want her dad to take the blame. Lying it was. "I'm sorry, Dad. I meant to call you. I think I must have eaten some leftovers that had gone off. I've been in and out of the bathroom for hours. I thought I'd feel better, but I must have lost track of time." Desperate times called for desperate stories about bodily functions that no one would want to examine too closely.

Except her father, of course. "Is that so? You and I ate together this morning, didn't we?"

"First breakfast," Rye replied, trying to sound weak. "I finished off an old cream puff as an early lunch."

"Hmm." Hardy Rye was not convinced.

A small bit of honesty would help. "I drifted off for a while, and I just woke up and I still feel terrible."

There was a long pause for parental evaluation. "When you see Wanda, you better grovel!"

"Give Wanda my love and take lots of pictures!" She hung up and dropped the phone onto the sofa. Pushing herself off the couch, Rye caught a glimpse of her reflection in the mirror. Her curls were sticking out everywhere. It looked like a bird had made a particularly fluffy nest on her head. She opened a can of chicken soup and grabbed the box of saltines from the cupboard. Hardy's soup would be better, but he wouldn't get away for a while. Might as well be convincing.

The knock on the door came as she sat down with her hot bowl of soup. Rye was determined to ignore it. She hadn't bothered to turn on any lights, and her friends expected her to be at the wedding. Rye knew that even Andy, Crystal, and Rafael had been invited when the couple came home early from their honeymoon. That left…Daniel, maybe?

The knock came again, this time more insistently. Rye pushed back from the table and stalked to the door. "What?" she growled as she threw it open.

To her surprise, it was Claudia with Noah Tesco. Noah was on crutches with his cast, but he didn't look as bad as Rye had feared after hearing about his accident the week before. Any cuts or bruises seemed to have healed.

Noah actually shrank back at Rye's tone, but Claudia just pushed past her. She wrinkled her nose at the smell. "What on earth are you cooking? It smells god-awful in here!"

"Dinner," Rye said.

Still staring at Noah, she calculated the impropriety of having him in her home. After a long moment, she stood back and let him pass. He stood awkwardly by the door while Claudia threw herself on the couch. Rye hated that her ex looked so good, especially when she herself was a mess. She had the sudden insight that this woman had deliberately played it that way.

"What are you doing here? I thought I made it clear last night that we were done."

Claudia shrugged. "I guess you don't want to hear what Wyatt said to Noah when Noah went to visit him in the hospital this afternoon."

"Fine." Rye sat down at the table. "Tell me what happened in the hospital, Noah."

"I don't know if it will help," he said.

"If there's any chance you can help find the shooter, it's worth trying," Rye replied.

"It's better than that," Claudia said smugly. "Tell her who the shooter was, Noah."

"I don't know for sure," he replied. "But I saw a couple of guys by the Dad Yolks truck, and a little while later I saw Mr. Eames—you know, Wyatt's dad? I saw him come out of the truck wearing, like, a hoodie over a baseball cap. I thought it was weird because it was so hot that night, and inside his truck it's a furnace. I worked there last year, you know."

"Tell her what Wyatt said," Claudia urged.

"He just kept saying, 'I saw my dad, I saw my dad.'"

"Surely his dad has been with him in the hospital?" Rye asked. "Maybe he just means—"

"No, that's the thing!" Noah said. "I saw his mom when I went to visit the hospital, but his dad wasn't there."

"I don't think we should jump to conclusions," Rye replied gently. "Maybe he was in the cafeteria or the bathroom. Maybe he had to run home to get a shower and change clothes or pick up something for his wife. Having a child in the hospital is one of the most stressful situations—"

"Tell her what you heard at the nurses' station," Claudia urged.

"I was wondering if the nurses could call facilities to help Wyatt's mom with the chair she was sleeping in. While I was waiting, I heard two of them talking about Colin—that's Wyatt's dad—about how no one has seen him. They have a couple of cops posted outside of Wyatt's room, and one of the nurses said he thought that was why. So I thought maybe Colin had something to do with the shooting, and now he's on the run. I mean, he loves his son. He wouldn't shoot him. But…"

"How well do you know him?" Rye asked.

"I worked for him, like I said. And I've known Wyatt since middle school. That's when we moved here. We used to hang out at his place sometimes, but not for the last year or so. He always likes to be out playing basketball."

"I was at the Cedars this afternoon, and I saw Noah, and he told me all this," Claudia interrupted. "I knew we had to come share this with you."

Rye ignored her. She looked at Noah. "You and Wyatt are friends. Did he ever say anything about his dad that would make you think he's violent?"

Noah shook his head. "No."

"Do his parents own guns?" Rye asked.

"Yeah, I think so. I saw the same gun safe my uncle has when we used to hang out at Wyatt's," Noah replied. "Plenty of people in our building own guns. It's not really a big thing. Like, it's weird if you don't have one."

"Why?" Rye asked.

"Why is it weird?" Noah sounded confused.

"Yes, but also, why do so many people have them? Hunting? Self-defense?"

"I don't know?" He fidgeted. "Can one of you take me to the closest bus stop? I've got to meet some friends soon."

"I can drive you," Claudia said.

"There's a bus stop right at the end of our driveway, Noah," Rye replied. "Can you make it that far?"

"Yeah."

"I know you don't want to get involved with the investigation, but if you called in an anonymous tip, it could help," Rye told him, opening the door and ushering him out. Rye watched him head down the driveway. Then she stomped back inside, not bothering to close the door.

"Get out," she said, unceremoniously wrenching Claudia up from the couch.

"What's your deal? I was trying to help!"

"I don't need your help. I don't want your help. I definitely don't need you bringing students to my house to discuss a violent crime. What if it gets back to the shooter? What if the shooter is Wyatt's dad, and he finds out that Noah was poking around? I don't want that on my conscience. Do you?"

"How would anyone find out?" Claudia ignored Rye's attempt to shove her toward the door.

"Did you drive him here from the Cedars? Where anyone could have seen him leaving with a teacher from the high school? What do you think people are going to say about that? You could be accused of anything! You could lose your job, Claudia."

"You're being so dramatic!" Claudia replied, pouting. "I thought that was my department."

"I don't even know you anymore," Rye said.

"Where do you get off judging me?" Claudia retorted, her cheeks heating up. "In the last year and a half, my girlfriend and one of my best friends were killed."

"I know—"

"Should I just get over it?" She shook her head. "I'm a good actress, but I'm not that good."

"Well, you haven't been practicing since you were seven years old," Rye said sharply.

"Plenty of people lose a parent!" Claudia replied angrily. "Not all of them use it as a crutch for the rest of their lives! At least you got a sister out of the deal— that's more than most of us can say."

"That's enough." A steely voice came from the open door. Camila. She stormed in and took Claudia by the arm, escorting her out the door, then throwing the deadbolt for good measure.

When she turned to Rye, her expression was furious. "How many times do I have to tell you to stop messing with her?"

"Claudia came here with Noah Tesco, telling me that Noah had heard something that might help with the case. I didn't ask for their help, and I told them to leave." Rye could tell from Camila's outfit—crisp shorts and a midriff-baring top paired with several gold chains to look effortlessly chic—that she had been at the wedding. Maybe she'd even saved a dance for Rye. "I told her off," Rye continued. "Maybe it will be enough."

"For her to stop calling when she knows you'll answer? I doubt it."

"I can stop answering."

Camila just shook her head. "That's not who you are."

Rye wanted to protest, but she knew Camila was right. It wasn't just Claudia. Rye didn't have it in her to turn away people asking for help. It made her good at her job, more patient with her students, and a friend worth having. It was also her Achilles heel, and Claudia was not the first person to figure out how to exploit it.

"I'm doing my best, Camila."

Her friend sighed. "I know you are." She looked Rye up and down critically. "You look terrible, by the way. Are you sick?"

Rye couldn't lie to her friend. "I told my dad I was."

"What will you tell Wanda?"

Rye shook her head. "The truth. Just…not today. I don't want to ruin the day."

Camila dropped onto the couch and patted the seat beside her. "You wouldn't be the first. Let me catch you up."

34

The alarm jarred Wanda awake. She'd had an awful night's sleep. She needed to wash the nightmare sweat out of her hair before church. She swung her legs over the edge of the bed, then realized she could feel vibration from her phone beside her. The screen read 5:30—a full thirty minutes before she needed to be up. It was a phone call, not her alarm.

The caller was Bellona Pond. Of course it was.

"Wanda, I am so sorry. Did we wake you?" The voice was Lara Alesci, one of the sweetest parishioners at Trinity and, inconceivably, Bellona's fiancée.

"I'm afraid you did, Lara. I was up late last night celebrating my sister's wedding."

A long silence followed that Wanda guessed was a muted conversation. When Lara continued, Wanda thought she might be outdoors. She could hear a static like wind. Must be chilly at this time of the morning on Cape Cod. "I'm sorry, Wanda. Bellona is grumpy this morning because we can't get married."

"What happened?" Was the friend officiant a no-show? Wanda was not driving to Cape Cod this afternoon, no matter what.

"We don't have a marriage license! We arrived on Friday to get ready for the Saturday rehearsal. I asked our friend if she had the license."

"Lara, you didn't get the license here?"

"No! We thought it was the officiant's job."

Wanda took a deep breath. "And the officiant correctly thought it was yours. She should have asked you! Not everyone knows what to do, particularly in different states. In Massachusetts a couple applies for a license no more than sixty days before getting married. It then takes three days to process. The officiant signs the license after the ceremony and mails it to the city from which the license was obtained."

"So you can't come down here and fix it?"

"It's Sunday. There is no fixing! Here's what I suggest. Have your wedding today. In the place of a declaration of marriage, the officiant can say this: 'Lara and Bellona, we have witnessed your promises and celebrate your love and the new life you will live together.' You will then kiss and have a wonderful party, because you *do* love each other, and nothing else matters. When you come home, you will get a wedding license, wait three days, come to the church office in your jeans, and I will marry you legally."

"This is terrible, just terrible."

A stink bomb was terrible. A threat was terrible. A flood was nearly a washout. A honeymoon interrupted by a child rejected and put out on the street was a wounded family. Wanda breathed deeply into her pastoral persona. "No, it isn't terrible, and it will become a memory that will evoke a lot of laughter. Today is going to be an amazing celebration of your love. The promises are real. The kiss is real. You will be surrounded by tenderness and love."

"Bellona is so upset. Maybe you should talk to her—"

"You can do this, Lara," Wanda replied. What she wanted to say was, *Not on your life will I have this conversation with your soon-to-be wife, the bane of three church committees!!*

"Are you sure?"

"Have a beautiful day!" Wanda chirped, then hung up, tossing the phone onto the bedside table. The nightmare headache was gone. Five June weddings, and the one that really reminded her what mattered was the one she didn't perform.

35

On Sunday afternoon, Rye decided she had better face the firing squad. She pulled up to Wanda's house with flowers from her own garden—not Hardy's, but the little plot she had started herself in the spring—and a small bowl of her preciously grown strawberries, along with whipped cream and Rye's special shortcake that even her father couldn't recreate.

She also had printed a photograph that Hardy had sent the previous week of Mickey, Rob, Stephen, and Lance. Blown up in glossy black and white, it looked as beautiful as anything a professional could have captured.

She knocked quietly on the door. In case no one was home, she had prepared a note and could leave her offerings on the porch. No such luck. She heard the dogs barking, and then Lance trying to push them away from the door as he struggled to open it without letting either one sneak out. Rye didn't have any hands to help, but she had been in this position enough times to know to use her leg to force the dogs back inside as she slipped in behind.

"You look nice," Rye said. Lance was dressed in clean khaki shorts and a polo shirt, his hair pulled back into a tidy bun.

"We had a wedding breakfast this morning after church," he said with a sigh, pulling at the neck of his shirt. "Not sure why we needed to have a second reception—" He trailed off as his mother swept into the room, looking elegant in cream linen pants and a rose-pink silk camisole. "Mom! I was just telling Rye what a beautiful second reception we had this morning!" Lance said, his tone chipper.

"I'm sure you were," Mickey replied, rolling her eyes. "You can get out of those clothes now if you want."

"Thank God," Lance muttered, already rushing for the stairs. The dogs, who had lain down for a moment, were up in a flash and following him up the stairs. The noise was, as usual, catastrophic, but it made Rye smile.

"He's such a good kid," she said.

Mickey was clearly appraising her. This wouldn't have been her first choice for meeting Wanda's sister. Although a shower had fixed her hair and Rye had French braided it to avoid any potential disasters from the predicted rain, she wore denim shorts and a blue V-neck tee. Next to Mickey, she felt severely underdressed.

"Winnie," Mickey called in a melodious voice that fell just on the wrong side of grating. "You have company."

Wanda came out of the kitchen wiping her hands on a towel, still dressed in what Rye thought of as her church clothes. She was followed by a man Rye presumed was the groom, and she smiled weakly at them, wishing her wrists weren't starting to hurt from the load she carried.

"Rye! Did I miss something? I wasn't expecting you, was I?" Wanda asked. "Today has been a bit chaotic, and I haven't looked at my calendar or my texts."

"No. I just dropped by to bring some gifts to you and the happy couple."

Rob was giving her a once-over that reminded Rye of her own father. She meekly followed the three of them into the kitchen, where Wanda took the flowers and placed them on the table.

"These flowers are beautiful," Mickey said. "What florist are they from?"

"I grew them," Rye said. She reached into her bag and pulled out the dessert she'd brought. "And these strawberries are from my garden. I tried to make clotted cream to go with this, but I couldn't get it right, so I brought fresh whipped cream instead."

"These are from Hardy's garden?" Wanda asked.

"I have my own little plot behind the barn," Rye replied. "It doesn't hold a candle to my dad's, but it's been a fun experiment for me." She pulled the last package out of her bag—the carefully wrapped frame— and handed it to Mickey. "I'm so sorry I missed your wedding yesterday."

"Oh yes," Mickey said. "The food poisoning is…all gone?" She looked like she might drop the gift if Rye replied in the negative.

"I actually just…" Rye took a deep breath and blew it out slowly. "I lay down after lunch and slept through my alarm. I was so mortified when my dad called that I lied and said I was sick."

To Rye's amazement, Wanda started to laugh. "Mickey, do you remember my high school graduation party? It was the same thing, except I'm pretty sure you were so hungover that you wouldn't have been able to stand up straight without a bowl in your arms." Wanda turned to Rye. "I love my sister, but the number of events she has missed—well, let's just say she shouldn't throw any stones."

Mickey sniffed. "I wasn't that bad."

"You were an hour late to Lance's baptism!" Wanda retorted.

"He was a baby! It's not like he knew the difference!"

"He wasn't the only person in attendance!" Wanda replied.

Mickey had finished unwrapping Rye's gift by that point, or the argument might have continued. She put a hand to her mouth. She turned to show it to Wanda and Rob.

Among the pedestrian shots of food, and flowers, and slightly awkward smiles that her father had sent, Rye had found a gorgeous shot of Mickey, Rob, Lance, and Stephen sitting together in Hardy's fully blooming rose garden. They were laughing, lifting their glasses to cheers, and the joy was palpable. When Rye had seen it, she immediately sent it out to be printed. She had even found a rose gold frame after Wanda had told her about the floral details for the wedding itself.

"Rye, that's incredible!" Wanda exclaimed.

Rye reached into the bag one last time and handed a smaller package to Wanda. Wanda looked at her questioningly, then began to unwrap it. Rob and Mickey were still exclaiming over their own gift and didn't seem to notice. In this frame was a photo taken in May of Wanda, Hardy, Lance, and Rye at the annual church picnic. It was a silly shot—Lance was pretending to strum a turkey leg, Wink and Figgy were jumping up trying to catch a taste, and Rye was giving Wanda bunny ears, but Hardy…Hardy was staring at Wanda with absolute adoration. It was a moment of intimacy that Lance's friend Leslie had caught on the fly. Rye didn't know what had prompted the girl to send it to her, but Rye had been grateful.

Wanda pulled Rye into a tight hug. "Thank you."

"I really am sorry I missed the wedding," Rye murmured.

"I had my hands full with everyone who did come," Wanda whispered. "And while I could have used your help with the stink bombs, Lance and Stephen stepped up admirably."

"It's our turn for a nap," Rob said, interrupting them. "But it was nice to finally meet you, Rye. We've heard so many stories."

"All disastrous, I'm sure."

Rob tapped the side of his nose and grinned at her. "I like to come to my own conclusions." He picked up the wrapping paper and tossed it in the trash as Mickey called to the boys that they were leaving. Wanda followed her out to assist in carrying packages to the car.

When they were alone in the kitchen, Rob turned back to Rye, his expression soft. "I was planning on not liking you, especially after yesterday. But the way Lance talks about you—it might not have fully convinced me, but his friends, too—they all love you."

"May I ask why you were determined not to like me?"

"Mickey knows Lance loves it here, but you and Wanda…you've been involved in some dangerous situations this year. It's hard for his mother to be so far away, knowing he could get hurt, or worse."

Rye opened her mouth to say that she and Wanda would never let Lance put himself in danger, and that the danger he had been in, he had thrust himself into without any sort of permission from them. Instead she nodded. "I understand. I also know that when Lance was living with Mickey, he was bouncing from school to school. He was hanging out with a…not great crowd, and he was taking care of his mother a lot more than he should have been. With Wanda, he's flourished. He wrote a play that was performed at a competition. He's made the honor roll every quarter, and he seems to actually enjoy spending time with my family, with a younger friend who needs a role model, and with Wanda. Lance is kind and creative and fun, and he has brought so much joy to all of our lives, and in return, Wanda, Hardy, and I have brought stability to his life."

"I agree that there have been a lot of benefits to his time here, but—"

"It's also given Mickey and you time as well," Rye interrupted, not wanting to hear where Rob might be going with his train of thought. "It's given Mickey and Stephen time to bond, and I think it's taken the pressure off of mother and son and allowed them to start to repair their relationship. I think Lance will have a wonderful senior year here, and I know he and Wanda want to come and stay with you in London for the holidays. That will give him time to explore England and make some decisions about his future, don't you think?"

Rob's expression had grown serious. "I do see a lot of your father in you. You have a way of saying things that makes it very hard to disagree."

"It's a skill I've honed my whole career," she said.

"You love Wanda very much, don't you?"

"I do," she agreed. "And it's important that I speak up for the people I care about, just in case they have a hard time doing it themselves."

Rye reached down and rubbed Figgy's ears. It was unusual for him to wander around without Lance. It was as if he sensed that whatever happened here might impact his beloved human's future.

"You're what I've heard referred to as a 'pit bull friend.' Loyal, but not without teeth."

Rye laughed with genuine humor. "Yeah, that's me."

"It's…refreshing, like ice in a beverage. I'm not used to the cold, but I could learn to enjoy it."

"I'm definitely an acquired taste."

Mickey called for Rob then, and he gave Rye a reserved smile and left her alone in the kitchen.

Rye sat down so that Figgy could put his head in her lap and get a proper ear scratch. "I don't know, my boy. If it comes down to it, will you help me barricade Lance's door?" Figaro looked up at her with his toothy doggy grin and woofed. The human decided to take that as a yes.

36

When Wanda returned to the kitchen a few minutes later, Rye had gotten two plates of strawberry shortcake ready. Daniel was with Wanda, and Lance and Stephen behind them, so Rye stopped making tea and started pulling out more plates. Lance moved to help her, picking up Wanda's favorite mug and putting it by her seat, and serving lemonade to the others, who didn't prefer hot drinks in the summer.

Figgy was alertly checking for crumbs under the table until Wink came in. Figgy immediately dropped down onto his dog bed and put his chin on the floor, watching as his alpha scouted the room. Lance gave both of them treats, and after everyone was settled, Wink joined Figgy for a nap.

"I didn't plan on having a confab this afternoon," Wanda said, licking whipped cream off her fork, "but since we're all here…"

"The sheriff's people have started asking me more questions," Daniel replied. "The shooting takes priority, of course, but they seem to believe there might be a connection."

"It probably has to do with the note I found yesterday at the church," Wanda replied. She showed them a photo. "Clearly someone does not want us investigating Jodi's death."

Rye pulled out a notebook where she had been jotting down notes on the case. "I have a rough timeline, starting with Jodi's brakes being cut and her death; then there was Noah Tesco getting swiped by that Suburban, which, if his friend Abbie is right, also made a second pass; someone going through Jodi's papers; the boys' fight; then the shooting of Wyatt."

"Didn't Noah tell you that Wyatt's father has been acting strange, too?" Wanda asked. "Not going to visit his son in the hospital is unusual. Though it's not impossible that he has some sort of phobia—I've certainly known plenty of people who feel sick at the idea of even entering the building."

"But to let that keep you from your son?" Lance asked. "I'm not an expert in detective work or good parenting, but that's extreme."

"It might not be the hospital—it might be the law enforcement presence," Rye replied. "Last I heard, Colin Eames hasn't given a statement."

"Was he there that night?" Wanda asked.

"His food truck was in the parking lot when Camila and I arrived to pick up Claudia, but he probably has a car," Rye said. "The deputies were rounding up everyone they could find, and I know they searched the apartments of the two victims. If Colin were hiding, they probably would have run across him."

"Unless he was at a neighbor's," Stephen pointed out. "The cops didn't have the right to search every apartment. People ran out to see what was happening.

They could have left their doors unlocked. He could have been hiding—anyone else could have been, too."

Daniel sighed. "And that area is heavily forested. It wouldn't be hard to disappear."

"What about the mechanics?" Lance asked. "You know, the women who kicked your butts?"

Rye's head was still tender. "Sam and Charlie? What about them?"

"I thought you said they lived at the Cedars," he replied.

"No, they have a little apartment above their shop," Rye corrected. "Sam's mother lives there, though, with Charlie's younger brothers. Sam offered to do the repairs on my car for free, but only after I mentioned that I thought her cousins might have been the culprits."

"Bribery," Stephen muttered.

Daniel nodded. "It could be."

"They must know something," Rye said. "Sam's mother told me that Jodi Franklin basically ruined Sam's chance to go to college. That's motive."

"But if Jodi's death is connected to the shooting…" Wanda paused, trying to collect her thoughts. "Was the shooting a warning? To silence anyone who knew anything? If so, it backfired. Now the authorities are more convinced that Jodi was murdered."

Rye nodded. "Noah's accident also seems more like a warning to me. It had the desired effect. He's refused to give any information about what happened. All the sheriff has is what Abbie said at the scene."

"If Jodi's death is tied in to the shooting, what was the motive for her death?" Stephen asked, rubbing his temples. "Someone wanted her dead, and either they wanted it to look like an accident or they got lucky and she put herself in the position to make it look that way."

"If Sam had nothing to do with it," Rye replied, "which we still don't know for sure, then Jodi knew something that we don't."

"It could have been a mistaken identity," Lance offered. "Jodi had dark hair, right? From behind, maybe she looked like someone else." He paused, clearly uncomfortable. "Claudia, for example, has been at the Cedars a lot. She has black hair, and they both have thin builds."

Wanda and Rye exchanged looks. "You're right. She has been there a lot, and there doesn't seem to be a girlfriend," Rye said. "And Thursday night, when Camila and I picked her up, she freaked out when she heard we were headed for the station." Rye pulled out her phone and showed them a photo. "Camila found a little bag of pills jammed down in the cracks of her back seat on Saturday morning. If she hadn't needed to install a car seat to give one of her nephews a ride, she might not have found it for a lot longer." She enlarged the picture to show them where the baggie had been found, stuck in the spot where the car seat would tether in. "I knew Claudia was struggling with her drinking, but I didn't know it was drugs, too."

"That's more pills than a person would buy for themselves," Daniel said, taking the phone. "It's more likely she's selling. Look, some of the pills are bagged individually."

"Camila told Ryan?" Wanda asked. Rye nodded. "Has Claudia been arrested?"

"The proof is circumstantial. Camila's sister-in-law grabbed the bag along with a bunch of other things from the back seat. Claudia's fingerprints are gone."

"Does Claudia know it's been found?" Daniel asked. "Because if she's selling, she can't afford to lose that stash. She might try to break into Camila's car to get the pills back." He looked grim. "If someone is expecting money from those sales, Camila could be in danger. Dealers can get desperate, especially if they're sampling their own product."

Rye hadn't thought of that. "I need to let her know." She noticed that Lance looked troubled. "What is it?" she asked him.

"Ms. Ramirez has been a good teacher this year. I know she's had a really tough time, but I never imagined...I don't know." He shook his head. "I guess I can see the erratic behavior. She was so helpful while my play was rehearsing, and when it was over, she boxed some of us out. We couldn't bring our lunches to the green room anymore because she was holding tutoring sessions—or at least that's what she said."

"She came back for the second semester part-time," Rye replied. "She didn't have enough hours to be tutoring on top of her classes."

"I thought it was weird because I saw some of the kids going in and out, and they weren't people I recognized from any of my classes in the department. We're a pretty close-knit group," Lance said. "These kids were more...sporty, I guess." His face lit up. "That's where I know that guy from!" He turned to Stephen. "Remember the guy who helped us out at the Cedars? I thought I recognized him from school, but I couldn't place him! He's, like, a coach or something."

"Mike Nifterick?" Rye asked.

Lance shrugged. "Maybe? I don't know his name. I just remembered his face." Rye scrolled through her photos and finally held up one she'd taken over winter break. "Yeah!" he said. "That's him!"

Rye showed the picture to Wanda, who shook her head, then to Daniel. "Mike and Jodi used to work together at Lincoln, and he told me they were still training together. I spoke to him about her death."

Daniel looked closely at the photo. "I've seen him, too. He's at the Cedars all the time. I thought he lived there."

"No," Rye said. "He has an apartment downtown."

"So two teachers—neither of whom live at the Cedars—now spend a lot of time visiting there? And have had private meetings with students outside of their department responsibilities?" Daniel shook his head. "That's definitely a red flag. Jodi could have known something about it. She knew both of them, right?"

"They'd all worked together at Lincoln," Rye confirmed. "I can't imagine Mike getting involved with drugs, or whatever Claudia is into. He talks all the time about keeping our bodies pure, and it seems like he's doing fine—he has a nice place, he's popular with the kids—"

"Maybe he's not involved," Stephen spoke up. "Maybe he and Jodi were working together, trying to figure out where the drugs were coming from and how to put a stop to it."

"That's a good point," Wanda replied. "We don't have enough information yet to go jumping to conclusions. Certainly not about Mike, and Claudia…She's a troubled woman. We can't rule out the possibility that she had purchased those pills to take herself." Wanda sighed. "Which is not great, but it would be better than finding out she was dealing drugs to students."

"I wish we knew what had been taken from my sister's apartment," Daniel said, clearly frustrated.

"Or what made her leave her apartment that night in the first place," Rye added.

Lance looked thoughtful. "You remember how when I first moved in, I asked if I could move my desk so that I was right by the window?" he asked.

"Sure." Wanda was trying without success to keep Figgy from crawling up into her lap, where he definitely did not fit.

Lance moved onto the floor so the big dog could flop over and get his belly scratched. "At first, it was just to have scenery to look at when I was bored—"

"But then those new neighbors moved in!" Wanda exclaimed. "Now it's like a soap opera every other day! You shouldn't be watching that!"

"Guess that means you *are* watching what I shouldn't be watching?"

"They don't seem to care about privacy," Wanda replied.

"Proves my point. Our neighbors aren't criminals, but maybe some of Jodi's neighbors are."

"You think this might have been a *Rear Window* situation?" Wanda asked.

"If she'd witnessed a murder, we probably would have heard about it by now, but drugs?" Daniel nodded. "I could see that."

"I have to go pick up my car tomorrow," Rye said. "Maybe I can talk to Charlie or Sam, find out if they know anything. I know they don't live there, but it doesn't mean they haven't heard things from Sam's mom or the boys. Madeline doesn't like me, but Sam and Charlie seem cool."

"I'll go with you," Daniel suggested.

"I don't think that's a good idea. They definitely don't like you."

"I could go," Stephen volunteered. "I promise you, no one ever feels threatened by me."

"Until you land a few punches," Lance replied. "Then they start taking you a lot more seriously!"

"There will be no need for punching," Rye said, "because I am going alone to have a polite chat." Daniel looked like he was going to object, but Rye didn't give him a chance. "I can't in good conscience send Lance and Stephen back to the Cedars, but Daniel, there's obviously something happening there. I was thinking you could move into Jodi's apartment so you can be there all the time without people getting suspicious. It would have to look legit, though."

"I have some boxes in my bedroom that have never been unpacked," Wanda offered.

The three men looked at her askance, but Rye nodded. "Me, too. Daniel, you could just grab those and do a couple of runs so people see you going up and down the stairs with them. Bring some clothes for yourself and set up shop. Maybe get to know your neighbors?"

"Technically her lease goes through the end of August, so I could do that," Daniel said.

"It might be dangerous," Rye cautioned. "In fact, I can almost guarantee that it's a terrible idea."

"Which is why you aren't sending the kids," Daniel replied. "This is my job, remember?"

"And we can't send anyone else without it looking suspicious. Rye and even Hardy are too well known around town to go undercover." Wanda sighed, looking unhappy. "But I don't love the idea of putting you into this position, Daniel."

He patted her hand. "I want to do it. You aren't forcing me into anything, I promise, unless your boxes are full of religious books."

Wanda shrugged. "I honestly have no idea! I haven't needed anything out of them in this long, though, so it's probably nothing too exciting."

"Will you keep us posted?" Lance asked.

"Sure," Daniel said.

Wanda brightened. "I'm going to meet those neighbors first."

"What? Why?" Rye asked.

"I am going to plan a memorial service for Jodi"— Daniel started to protest, and Wanda lifted a hand to forestall him—"because I have plenty of parishioners who would expect me to have a service for her. She was prickly sometimes, yes, but she was also brilliant and helpful to many people in the community."

"But what does that have to do with her neighbors?" Stephen asked.

"I'm going to canvas her neighbors at the Cedars asking for memories they have and letting them know they are welcome to attend." Wanda grinned. "People tend to let their guard down around me. They think I'm the same as a priest and that anything they tell me is automatically confidential. I don't feel the need to disabuse them of the notion if it helps our case."

"That's pretty clever," Stephen said. "And sneaky."

"If it gets us a few more leads, I say go for it," Daniel agreed.

Rye looked a little nervous. "Are you sure you want to do this? The Cedars has been a powder keg since Jodi's death. I don't want you in the middle of that."

She held up her scout's salute. "I promise I'll be careful."

Rye just glared at her. "That doesn't work on me. I know the Girl Scouts didn't want you!"

"Fine," Wanda said, holding up one of Figgy's paws. "I pup promise you I will be a humble servant of God, making every decision with prayerful consideration and using an abundance of caution."

Wink barked, just once, from his bed. "I agree with him," Rye said. "You are not to be trusted."

37

THERE HAD BEEN A DAY WHEN MICKEY PUT LANCE ON a cross-country flight to Massachusetts to arrive more or less unexpectedly at Wanda's door. Meanwhile, Mickey flew to Europe with a scam artist she was infatuated with. She had not asked Wanda's permission then. In fact, she had not even told Wanda that Lance was coming to stay until he was already in the air on the way to the East Coast. Mickey had been shocked when Wanda had needed her to arrange for high school admission, insurance forms and health data—shocked that sending a teenager to live with her sister would involve as much work as it did.

Mickey was a very different person than she had been a year ago. Wanda thought of her sister now as self-orbiting rather than self-centered, and she respected Mickey's efforts to change old habits. Wanda knew that she had not had a hand in Mickey's changes— but Mickey, without meaning to, had a major hand in Wanda's.

As different as her sister appeared to be, sitting at Wanda's kitchen table, chatting and laughing with her new husband, Wanda felt just as changed. Mickey had chosen a partner, stability, a lifestyle that was less show and more tell. Wanda had received chaos bundled in the form of one lanky adolescent.

She had lived her life cautiously, a little fearful about extending her heart after two divorces and many years alone, but now she sat surrounded by a "family" she adored. It was noisy. There were muddy paw prints on the floor, crumbs on every surface, and enough hoodies and sneakers scattered around on any given day to make it look like Wanda was hosting a youth group out of her living room. Which, to be fair, wasn't far from the truth.

And when Mickey announced, rather than asked, that Stephen would be staying for the summer to work with Lance at the funeral home and take some trips around New England, Wanda didn't even blink. At this point, one boy more or less in her home would not make a notable difference to her. Also, she had found out that as handy as Lance was in the kitchen, Stephen was equally talented with laundry. It meant that for the most part the scattered clothing smelled fresher than that of the average teen.

This morning, Rob had taken a play out of his wife's book and told them that Lance would be coming to stay with them for the winter holidays. Wanda watched her nephew out of the corner of her eye. He seemed pleased by the news, so she smiled.

"What about Aunt Wanda?" Lance asked.

"Two visits with my sister in a year?" Mickey pretended to ponder. "I do have a list of places I'd love to show you—"

"Don't say 'for shopping'!" Wanda said with a laugh. "I want a day in London, a day in Oxford or Cambridge, and I want to step foot in Scotland. The rest will be at your cozy home in Berwick-upon-Tweed!"

"Walking to Scotland from there wouldn't be a problem, but we're thinking of moving south. By the time you come, we plan to be much nearer London, and to where Stephen goes to school. You can help us find a new church! Wanda, you will have to stay for a month at least."

Mickey and Wanda hugged fiercely, and Rob gave her a friendly squeeze and whispered, "Don't let Hardy and Rye drag you into danger. Stay safe, for Lance."

"I will," she whispered. Behind her back, her fingers were crossed.

WANDA WAVED THEM OUT THE DOOR, PRAYING THEY wouldn't be late to their flight in rush-hour traffic. She drank another cup of coffee and thought about how she had discovered so much about being a sister in a visit not much longer than a week. At the same time, she had discovered how much she could be a parent even though she would never have the official title of "mother."

Back to the investigation. She got dressed in her casual clergy best. Talking with unchurched strangers was the only time she wore a collar. She needed instant trust when she knocked on doors at the Cedars. Her tab-collar blouse was light blue, and she paired it with a plaid skirt and a lightweight cardigan. Professional but not threatening.

First, she knocked on both boys' doors to remind them that they were due at Fairchild's at nine o'clock for an eleven o'clock funeral. Wanda gave more details to Lance. "Dogs need to be fed. Wink's been walked, but Figgy needs some exercise. I need to swing by the church office after I'm done at the Cedars, so I'll see you for supper—it's your night to cook!"

Wanda trusted that the groans emanating from their rooms were confirmation enough, but she smeared a finger's worth of peanut butter on her nephew's sock and let the dogs in as she headed out. It was always good to have insurance.

38

RYE DIDN'T HAVE TO BE AT HER FIRST MEETING UNTIL eleven, so she slept in before heading over to the garage to pick up her car. As a kid, she had taken the bus all the time. It was the only one in town, but still, they had one, and that was a point of pride to many. It did a loop around Stone Ridge, and although it wasn't always convenient to where Rye had needed to go, she'd enjoyed the independence it had given her as a teenager. The city had only raised the bus fare once, from fifty cents to a dollar fifty. There was such an outcry over it that they'd backed down to a dollar, and a dollar it had stayed. With a student or senior ID, the bus was free, so when Rye got on at nine thirty, there were only a few seats left.

She plopped down next to a woman who looked vaguely familiar, although she was too old to be the parent of a student. Rye spent the next ten minutes being reminded that Shelley was an usher at Wanda's church, and about the few times Shelley had seen Rye at church, and the many times she hadn't, and wasn't it nice that Rye's father was there so many Sundays? This last bit was news to Rye.

When she excused herself to get off the bus a few blocks from her destination, Rye had to promise to make it to the service on Sunday. She knew Shelley would be watching for her. She'd love to see the expression on her father's face if she asked for a ride to church with him.

When she arrived at the shop, there were a few people in line ahead of her. She had spotted Charlie and another woman in the bay as she walked in, but Sam hadn't noticed Rye yet. The window had already been replaced. If Rye hadn't been in the middle of it, she wouldn't have known a fight took place. Everything was spotless.

The last time she'd been in, Rye hadn't noticed all the photos on the wall, stuck up on a bulletin board next to advertisements for motor oil and windshield wiper fluid. The picture that caught her eye first was one of Sam in her graduation robe. Rye had worn the same style back in her day, and a few weeks ago she had applauded as the graduates crossed the stage in them—white for the girls, purple for the boys.

Sam looked happy, arms wrapped around her mother, both women beaming for the camera. Sam held her diploma up with great pride. It must have been a momentous occasion, only sullied by the fact that Sam's college dreams had been taken from her by Jodi Franklin.

Rye looked up as the bell on the door rang. She was alone with Sam, who was writing up a receipt. "Car's ready out front," Sam said without looking up. "Once you're done spying on me, I can get you the keys."

"I was just looking at your graduation photo. You look really happy with your mom." Rye didn't mean anything by it. She certainly wasn't expecting the slight crack in her voice. Her own mother had disappeared long before high school, and of course her father had been there, just as giddy with pride as Sam's mother.

Sam walked over and studied the picture. She pointed to another with her mother. The two of them were standing right outside in the parking lot. Sam was smiling, but her mother looked serious. "That was a week later, when I officially took over the shop. I've been working here since I was fourteen, but when the scholarship fell through, I decided I would rather start here full-time than go into debt. My mother didn't want that for me, but she handed over the keys. Told me that Charlie and I were ready to handle the shop by ourselves."

"So she doesn't own the shop anymore?" Rye was surprised. It had sounded like Madeline still needed the money to raise her nephews.

"She owns a third of it," Sam said with a shrug. "Doesn't do much anymore, although when we're busy, like recently, she'll take over at the desk while I help Charlie in the bay."

"Is it the pre-vacation rush?" Rye asked.

"What do you mean?"

"You said you were busy. Don't people usually come in at the beginning of the summer to get a tune-up, fluids checked, that sort of thing?" Rye had learned to repair a lot on her own car in high school under her father's tutelage, although the bodywork her car had required this year was beyond her abilities.

"No, mostly catalytic converter cages or replacements," Sam replied. "Theft has gone up again. We had about a month or two in the winter where we were hardly seeing anyone for replacements. Business was pretty slow, actually, and then all of a sudden it seemed like half of our appointments were covering one of those two repairs. It's a huge national crime trend, which people unfortunately don't know about."

"Good for business, I guess," Rye said. Her father had pointed out the story in the paper last week, and Rye had made sure Sam added a cage on her car while it was in.

"The replacements, sure. The cages themselves are pretty cheap if you want to install yourself," Sam replied. She quirked an eyebrow. "You owe me three hundred fifty for yours." Rye handed over her card. "I mean, I feel bad for people, but, like I said, the cage is cheap compared to putting a new converter in. Seems like more folks would want to do it, but I think they all have that 'it won't happen to me' mentality."

"Until it does."

"Exactly. Then they come in here complaining about how expensive the replacement is with the labor. I just tell them they can call around. We have the best prices."

"I saw that you offer classes." Rye tucked her card back into her wallet. "Why teach people how to fix their own cars? Doesn't that cut down on business?"

"We teach girls and women how to do some simple fixes. We don't make much off of the people coming in to get their oil checked or wipers changed out. If women want to come here to learn from us rather than look it up on YouTube for free, all the better. They bring their cars back here when they need a bigger repair because they know us. That's what Charlie is doing right now." She nodded toward the bay.

"They have reason to like you." Sam really had started to grow on Rye. She had a good head for business.

"And they trust that we're telling them what's wrong with the vehicle without selling them a half dozen other add-ons at the same time. I like repeat business. I like customers who hear about us from their friends. This is a small town, and whatever you may think of me and Charlie, we're a part of the community. We like it here."

"Why do you think I don't like you?" Rye asked.

"Because of what happened with Ms. Franklin's brakes," Sam replied in a matter-of-fact tone. "You know what's funny? I liked her. I know she's not—she wasn't—popular, but she was smart. In her class, she wasn't afraid to get into ideas that were usually just brushed aside."

"Even after she ruined your chance at getting the scholarship?" Rye asked. "I'd be upset—more than upset—if someone had stolen my chance to get out of here."

Sam laughed. "That's the thing, though. I never dreamed of getting out. That's what my mom wanted for me, but I love it here. I have my family, my friends, and I love this corner. It was a little embarrassing, yes, but Mom continuously complaining—that's the worst. Besides, I'm taking some classes at UMass Lowell in the fall."

Rye was impressed. She spent a lot of time talking with juniors, seniors, and their parents about after—high school plans, and few were as pragmatic and happy as Sam seemed to be.

"My mom built this place, and then she gave it to me. There's nothing I could've learned at school that would mean more to me than that. And I *am* going to give her a university graduation to attend. It may take six or seven years, but that's okay." Sam leaned toward Rye and lowered her voice. "I was actually a little grateful to Jodi Franklin. It meant I never had to tell Mom I didn't want to leave."

"But Jodi's brakes—"

"Someone messed with them, for sure, but it wasn't me, and Charlie knows how I feel. She wouldn't risk this place when she knows I wasn't even upset about what happened."

Rye picked up her keys from where Sam had placed them on the counter. "Thanks. And for what it's worth, I'm sorry for your loss. I've had a couple teachers like Jodi Franklin, and I sometimes feel like they're still keeping an eye on me, making sure I keep my nose clean."

Sam laughed. "If this is you keeping your nose clean, I think we're all lucky those teachers are keeping you in check!"

39

Wanda had been to the Cedars in the past, visiting parishioners and "friends." More than a hundred people, many of whom lived in the area, frequented the weekly free supper at Trinity Church. There were four menus for the month—chicken pot pie, chili (replaced by hamburgers in the summer), pasta and sauce with meatballs, and tuna casserole. All menus were soft for those with few teeth. Guests were "friends" if they chose not to go to church and parishioners if they did. Wanda visited and checked in on members of both groups when she learned there were illnesses or special concerns.

The fourth floor of the Cedars was where older folks preferred to move, avoiding the noise of families and the music of young adults. No one was home in the endcap apartment, but across the hall from Jodi's place was a surprise.

"Pastor Wanda, come in! What brings you here?"

"Martha, lovely to see you!" Martha Snider organized Trinity's weekly suppers. She was healthy as a horse, so Wanda had never had cause to visit her at home, even though the woman must be close to eighty. Martha owned aprons with every kind of bird possible. Today she was modeling one that read "Honkers" across the top and had a variety of geese painted underneath. Wanda wasn't sure whether Martha was in on the joke or not, but it made her smile. It didn't hurt that the apartment smelled of chocolate chip cookies fresh out of the oven.

"I'm getting some dessert ready for tomorrow. Would you like to taste test the cookies?"

"If you twist my arm!" Wanda said, laughing.

Martha went into the tiny kitchen to get a plate, a small glass of milk, and a warm cookie. She said something, her back turned to Wanda.

"I'm sorry. What did you say?"

"What brings you here?" Martha repeated, turning to face Wanda.

"I'm helping to plan a memorial service for Jodi Franklin. I'm looking for folks who would like to share an anecdote about her or tell me a story that I can share. I didn't realize you two were neighbors."

"Jodi was my fish sticks lady. Every month she would bring me enough boxes to feed those who don't care for the tuna casserole. Tuna casserole is easy to make but a dated taste. I usually had enough fish sticks still frozen I could also send some home with families who would need another dinner. I don't know what I'll do now. I can't afford to buy them myself, but people have come to rely on them."

"I didn't know she was so generous."

"She was a very private person. She and I got into plenty of disagreements, let me tell you! She was stubborn as a mule, that one, and thought she knew everything, as though I wasn't old enough to be her mother!" Martha shook her head. "But she had a good heart. People didn't know that about her, and I'm sorry for it now. She deserved recognition for all the little kindnesses she did."

"I'll be sure to mention it at her service," Wanda replied. "But also it's enough that you knew and appreciated her so much."

"It made up for how nosy she was," Martha declared, standing up as her timer went off. She pulled another batch of cookies out. "Mark my words—people will start to notice now that she's gone. No new books in the little library outside Trinity. Fewer donations brought to the food kitchen. They might not know why things are a little worse, but they will be."

"It sounds like she did a lot for the community without needing any recognition."

"Oh, yes," Martha agreed. "She even paid the electricity bill for the girl at the other end of the hall. But do you know how she found out about the overdue notice? She would go through any mail that was left on that little table downstairs. Plenty of people leave things there, too—bills they can't pay, notices of eviction. If we got to talking, Jodi would tell me about all of them." She popped another tray of cookies in. "She could spill the tea, as the young folk say. I wish I could do more, but if I get to chatting, I'll lose track of what I'm doing here."

Wanda nodded, guessing it was dismissal. "Thanks for your time, Martha. When Jodi's brother decides on a date for the service, I'll be sure to let you know."

"You do that," Martha replied. "I have plenty I could stand up and share!" She said something else, but her back was to Wanda again, and she didn't catch it. Wanda gave the older woman a gentle hug. She gladly accepted a baggy with two more cookies inside and promised that she would try to find a person to help with fish sticks.

In the hallway, she turned her hearing aids up as high as she could. She was failing to understand people, and that was the most important thing in the world. Be a detective? She might not even be able to be a pastor if this kept progressing.

No. That was just the ableism demon that had somehow jumped off the pages of her old ministry textbooks and lodged inside her brain. She could still do this, but maybe Lance and Stephen were right. Maybe she needed to start making some changes.

The next stop was Jodi's next-door neighbor. Wanda knocked and waited, then knocked again. A loud, disgruntled voice shouted, "I'm coming. Better be worth my time."

Oh, dear. Wanda plastered on an exceedingly pleasant smile.

Too pleasant. The opened door was almost shut in her face. "I don't want to buy anything or get the *Watchtower*!" The loud voice of a very tall thin man using a walker went right over her head.

"I'm not selling anything. I'm Reverend Wanda Duff from Trinity Church, and"—she put her hand out to stop the door from hitting her in the nose—"I wanted to talk to you about Jodi Franklin, if you have a minute?"

The man was still eyeing her suspiciously, but he didn't attempt to lock her out, so she continued. "Jodi's brother, Daniel, would like to plan a memorial service, but he doesn't know any of Jodi's friends. I told him I would ask her neighbors if they had any stories to share, either in person at the service or to me."

His face brightened, and Wanda was hopeful he would be able to tell her something she didn't know, but he turned and shuffled backward on the walker, grabbed a paper bag, and shuffled back. "Here, you take this. It's her mail. I always used to pick it up for her when she was away, and so I just kept on doing it." He handed Wanda a little mail key from the hook beside the door. "This is hers. I went in and got it after I heard about the accident." He took a moment to study the other keys, then pulled one down and gave it to her. "I suppose I won't need her house key anymore either. But I'm keeping the magazines. She always let me have them after she was done reading, and, well, she's done reading now, isn't she?"

"Oh, well, yes, I suppose so." Wanda looked in the bag.

"That big envelope in there? She sent that to herself. She was always doing that when she went on vacation. She liked to pack light, you know, so she didn't have room for souvenirs. She would mail herself little packages. I told her she should save herself the money and buy a bigger suitcase, but she never listened to me. I don't know where this last one is from. She hasn't gone away for a while."

"It sounds like you knew Jodi pretty well, then?"

"Not really." He paused. "Well, not by choice. She would bring dinner sometimes. I never asked for that, mind you."

Wanda could see behind him into the apartment. It was as sparse as many nursing home rooms she'd visited, and she hoped someone besides Jodi checked on this man every once in a while. "Maybe she was lonely," Wanda suggested. Maybe Jodi knew this man was, too.

"Well, she certainly never had any gentleman callers, if you know what I mean. Our bedrooms are back-to-back, and I never heard any funny business going on." Again, he paused. "Except the day she died, of course. People were banging around in there. I woke up, and it sounded like somebody was slamming doors. I didn't know she'd passed at that point, of course."

"What time do you usually go to bed?" Wanda asked.

He raised his eyebrows at her. "At my age? Whenever the mood strikes, but that day I remember it was early. I had a cold, and Jodi had brought me some soup for dinner around four. Not that I asked for it, but she said she heard me coughing. Always in my business, that one."

"Do you happen to remember what time you woke up from the noise?"

"Why? Is that important for your service?" This man was sharper than Wanda had given him credit for.

"I was just curious. Her brother said her apartment was a mess when he first went in."

"Jodi's apartment? A mess?" He let out a wheezy laugh that turned into a cough. "Never in my life did I see a hair out of place! She had the ADD, you know." He nodded sagely.

"Could you mean…OCD?" Wanda asked after a moment.

"That's it. I know she must have. She would come and tidy my place, too, not that there's much to do, but she would wash my sheets and towels, that sort of thing."

"If you don't mind my asking, do you have anyone else who looks in on you? We have a group of people at Trinity who love to stop in and visit." She held up a hand, seeing he was about to protest. "It's not a religious thing. Many people in the group are lonely, like Jodi was, and it gives them something to do. They might bring cookies sometimes, or books from the library, if you enjoy that sort of thing?"

He harrumphed. "I don't need looking after, if that's what you think."

"Not at all," Wanda replied. "You would be doing them a favor."

"Cookies, you said?"

"All sorts of baked goods, and if you have a favorite, some of them are happy to make something new."

He was hooked. "Fine. I'll give you my name and number. You make sure they call first, though?"

"Of course," Wanda said, taking a little notebook and a pen out of her purse. "I'll be sure to tell them you enjoy magazines, too. I know plenty of people have no idea what to do with issues once they've been read. If you want them, you'll have plenty to choose from."

He handed back the notebook where he'd scrawled *Dave Greenwald 555-618-9000* in shaky handwriting.

"Do you have email as well, or do you prefer to be reached by phone?"

"How old do you think I am?" he asked. "Of course I have email, but I hate to check it. They can call."

Wanda smiled. "It was lovely to meet you, Mr. Greenwald."

He started to shut the door, then pulled it back a few inches. "How will I know when Jodi's service is?"

"I can call and let you know if you'd like."

Dave Greenwald let out another wheezy laugh. "You do that."

WANDA STRUCK OUT AT THE NEXT TWO APARTMENTS. When she reached the last door on the right, her knock produced a little scuffle, and a woman in her early seventies opened the door, dressed for going out.

"Come in, come in, you'll let the boys out!"

Wanda let herself be swept in and the door shut hard behind her. The "boys" were kittens, and Wanda was quickly introduced to Hobbes and Tigger. The woman was short enough that she looked five-foot-one Wanda in the eye, with short light brown hair streaked with white. She politely unbuttoned her coat and sat down in a chair, gesturing to the matching sofa. Wanda was quick with her prepared speech about Jodi.

The other woman introduced herself as Carrie Smith, a retired business teacher from Lincoln High. "I used to teach typing and shorthand, but by the time I retired I was teaching word processing and office technologies. I'd already been there fifteen years when Jodi arrived. She didn't socialize much, but she was never rude. And when she heard I was looking for a more affordable apartment for my retirement, she put in a good word for me. I really appreciated that."

Wanda nodded. All the neighbors seemed to agree about Jodi's character.

"She loved charity runs, and she knew so much about each charity that it made it almost impossible not to sponsor her! She loved the run but believed in the causes. I think that was easier for her than relating to people." Carrie looked embarrassed. "You know, we live on the same hall and go to the same gym, but it was a week before I realized she was the one who had died! I don't get the paper anymore—too depressing—and I just figured it was one of the young men downstairs. We have a few troublemakers. A teacher can always spot them, you know."

"A minister, too," Wanda agreed.

"I heard about it when I went to get dinner from Colin's truck. Have you tried it? The food is great, and he's just about one of my best friends these days. His son is in the hospital after that horrible shooting. Thank goodness I was visiting my brother when that happened."

"I have to admit I haven't tried the food from Dad Yolks yet. Is it worth it on a pastor's budget?"

Carrie laughed. "I may be biased. I hate cooking, and I can't stomach those microwave meals. I eat a salad for lunch, and most nights I get dinner down there."

Wanda took a swing. "You must miss him. I'm sure he's been at the hospital with his son the last few days."

Carrie gathered her purse and stood. "I hope you catch Jodi's killer, dear."

Wanda was startled. "What?"

"How many clergy detectives do you think we have in this town?" Carrie pushed her glasses down her nose and studied Wanda the way she must have done to many a fibbing student. "I know all about you—just hadn't had a chance to put a face to the name."

"I really am planning a service for Jodi—"

Carrie waved a hand. "I know you are. And I know that you know Colin Eames is missing. I don't know where he is, and I hope to God he had nothing to do with anything that's been happening around here. He's a good man and a good father. I know him well enough to say that." She frowned. "But I also know that even good men get desperate sometimes. Even they have to protect their families by doing things they never dreamed they would have to do."

"Was Colin doing something like that?"

"I really don't know," Carrie replied. "I just know that the last few months, it's been…worse around here. My car got broken into, and someone stole the catalytic converter off it. I'm not the only one, either." She tapped the side of her nose. "Jodi was one of my few friends around here without fur, and I'll miss her, but I can't say I'm surprised."

"What do you mean?"

Carrie led Wanda to the door. "Have you been to the apartment at the end yet?"

"No, not yet."

"Come on." She took Wanda down the hall and knocked on the last door, then shouted through it. "Jewel, this lady, Wanda, is my friend. You can talk to her."

And then Carrie was gone. Wanda wanted to ask her what she'd meant when she said she wasn't surprised, but the door opened, and a young blond woman was standing there. Wanda immediately noticed the woman was missing her two front teeth. She had a little boy attached to one leg and a baby, maybe five or six months old, wrapped against her chest.

"I'm Jewel Fisher," she said. "Won't you come in and sit a while?"

Jewel swept toys off the chair that wasn't covered in laundry in the process of being folded. "I'm just going to turn on *Daniel Tiger*."

Wanda squatted down—she would never tell Hardy how grateful she was for his insistence on squats in her workouts, but it sure helped right now—and waved at the boy. "I'm Wanda."

His lip quivered, and he grabbed his mother again, almost pulled her over as she tried to set up an old laptop for him.

"This is Texarkana. Say hi, Tex."

"Hi, Tex," Wanda parroted in a silly voice.

The boy straightened. "No! I say it! Hi, Tex!" He jumped on the couch, knocking over several piles of laundry.

Jewel swore quietly, then covered her mouth. "Sorry! I just got those folded." She sighed and put the laptop in front of her son.

"I live with a teenage boy. I promise you I have seen way more laundry and heard much worse words," Wanda replied. Jewel smiled tentatively. "I love your son's name. It's beautiful. Is it a family name?"

"I named him after where I was living when my boyfriend got me pregnant."

"Texas side or Arkansas?"

A real smile this time. "Texas. Have you been?"

"Years ago, my first husband and I drove through on our honeymoon. It's a big change living here, I would imagine."

"You can say that again." Jewel bounced the baby. "This is as far away as I could afford to get. I had Missy here at the Stone Ridge hospital. Do you know Martha Snider? She helped arrange housing for me."

"Martha is a member of my church," Wanda said. "She's a wonderful woman. In fact"—she reached into her pocket and pulled out the cookies—"I just saw her a few minutes ago, and she asked me to give these to you."

Tex's face lit up when he saw what Wanda had. "Cookies!"

"One for you and one for your mama!" Wanda replied.

"She must be baking for spaghetti night tomorrow," Jewel said.

Wanda reflected that there were a lot of connections on the floor, and that was probably true of the rest of the Cedars. It was like a little village. "I've been knocking on doors because I'm helping Daniel Franklin to organize a memorial service for his sister, Jodi."

Jewel stroked Missy's hair. "Jodi Franklin saved my life. I hope whoever killed her gets life in jail."

"You don't think it was an accident?"

"Heck no! Some people around here thought Jodi was a snitch, but she was a good woman. A couple of weeks ago, my no-good sister told Tex's dad where I was. He drove all the way up here and did this." She pointed at her teeth. "Now I need to get some sort of partial denture. Jodi was helping me with that, too." She looked like she might cry. "Anyway, he came up here and found me at work. I work at the Shaw's Market, you know, and he went through the whole place looking for me. We had it out, and he hit me right in front of everybody. Jodi helped me get a restraining order, and she told me the judge won't let him have custody, since he's been in jail a bunch of times."

"That must have been scary."

Jewel shrugged. Wanda expected this wasn't the first time something like this had happened to the woman, but it might have been the first time someone stood up for her. "Jodi was always helping me. She said she thought I could get my GED when the kids are a little bigger. She was going to help me study for it." Now Jewel did start to cry. "She bought me diapers and formula when I came up short. Not just once, either. Whenever I needed it."

"There's no replacing someone like that," Wanda said gently. "Jodi was one of a kind."

"I'm not the only mom she was helping either, I don't think. She reported some people, and I know they weren't happy about it—not even the mothers, because they said now they can't make rent."

"It sounds like Jodi really knew what was happening around here."

"Most of us think she found out something somebody didn't want her to know," Jewel replied. "Don't go telling the police, though. If people knew I said something, we'd have to get out of here quick."

"All I heard you say is that you want folks at the memorial service to know that Jodi Franklin looked out for people, especially women and kids who were down on their luck."

Jewel looked at Wanda for a long time and then broke eye contact and nodded. "I don't know what I'll do without her."

"I'll be at our community meal tomorrow night. If you're coming, I can connect you with some other people there who could help."

"I'm not religious, though."

"I told Mr. Greenwald in 4C the same thing—it doesn't matter one bit. The people I'm talking about are the kind who have extra love to give. They like to bring a meal or watch some babies for a few hours while you go out. They'll drive you to appointments if you need that, and just keep you company if you get lonely." Wanda shrugged. "They've saved my life a couple of times this last year."

Jewel thanked her, and Wanda left, hoping she would be able to connect a few of these neighbors who had depended so much on Jodi's kindness.

Generous with causes and fish sticks, a focus on helping endangered women or children, and known to be into people's business—Jodi had a lot more going on in her life than her brother had known. Wanda wondered if the sheriff's office knew all of this, too. Did they realize Jodi was the kind of woman who might run down the stairs to help a person in a domestic dispute?

Wanda had a lot of information that she needed to share, but she was going to see what Jodi had mailed herself first, right after she made her final visit of the day with Madeline Gayle.

Hardy was waiting for her when she got home. Wanda blurted out everything. Maybe it was pride, but mostly it was to stop playing detective and go back to wedding plans…at least until Mickey and Rob left town. Hardy took the envelope and, without opening it, said, "This goes to Ryan. Whatever it is, you don't want to know it."

BY THE TIME RYE GOT BACK FROM THE DISTRICT office on Tuesday evening, she was more than ready for the run she'd scheduled with Camila and Ryan. She was changing into shorts and a T-shirt when her phone dinged.

> Change of plans. Wedding stuff. Want to join?

The message was from Camila.

> Pretty sure your mother would hate that.

Rye sent her reply as she went to answer the knock at the door. Ryan stood there, earbuds in and already sweating.

> Ryan just arrived. Want me to send him?

> No. Meet later?

> Definitely.

Rye tucked her phone into her armband. "Hey. Camila says she has wedding stuff to do."

"Okay," Ryan replied, stepping past her to fill his water bottle up.

"Did you run here?" Rye glanced out into the driveway for Ryan's car.

"Yeah. Tyler and I were hauling some beams in his truck earlier, and he needed to use my car tonight." Ryan splashed some water on his face. "It's hot as Hades out there, too. You ready to sweat?"

"After the day I've had, I'm ready."

They headed out on the old cart road that ran behind her dad's property. She nodded her head at an almost hidden break in the path, and Ryan followed her up the first steep incline. He had an advantage, since his legs were already warmed up, but Rye had run these roads since she was a kid, and her legs adjusted to his pace soon enough.

"Bad day?" Ryan asked as they reached the top and started a long decline into farmland owned by one of Hardy's neighbors.

"Just long."

Ryan chose that moment to peel off his T-shirt and stick it into the waistband of his shorts. If there was one thing Rye could say for sure, it was that Ryan managed to look better now than he had as a young deputy—which, she realized, was the last time she had seen him so relaxed.

She stared resolutely ahead. "Where are you on the shooting?"

"You know I can't discuss an open case."

"Can you at least tell me if you think it was connected to Jodi Franklin's death?"

"Not really, no."

Rye sighed. "Not really because it's not connected, or not really because it is, and you can't tell me?"

"What do you think?" Ryan accelerated as they neared the bottom of the hill.

"Daniel says you've been talking to him again. You wouldn't do that if you didn't suspect that there might be a connection." Rye intentionally pulled back her pace when they hit the uphill, and after a minute Ryan fell back and joined her.

"What else did he tell you?"

"He's going to move into Jodi's apartment until her lease is up so he can keep an eye on things."

"What's he looking for?"

"What did he tell you when you questioned him?"

Ryan started to increase the pace again until neither of them could easily speak. When they reached the top of the hill, they were both gasping. Ryan held up his hand to call for a stop.

"Why won't you help me out?" she asked. "You don't want to investigate Jodi's death. I do. You have a much more important shooting to deal with, and I don't want to touch that."

"This isn't a negotiation," he replied, wiping his face with his shirt. "You want to come work for me? Take the proper steps."

As Ryan well knew, she had attended the police academy in Texas during her gap year before college. When she decided to get her master's in education instead, she'd put aside any thought of joining the police force, and she certainly wasn't going to be calling Ryan Phennen "boss" anytime soon. "I just want to help Daniel get closure. If it was an accident, fine. But I want to be sure."

"I hear that, but I can't give you anything."

Rye turned and started walking back the way they'd come as the first big drops of rain began to fall. "Fine."

"Are you pouting now because I'm doing my job?"

"When it rains, this road is the first thing to wash out. I don't want to be knee-deep in mud." She bit her lip. "Can you tell me about the catalytic converter thefts at the Cedars, at least? When I picked up my car, Sam mentioned it."

"We have someone working on that."

The rain had started to come down harder, and already the path was too slick to run on without risking injury. "From that neighborhood, or in general?"

"From the Cedars. Two buildings, twenty-four apartments each. Nothing that wasn't in the paper." Suddenly Ryan grabbed Rye's arm as he went down hard. Rye might have been able to catch him, but he'd slipped on the steepest part of the hill, and they slid the rest of the way down in a tangle of limbs and curses.

When they stopped, both lay there panting as the rain soaked them. Rye pushed herself up. She waited for Ryan to pop up next to her. When he didn't, she looked down and realized there was blood mixing into the mud around him.

"What happened?" She scanned his body for injuries.

Ryan slowly rolled over and showed her his back, sliced up by rocks. Rye didn't have a scratch. He must have been holding her more tightly against him than she'd noticed.

"Can you stand up?"

"I think so," he said with a groan, rolling over onto his stomach. He pressed himself to hands and knees, then rose shakily to his feet.

Rye slipped her arm around his waist. They still had a long walk home. Even if she called for assistance, there was no way to get a car along this path. Ryan winced but put more of his weight against her as they started to move slowly. After a few minutes, he started shivering, the rain cooling them both quickly. Rye wracked her brain for something to distract him.

"Do you think Camila's wedding duties would have been more fun than this?" she asked.

Ryan let out a rough chuckle. "Have you met her mother?"

"She is not in my fan club."

"Or mine." He winced as they started to climb the last hill back to the main path. "I've had dinner with them a few times. They love Tyler, which is great."

"Who doesn't? He's basically a golden retriever puppy."

"As opposed to me?"

"Canine, yes, different litter," Rye said. "You're more of an Irish wolfhound. A bit of an acquired taste, but loyal." She thought about this as they walked under the trees that lined the main cart road, remembering that an Irish wolfhound had saved her and Wanda's lives the autumn before.

Ryan broke into her thoughts. "So what about you?"

"An Akita," Rye replied without hesitation.

"Oh, yeah?"

"They're known for their strong-willed and independent nature. Bred to be guard dogs, but they're not aggressive by nature. Just…wary."

Rye felt rather than heard the rumble of his laughter. "That sounds right. Courageous, too, I've heard."

"Now you're a dog expert?" They were almost home, but she could feel him flagging.

"I had an Akita when I was a kid," Ryan said. "Before Tyler was born, before my mom was strung out. My dad bought her for my ninth birthday."

"I thought he wasn't in the picture."

Ryan shook his head. "He drove long-distance hauls. He liked the open road a lot more than he did having a family. But when he'd come home, if my mom didn't immediately throw him out, he'd usually bring some sort of extravagant gift for us. That year, it was Evita."

"You named your dog Evita?"

"No, she came with the name. Never would answer to anything else. Like you said, strong-willed." Ryan winced as he slipped, and Rye tightened her grip to keep him from falling again. "After my mom got…sick, my dad came back and took Evita. Said we couldn't take care of her."

"How old were you?"

"Thirteen. Almost fourteen. That was my birthday gift that year. No more dog."

Ryan had survived so much. He'd taken care of his brother after their mother died, lived in a car, gotten his GED, and then gone to the police academy. Rye was certain the day he lost his dog was the official end of Ryan Phennen's childhood.

"I'm not sure Tyler even remembers, or if he does, maybe he thinks Evita died. I don't know." Ryan paused. "Tyler's the reason I made it through. He has this warmth that draws you in even when it feels like there's nothing left." He started hobbling toward Rye's front door. "So it's okay with me that Ana loves him, that everyone loves him, because he saved me when I had nothing left."

Rye got out her first aid supplies while Ryan took a shower. She heard the water turn off and went to the bathroom door. "I forgot to tell you that spare towels are under the sink."

"I used yours" came Ryan's response.

"You better not have bled all over it," she teased.

The door opened, and Ryan emerged wrapped in her green-and-white-striped bathrobe. It barely fit. Rye made sure to avert her eyes as she handed him some clothing she'd grabbed from her father's dresser. Ryan took it and retreated into the bathroom. When he opened the door again, he wore athletic shorts and a black rec league T-shirt.

"Why did you put the shirt on before I had time to check your back?" Rye asked. "I have to make sure I didn't miss any debris and then bandage it."

"It's fine."

Rye sighed. "Take. Off. Your. Shirt."

"I thought that was my line," Camila said from the doorway. She was dressed in a black linen mini dress that looked the worse for wear after the storm.

Rye tugged on the bottom of his shirt until Ryan started wiggling out of it. Blood was already causing the fabric to stick to his wound.

"I thought you had dinner with your family after the walk-through," Ryan said, his voice muffled through the fabric.

"Rye texted me. Also, it was a wedding counseling session for the whole family with Wanda and Father Paul. I did not mind missing out on dinner after that get-together, trust me."

Rye checked to make sure she hadn't missed any gravel, then slathered on Bacitracin and covered the worst cuts with waterproof wound dresings. "This should protect it as long as you don't pull any stupid cop tricks."

Ryan rotated his shoulders gently and winced. "I doubt I'll be getting into anything too dramatic for a day or two."

Camila rolled her eyes. "Sure, buddy. Just a day's rest is all you need."

"Who said anything about rest? I have an open investigation into a shooting. I'll be lucky if I make it home to sleep." Ryan was trying to maneuver the shirt back on, but it took so long that Rye threw it in the general direction of the laundry basket and traded it for an old button-up he didn't have to pull over his head.

"How did that interview go?" Camila asked as she helped Rye set the table for a quick meal. "Ryan interviewed Noah Tesco's girlfriend. It's Abbie…something. Ana had her in class."

"I can't talk about an ongoing investigation," Ryan said, scooping up some curry that Rye had microwaved for them.

"Apparently Abbie saw everything," Camila continued, ignoring him. "Ana saw her at the store the other day and asked if Noah was doing better. Abbie just broke down."

"Camila—" Ryan tried to interject.

"She was so freaked out by the whole thing, because she thought she recognized the guy driving, but then Noah told her she didn't."

"How would Noah know what she saw?" Rye asked.

"That's the thing—Abbie told Ana that she *did* know the guy but that Noah told her not to tell anyone because she was wrong. But at the time she hadn't even described him. So he must know who the driver was, too."

Rye stopped spooning rice onto her plate. "Wanda agrees that Noah is afraid. If he knows who hit him, or Abbie thinks she knows but he doesn't want her to name him, it has to be because Noah doesn't think catching one person will make any difference."

"Except to put a target on his back," Ryan added. "I thought Abbie would tell us, and she hasn't. I think she wants to, but—" Suddenly he realized he was confirming all Camila's conjectures. He rubbed his forehead like he had an awful headache.

"But if Noah's right, then keeping quiet is the safest thing to do, at least according to teenage logic," Rye finished.

"So Noah and Abbie know who killed Jodi Franklin and just won't tell the sheriff?" Camila asked. "Noah's been attacked once, and his best friend was shot!"

Rye shook her head. "The person who hit Noah might not be the killer. He might be part of a larger organization—one that Noah, at least, recognizes." She ticked off this possibility on her index finger. "Or one person could have killed Jodi, another hit Noah, and a third shot up the Cedars and nearly killed Wyatt." Another finger. She looked at Ryan, but he wouldn't meet her eyes. "You aren't looking for a murderer. You're trying to bring down something bigger."

"The drugs we found?" Camila asked.

"What about all of those stolen catalytic converters?" Rye mused. "Could it be both? No. That doesn't make any sense."

"Two separate problems!" Camila replied. "No wonder you're not getting any traction. There are too many distractions."

Ryan stood up abruptly. "I need to get back to work. Camila, are you giving me a ride, or should I call someone?"

"I can bring her home later if you think you're okay to drive," Rye said.

"I'm fine." He held out his hand, and Camila tossed him the keys.

"Don't do anything I wouldn't do," Rye said as he turned to leave.

"There's something you wouldn't do?" was the last thing they heard before he hobbled out the door, pulling it behind him. The dramatic gesture was diminished when Ryan caught it before it slammed, allowing it to close silently behind him.

41

WANDA CALLED A MEETING IN HER OFFICE AT THE church after Wednesday Bible Study. Hardy and Rye, Lance and Stephen, Daniel, and Martha Snider. After she had done introductions, she began. "We need to talk about what's going on at the Cedars. I asked Camila to come as well, but she needed to be with her family. She gave me an important clue, though, and I think it's a good place to start."

"Not with a prayer?" Martha asked.

The rest of the group looked uncomfortable, but Wanda was game. "God, help us to understand the pieces of this mystery so we can stop any further harm to this community. Thank you for Jodi's witness. Please be with Wyatt's medical team. Help us to find Colin. Help us figure out who killed Jodi and who is pulling the strings and stop them. Amen." She straightened. "What kind of a place is the Cedars?"

"It's a community," Martha answered. "People take care of one another."

"Maybe once, but now it's a last resort for housing, full of drug addicts and petty criminals," said Daniel.

"Martha, have you noticed that more people have been hanging around outside the buildings? People who aren't residents of the Cedars, I mean?" Wanda asked.

"There have always been kids out there, playing on the lawn or on the basketball court. We got a new hoop installed this spring, and that's been popular. There are some new boys who moved in with their aunt last year—I see them on the stoop all the time."

"Madeline Gayle's nephews?" Rye asked.

Martha shrugged. "I'm not sure. I introduced myself, but they just mumbled something and walked off."

"What about adults?" Wanda asked.

"Oh, yes. The food truck has been very popular. Colin Eames runs that, you know. I think a lot more families come down to get dinner, and then I see people chatting. A lot of men, which is nice to see, but most of them don't live here. You hear about the male loneliness epidemic, and it's good to see them out there having a good time. It gets a little loud sometimes, but I'm a deep sleeper. My across-the-stairwell neighbor, Dave? He sleeps terribly, and he's told me he can hear them sometimes until two or three in the morning, if you can believe it. He said he's seen plenty of fights at night, too."

"Have you noticed more visitors?" Wanda asked.

Martha nodded. "I chalk that up to the truck being here just about every evening. People love a food truck, and there aren't many around town."

"Claudia's been going there a lot, and she's vegan," Rye said. "So she isn't going for the food. She claims she knows people at the Cedars, but she's never given me any names."

"Plus Camila found those pills in her car after you drove Claudia to the station," Hardy pointed out. "This 'friend' could be her supplier, and she could be selling as well."

"So there are residents and outsiders," Wanda said. "But this isn't the only place in town to hang out, so what makes it special?"

"Privacy," Daniel suggested. "It's on a dead-end road surrounded by undeveloped forested land."

"And the neighbors are tight-lipped, especially with law enforcement," Rye added.

"It's ideal for drugs," Daniel said. "I hate to burst Martha's bubble, but those 'friends' you've seen outside are definitely dealing. I suspect they're moving drugs and cash through the food truck."

"I don't think Colin would do that," Martha protested.

"He might be under pressure to help," Hardy said, laying a hand gently on Martha's arm. "This is all supposition, but it is a good guess. There isn't much regulation of those trucks. They don't tend to pass through weigh stations, and a lot of cash moves through for regular sales. Maybe he was asked to 'help' once, took money for it, and now he can't get out."

"Maybe the shooting was a warning," Lance mused. "If Wyatt was targeted, someone could be sending a message to his father because Colin was trying to back out."

"But who, and why?" Wanda asked.

"It could be whoever's in charge," Hardy replied. "It could be a rival dealer. Maybe Colin's 'boss' encroached on someone else's territory, or maybe someone else wants to move in on his."

"Or maybe whoever killed Jodi is warning witnesses to keep quiet," Rye pointed out. "Although, in doing so, they're drawing a lot more attention to the Cedars than they planned."

"Which means they're getting desperate," Hardy said. "And should be considered extremely dangerous."

"When Camila and I were talking last night, we realized that there might be another factor muddying the waters," Rye said.

"The catalytic convertors?" Wanda suggested.

"Yes. The number of thefts at the Cedars is almost comically high," Rye confirmed. "Sam said business is booming, and most of her customers are coming in to get a cage or a new converter."

"Do you think she could have something to do with it?" Hardy asked.

"Sam? Not after talking to her, no. But her male cousins? Maybe. I may have no proof that they defaced my car and stole my tires, but I don't know of any other student who could pull that off in such a small window of time without getting caught."

"Two young men at the Cedars have been 'warned' through physical assaults, and a woman has been killed," Wanda said. "Rye's car got almost destroyed right in the high school parking lot."

"Lance and Stephen were assaulted, too," Hardy pointed out.

"That was just over some girls, though," Lance said. "Those guys were being jerks."

"But when that teacher—what's his name, Nifterick? When he got involved, they backed off," Stephen replied. "I don't know about here in the States, but most guys my age don't care what some teacher tells them to do at school, much less anywhere else."

"Mike Nifterick?" Martha asked. "I know him. He used to work with Jodi and our neighbor Carrie. He's come around a lot recently, now that you mention it. I know he and Jodi were doing some training for her

Grand Canyon trip, but once she passed, I figured I wouldn't see him again."

"Why did he come to the Cedars instead of Jodi meeting him at the school track?" Rye asked.

"Well, I've heard that there are some paths in the woods behind our buildings. Maybe they were using those? I don't really know, but he started coming a few months ago, and they would go off for an hour or two. I think things were a bit tight for him, because he started staying for dinner with Jodi," Martha said thoughtfully. "She loved to cook—not like me, for a hundred people at a time—but new recipes. She mentioned something about his position at work getting reduced. But I've seen him at the food truck the last few weeks, and it's not the cheapest, so maybe he got a second job."

Wanda glanced at Rye, who shook her head slightly. Mike's position at the school had been cut to part-time, but she hadn't heard anything about him getting other work. "I hate to suggest it, but is it possible he's started hanging out with some of Claudia's…friends?"

Rye nodded grimly. "I was thinking the same thing."

"Also, if he's been in Jodi's apartment, he could have seen what *she'd* been seeing," Daniel said. "All he would have to do is glance out of either one of her windows, and he'd know she had a view of everything happening at the Cedars."

"And if she were taking notes and left them out by mistake one day," Wanda replied, "he might know exactly what she suspected."

"We can't jump to conclusions," Hardy said. "We should share all this with the sheriff's people and see what they do with it."

"Probably nothing," Daniel muttered.

"Investigations like this take time," Hardy said. "I know it's frustrating, but this requires a delicate touch."

"I know," Daniel replied. "I'm just…I'm frustrated."

"What are you doing for dinner?" Martha asked him, reaching out and taking his hand. "We have our spaghetti supper, open to the community, and I could use a hand pulling it together. Jodi would sometimes fill in if another volunteer couldn't make it."

"I don't know. I have a few loose ends I was going to take care of—"

"Later," Martha said. "For now, give me a hand. I can tell you some stories about your sister that will curl your toes! She could be a real hoot sometimes!"

"Lance and Stephen promised to help me out in the garden," Hardy added. "Part of their community service for sneaking around the Cedars last week."

"I need to get going, too," Rye said. "Wanda, let's meet for breakfast tomorrow, and then we can go to the station, okay?"

Wanda felt like she should go to the station now, while it was all fresh in her brain, but the dogs needed to be walked, and she had a bulletin to write, not to speak of a wedding to polish. "That sounds good. Harvey's scones can fortify us for the road ahead."

42

AFTER RYE'S FAVORITE DEFAULT DINNER OF TEXAS spicy chili, from-scratch cornbread, and mint frosted brownies, Ryan and Camila had fallen asleep on the couch watching *Adventures in Babysitting*, one of Rye's favorite old movies. She finished cleaning up the kitchen and was about to wake them when she got a text from Wanda.

> Are Lance and Stephen still with Hardy?

Rye typed back quickly.

> I haven't seen them. Why?

The phone rang. Rye hurried outside. She pulled the door closed behind her and answered the call. "I had dinner plans tonight. I didn't check to see if the boys stayed to have dinner with my dad."

"Can you check?"

Rye was already jogging across the lawn toward her father's house. The door wasn't locked, which wasn't unusual, but the porch light wasn't on, which was. She hurried to the kitchen. It looked like there had been dinner, but everything was in disarray now.

"Wanda, they may have been here, but something's happened." She left the kitchen—food on the counter and at least one broken plate on the floor,—and hurried upstairs, turning on lights and calling for her father. Nothing. Rye ran back downstairs and out onto the porch. Hardy's car was in the driveway.

"Dad's car is here, but not Lance's. There's a mess in the kitchen. Is there anywhere else the boys might have gone?"

Wanda was in full-blown panic mode. "They would have texted."

"Use Find My Phone," Rye replied as she banged into her house.

Ryan sat up at once, already alert. Camila was groggier. Rye explained as quickly as she could, leading them across the way to Hardy's house. Now that she was looking, she saw tire tracks next to her father's car. Could be from Lance's car. It was hard to tell.

"I'm going to try to call my dad," Rye told Wanda. "Are you okay to drive?"

"I don't know."

Rye knew her friend still struggled with memories of a car crash she'd been in during their first case. "Sit tight. I'm coming to get you."

She hung up and called her father, once, twice. Straight to voicemail. Ryan was on the phone with someone, and Camila gestured to Rye to step back into the kitchen. On the edge of the table, there was a dark spot. Dried blood. It wasn't a lot. It could have come from the same accident that had caused a plate to fall and break into pieces at their feet.

Ryan started pushing them both back out the door. He took his mouth away from the phone. "In case this is a crime scene, I want you out of here."

"I need to go get Wanda anyway," Rye said.

She grabbed her keys and locked her door. Camila followed her across the yard. "I'm coming with you."

"You sure?"

"You're not coming straight back here with Wanda, are you?"

"What makes you say that?"

"Your father, Lance, and Stephen are missing. There's no way you're coming home to twiddle your thumbs."

They got into the car, and Rye pulled out, turning the wipers on as the rain picked up. She grabbed a hoodie from the back seat and gave it to Camila to pull over her T-shirt. "I want to check in with Daniel. I tried calling him after my dad, and there was no answer."

Camila was quiet for a few minutes as Rye navigated through the quiet streets. "Ana's pregnant."

Rye had been slowing for a stop sign, and now she slammed on the brakes. "What? That's amazing!" She looked at Camila's face. "It is, right?"

"She told our parents tonight. It didn't go well."

"But your parents love kids. How many grandchildren do they have already to moon over?"

"Ana and Tyler aren't married yet. My parents are…conservative about that sort of thing, especially my father."

"They live together," Rye pointed out.

"My parents didn't know that either. I thought Ana told them, but no. My father thinks they should call off the wedding. He says he won't pay for it, and he wants to go home."

"But Ana and Tyler will make amazing parents! He wants to throw away his relationship with them over a timeline?"

"He's humiliated. Ana told everyone—our whole family—so there's no way to spin it."

They pulled up in front of Wanda's house, and Rye texted that she was there. "How do you feel about it?"

Camila stared out at the rain. "I'm happy for her…and also, I don't think I want to have kids, which means this is always something that will be between us. Neither of us will fully understand the other's life after this."

"Are you kidding? Have you seen Wanda with Lance?"

"What do you mean?"

"Someday you might be that kid's everything," Rye said. "And even if you're not—even if Ana and Tyler parent more perfectly than any parents ever have—they will never be able to replace the very distinct love their child will have for you."

"But Ana—"

"—will never stop being your twin sister. You didn't really believe you would have symmetrical lives, did you?"

"No, of course not."

Rye reached out and squeezed Camila's hand. "This is a new twist, that's all."

"I know you're right, it's just…it's harder than I thought it would be."

"I know," Rye said. "And I've got you, okay?"

Camila gave her a look that Rye interpreted to mean, *Your track record isn't exactly spotless.* She was right. And also, she was wrong.

Wanda hurried out her front door down the ramp. "We need to go to the Cedars," she said as she buckled up.

"That's the plan," Rye replied, and put the car in drive. She didn't add that the location was as far as she'd gotten in the plan.

43

By the time the women reached the Cedars, the rain had passed, and the stars were out. Rye wanted to head straight to Daniel's apartment. The chance that the boys and Hardy were there was slim but not impossible. Wanda offered to speak to Madeline, since she hadn't been home when Wanda had visited the other day. She could use that as an opportunity to check out the second floor for any sign of the men. Rye knew Wanda had been training in self-defense for months, but she was glad when Camila opted to follow the older woman downstairs.

When Rye reached the fourth floor and Daniel's door, she could hear laughter inside. Not teenagers, though— it was a woman's voice she heard, and one she recognized. Rye knocked twice, then paused, then twice again. She and Daniel had arranged the signal more as a joke than anything else, but now she was glad they had it. After a minute, she heard footsteps, and he opened the door. He looked different. It took Rye a moment to realize that was because he was smiling. She hadn't seen him look even close to carefree since they'd met, but when the smell reached her, she realized why.

Claudia sat on the couch, curled up around a purple bong that Rye had seen in the other woman's apartment. The air was thick with incense and pot smoke, and Rye coughed. The contact high from that room would knock her out.

"Rye!" Daniel exclaimed, reaching out and giving her a hug. "Why didn't you tell me you were coming? I would have ordered enough food for you to join us."

Rye glanced behind him. On the table, there were enough containers of takeout Indian to feed the whole floor of this building. "I'm looking for Lance and Stephen. Have you seen them?"

Claudia had wandered over, and although Rye knew from her red-rimmed eyes that she was high, she also knew Claudia got high often enough that it didn't dull her senses as much as most—as much as Daniel, to be sure. Claudia leaned in and gave Rye a kiss on the cheek, which Rye instinctively pulled away from. Claudia turned to Daniel with a smirk. "She doesn't like to party."

"This is more of a memorial," Daniel replied, trying to pull Rye into the room. "Did you know Claudia was one of Jodi's students?"

"One of her colleagues, you mean?" Rye held her hand up to her nose. She was starting to feel a little dizzy from the fumes.

"No, she showed me a picture! She was in one of Jodi's classes!" He turned to Claudia. "Where was that photo? On your phone, right?"

Rye didn't have time to react as Claudia brought a lamp from the end table beside her up and swung it at Daniel's head. He ducked, but it grazed him, and he lost his balance, going down like a sack of bricks. Claudia shoved past Rye and tore down the stairs. Rye bent to check Daniel, but he was already struggling to get up. She raced after Claudia. By the time she made it down to the ground floor, there was no sign of the woman.

Rye took the stairs back up two at a time, careful to watch for any signs of movement, but the building was eerily silent tonight. Slightly out of breath, she sent a voice text to Camila and Wanda to give them a brief update, then hurried down the hall to check on Daniel. He was gone, with broken shards of lamp to show where he'd fallen.

Now that some of the smoke had dissipated, Rye could see that there were papers strewn around the apartment. The window was open, and the wind took another pile from the desk as Rye watched, blowing its contents everywhere. She didn't want to call out for Daniel or alert anyone else that she was around, so she eased inside, checking the little kitchen and bathroom first.

Rye heard a sound from the bedroom. It was soft, and if the building hadn't been so still, she might not have heard it. She glanced around. The only makeshift weapon she could find was a dirty frying pan on the stove. She grabbed it and crept toward the door. She heard the sound once more. As she reached for the handle, the door flew open, and Daniel staggered out, holding a hand to the spot on his temple where a goose egg was forming. In one hand, he raised a gun at the same time Rye raised the pan. They froze in an almost comical tableau, staring at each other. "Did you catch her?" Daniel holstered his gun.

"She got away while I was checking to be sure you weren't dead."

"If I'd been dead, it wouldn't have mattered if you'd checked on me," he muttered. Daniel turned and spoke in his normal voice. "Boys!"

Lance popped out of the closet, and Stephen shook dirty clothes off himself. He had literally been disguised as a chair, and Rye hadn't noticed. "When Daniel heard Claudia knock, he told us to hide in here, just in case. Chair is my go-to disguise."

"You didn't answer our texts," Rye said, relief filling her chest.

"They were on silent—not even vibrate, in case we tipped her off," Lance replied.

"I couldn't move," Stephen said by way of explanation.

Rye spared a moment to hug each of them. "I think you'd better stay here. Lock the door behind us and then stay in the bedroom. Don't go near the windows or turn on any light until we come back for you, okay?"

Stephen and Lance nodded, and Daniel took the lead as they exited the apartment. The hall was empty. Rye realized she was still carrying the pan. Oh well, it would be better than nothing, she supposed, as she followed him down the stairs.

"Should you be operating a firearm while you're high?" she asked softly as they crept along, listening at each door.

Daniel pulled at what Rye thought was a septum piercing and showed her a little white device. "I have allergies, so I use these nose filters a lot. Doesn't keep it all out, but it helps. Also I provided the baggie, and it was a weak strain."

"It smelled dank."

"I didn't say it was a good bag of weed, did I? It's what the high school students sell to each other here. Not the good stuff their parents buy."

"You've seen kids selling since you moved in?"

"Before that. Since the first time I came to go through Jodi's things. They're not exactly subtle," Daniel said. "I've watched Colin Eames pull up every night—well, until the shooting—and every night there was a constant flow of people, including your girl, Claudia. I went down and got some dinner tonight. The food was fine, but nothing that should attract that kind of crowd."

"It's definitely a front, then?"

"No doubt," Daniel said grimly. "And if I figured it out in just a few days, there's no way my sister didn't."

"But she didn't have proof?" Rye held up her hand as she spotted Camila flattened against the wall. They could hear Wanda's voice. Wanda came out, saying goodbye to Madeline. Rye glanced back at Daniel, but his gun had disappeared, and she was left standing with a frying pan.

"Madeline, hi!" Rye said, trying to keep her voice normal. "Good to see you."

"Is it?" the older woman asked.

"Of course." Rye tried unsuccessfully to hide the pan behind her back. Daniel and Camila had vanished around the corner. She gave Wanda a look that she hoped communicated urgency.

"Oh, good, Rye. You found that pan you lent your friend?"

"Yes," Rye said after too long a pause. "I didn't even ask her to wash it." Rye said, trying to sound like carrying around greasy pans was something she did every day.

"Madeline, again, I so appreciate your willingness to help with the fish sticks for the Community Supper," Wanda said. "I'll tell Martha Snider. I know she'll be grateful."

When the door closed, Wanda turned to Rye and spoke loudly. "I'm glad you got my call. Thanks for the ride home." After walking twenty feet, the pleasant pastor's face was gone. "Hardy's in there."

Rye froze. "What do you mean?"

"Madeline's nephews and an older man are in that apartment. The old guy is armed, revolver in his pants pocket, it seemed to me, and something bigger under his arm. Madeline seemed a little afraid of him." Wanda took a shaky breath. "She let me come right in, though. I talked to her about lending a hand with the church supper. I laid on my admiration for Sam, too—I hope you don't mind that I threw you under the bus."

"Get to the part about my dad."

"At first, I thought I was hearing the pipes, but then I remembered Hardy taught me about this knock he used once when he…never mind. A story for another time. Anyway, it's subtle, and the sequence is long to make it less noticeable. He played it for me on the piano a few times, though, and it stuck with me. It started about a minute after I got inside and only stopped when one of them got up and went into the bedroom." She looked around Rye. "Where's our backup?"

Rye stared at her. "We are the backup."

"You didn't call Ryan?"

"When was I supposed to do that? Before or after Claudia hit Daniel on the head and ran off?"

"What?" Wanda's voice was strangled. "We're alone?"

"The boys are upstairs. They were with Daniel but hid in his bedroom when Claudia arrived. They were coming after Hardy to help him but couldn't get out with Claudia there."

Rye was already dialing. "No answer from Ryan. I'll try Tyler." She waited for a minute, then hung up. Her phone buzzed, and she answered it. "Ana? Yeah. Yeah. Okay. Yeah. Can you keep calling for me? Tell them…yeah. Okay." Her expression was bleak. "A fuel truck overturned on Route 3, right at the entrance on Oak."

"Oak's the only road that cuts down here," Wanda said.

"There's no way for cars to get in or out right now," Rye confirmed. "And apparently all units were called to deal with it. Multiple vehicles were involved in the accident. It's stopping traffic in both directions. Sounds bad."

"We need a plan," Wanda said. "If no one is coming to save us, it had better be a good one."

MICKEY WAS GOING TO KILL HER, WANDA THOUGHT AS they retreated to Daniel's apartment. Wanda had promised she would not let the boys get into any trouble. She didn't know what had happened at the house, but Hardy had been brought here, and Lance and Stephen managed to follow him. She knew it would definitely qualify as trouble.

A part of her was frozen in fear, but she had years of practice pushing that aside. She'd had too many parishioners who needed mental health intervention or who had been accused of spousal abuse banging on her door wanting to "explain." Over the last year, Wanda had gone to therapy and self-defense classes so that she wouldn't have to feel helpless when situations got out of hand, but this was testing the limits of her new education. If anything happened to Hardy, she didn't know if she could handle it. And that made her...angry.

Daniel and Camila were in the apartment when Rye and Wanda got upstairs. Wanda ferociously hugged the boys while they tried to formulate a plan to rescue Hardy that wouldn't involve anyone getting shot. Daniel wanted to storm the place, but Rye pointed out that between the four of them they had one gun to however many might be in Madeline's apartment, and that was a sure way for people to die.

She wanted to wait until the middle of the night and break in without engaging in a standoff. Safer, but impractical, since anyone holding a hostage—especially a hostage like Hardy Rye—would have someone armed awake. And if that person was one Madeline's nephews, foolish and potentially drunk, there could be trigger-happy behavior.

Camila thought they should wait for help, but Rye pointed out that any sign of the cops could escalate the situation quickly, even if they got the message and came on foot.

Wanda had been pacing back and forth, trying to come up with an idea that didn't involve her getting shot while rushing into the apartment. It had all begun with looking out the window, and so she paused there, allowing the breeze to cool her. Later she might have called it a Breath of God, but at the moment, all she said was, "Sam!"

"You think Sam's involved?" Rye asked.

"Sam and Charlie are outside playing basketball. They definitely weren't in the apartment earlier," Wanda replied. "But they could get us into the apartment if we come up with a good reason."

"They could still be involved," Daniel said. "They seemed like the violent types to me."

"I'm pretty sure you seemed the violent type to them," Rye replied.

Wanda ignored Daniel and looked at Rye and Camila. "Look, ladies, I've seen Camila on the court. Here's my idea, but fifteen minutes is all you have."

45

"ARE YOU SURE YOU'RE OKAY WITH THIS?" RYE ASKED Camila as they headed down to the basketball court. "It would be fine if you wanted to stay upstairs—"

"And let you try to impress them with your basketball skills?" Camilla snorted. "We want this to be believable, right?"

Rye just shook her head and led them out onto the court where the younger women were playing. "Hey, Sam! I thought that was you."

Sam looked up and waved. Charlie kept sinking baskets without acknowledging them. "Want to play Horse?" Camila asked Charlie.

Charlie looked her up and down appraisingly, clearly enjoying the view. Rye pushed down a wave of jealousy because they had a job to do. All the better if Charlie was distracted.

"Sure," Charlie agreed, spinning the ball on her finger, then throwing it up and swishing it without looking. She bounced the ball to Camila, who took the same shot, although without the practiced ease of her competitor. "You want in, Sam?"

"Nah," her cousin said, grabbing a seat on the bench at the edge of the court. "I'm beat."

"Mind if I sit?" Rye asked.

Sam waved an arm toward the splintery wood. "It's all yours."

"Thanks. Is your cousin any good?"

"Is your girlfriend?"

"She's not my—" Rye started to say, then stopped herself. "Yeah, she's pretty good," she said instead.

"Winner gets a round of drinks," Sam called to the two women on the court. Rye could not believe her luck. She'd thought she would have to twist Sam's arm to convince her to bet on the match.

After ten minutes back and forth, Rye was starting to question that luck. Charlie and Camila were too well matched. Both women missed four shots each, but only by grudging degrees, and Rye was losing hope. At this rate, they'd be head-to-head until the sun came up. Then Charlie nearly pulled off an impossible shot. She'd been dribbling down the court toward one basket when, without stopping, she'd popped the ball over her head toward the basket behind her. It was close, too—the ball sang along the rim before slipping out—and Rye heard Charlie swear. To win, Camila only needed to make the shot. She was good, but this was a Hail Mary.

If there was another round, Rye would crawl out of her skin. The kind of person who could get the jump on Hardy Rye was not some run-of-the-mill thug. It would have to have been someone Hardy knew—someone he would have invited inside while the boys were finishing the garden chores. Someone like Mike Nifterick. Mike had been to Hardy's after Rye and Wanda's first case. He would know the house. Rye didn't want to consider it, but she couldn't think of a better person for the job.

Unless it had been Claudia, but Rye didn't think her ex had the physicality needed to threaten and overpower Hardy.

She focused on Camila, holding her breath as her friend started to lope down the court. At the far end, she let the ball fly. All four turned to watch it catch the rim and drop gracefully through the net. They all cheered, caught up in the moment.

"Thank God," Sam said, stretching. "I'm ready for that drink. Do you guys know the Thirsty Tortuga? It's a bit of a drive, but we love it! Key West themed, and the drinks are cheap."

"You didn't hear?" Camila pushed her hair off her neck. "A tanker turned over up the road. No one's getting in or out of here until the accident is cleared up."

"Daniel just moved into Jodi's place, and his fridge is bare, or I'd offer to grab us a few beers," Rye said.

"No." Sam waved the suggestion away. "We made a deal. My mom has probably got a bottle of wine she'd give us, if that's okay?"

"I thought your mom was busy tonight," Charlie said. "Some book club or something?"

"My mom hasn't read a book since I learned to read Dr. Seuss to myself," Sam retorted. "I'm sure she won't care if we pop in for a minute."

Charlie held up her hands. "You tell her it was your idea."

"I don't know why you think my mom hates you," Sam replied as they headed to the first-floor apartment.

"Because she thinks I'm trash and drag you down." Charlie was straightforward.

"Hates me, too," Rye added. "But she likes Camila, so we can just take cover behind these two." Not literally, she hoped, as Sam pushed open the door.

"Hey, Mom, we're just grabbing a bottle of—" Sam stopped as they took in the scene before them. Madeline was awkwardly holding a gun on Daniel, and Wanda stood with her hands raised. Charlie's brothers were on alert behind Daniel. An older man, heavily muscled and armed, swung his gun toward the newcomers. Wanda took advantage of the distraction, ducking sideways and bringing her arm down hard on the wrist of the boy closest to her. Madeline and the stranger swung in her direction, giving Daniel an opportunity to slam his hip against the older woman. A shot went off wide as the sole gunman swung his weapon back and forth.

The door to the bedroom burst open, and Hardy charged out, arms and legs untied, holding what looked like a silver jewelry tray in front of him. It deflected a bullet, but the second shot caught him on the upper arm. Rye screamed and without thinking threw herself at the stranger who'd shot her father, smashing his hand over and over against the old metal radiator until he dropped the gun.

Wanda grabbed for it, but the man was faster, getting his fingers on it just in time for Rye to land a blow to his kidney. He screamed and jerked, shooting again, this time into his own foot. He dropped the gun as he fell forward, and Wanda retrieved it. She threw herself into the bedroom, where Rye could hear her calling dispatch, yelling that they'd better drive an ambulance over a few lawns if the road was blocked, because they needed to get here now.

Daniel and Madeline had taken their fight into the hall. Rye glanced at Camila, who knelt on one of the boys' backs. The younger two stood back against the fridge, hands up.

A roll of duct tape had been left on the windowsill near where Hardy was standing, and Rye could see from her father's wrists that it had been used on him. Keeping her knee jammed into the shooter's back, she gestured, and he tossed it to her. She lashed the duct tape around her captive's arms and feet, ignoring his screams about his own gunshot wound. Tempted to kick his foot for good measure, she refrained with effort.

"Dad? Are you okay?" Rye kept her voice even as she moved beside him. He'd pushed himself up against the wall and was holding his hand over the wound. Blood was seeping out, but it seemed to have slowed.

"Flesh wound," he muttered. "I'm fine. Help Daniel."

Rye stood. Wanda nodded and knelt beside Hardy to wait for Ryan and his deputies, the gun trained on the two teens in case they decided to try something stupid.

Outside the apartment door, Sam was screaming at her mother to stop, but Charlie held her cousin back. The commotion had caused doors to open, then close again just as quickly when people saw Madeline had a gun that she clearly didn't know how to use. She let off a wild shot, but Daniel dropped flat. Charlie caught the bullet in the arm she was holding around Sam and was thrown into the wall. Sam grabbed her cousin to try to hold her up, crying. In the commotion, Madeline let off another, this one pinging the metal railing on the stairs.

Rye followed the sound, and she saw Claudia standing there, looking down as blood spilled from her thigh. Claudia started laughing then, even as she crumpled and slid down two steps. Her laughter was shrill and hysterical as she pressed the papers in her hand against her leg. Madeline pointed the gun at Daniel, and Rye felt more than heard herself scream when she pulled the trigger.

Nothing. The chamber was spent. Madeline stared at it as if she wondered how it had gotten in her hand. She dropped the gun, looking as though she was coming back to herself, but Rye was already in motion. She plowed into Madeline, pushing her over the railing into the bushes below.

There was a brief silence, and then Madeline started yelling. Daniel limped past Rye and Claudia in a daze, his own gun drawn, and surrendered to the squad cars that began to stream into the parking lot. Sam was half dragging her injured cousin toward the sound of sirens.

Rye knelt down beside Claudia, afraid to touch her in case the fall had damaged her spine. "How bad is it?"

Claudia's hysterical laughter had subsided into groans, and her face was streaked with tears. "Everywhere," she whispered. "It's bad everywhere." She put her hand up to her heart, fingers covered in sticky blood.

Rye held her hands over the wound in the thigh and applied pressure. If it had been an artery, Claudia would be gone. As it was, she was losing blood, but it wasn't gushing. Rye didn't know if the medics had arrived or, if they had, how they would triage Charlie, Madeline, Hardy, and Claudia. So many people needed help, but right now, she just focused on keeping her hands in place.

"I killed her, you know," Claudia croaked. "Jodi Franklin."

Rye froze. "What?"

She waved the bloody sheet of paper in Rye's face, but Rye couldn't take it without moving her hands. "I could have grabbed her, maybe pulled her back." Claudia spasmed from the pain, and it took a minute before she could speak again. "But she ruined my life twice. Once when I was a senior and she failed me like she failed

Sam, and then later…It was worse when we worked together at Lincoln. I thought we might be friends. I have a trans brother, and she has a trans brother. We could talk about it. But she didn't want anything to do with me. I'd listen to all of her little jabs, and I had to take it because she knew things…"

"So you came to Stoneridge," Rye filled in, with a sick feeling at how sloppy school hiring could be.

"I couldn't stand seeing her smug face every day." Claudia growled as Rye pushed down a little harder on the wound. "And then I found out she and Mike were friends, so I still had to see her. I told him…I told him not to hang around with her. That she would figure out what was going on."

"That you and Mike were dealing?"

"When my friend told me I could get what I like cheaper here from Colin's truck, I started hanging out. I got an offer to sell a little on the side. Nothing big. Just enough to cover the therapy bills."

"Jodi wasn't stupid," Rye replied. "She figured it out."

"She told Mike she had evidence! She had pictures of me buying drugs! That she would get me fired, get the truck shut down. She didn't know how much further this all goes."

Rye felt more blood seep through her fingers.

"It wasn't like I was a criminal. Mike took advantage of the situation when he found out what I was doing. He needed the money and asked me to hook him up, to help him get product." She shook her head. "He didn't want to sell to kids, though. I told him my dealer wouldn't need him, but Mike got the mothers here eating out of his hands. Then he started taking it to gyms where he was teaching kickboxing, kettlebells, and Boot Camp."

"Did Jodi know about what Mike was doing?" Rye asked.

"I don't think so. She was trying to convince Mike to help Colin get out of this mess, so probably not."

"Help Colin get out of what?"

"She wanted Colin to escape the people he owed money to. That's why Colin was dealing. He could take his family and get out of here. She said Wyatt would get hurt if Colin let them keep using the truck to move product."

"She was right," Rye said softly.

"But Colin knew, same as I do, that they would kill him if he tried to leave."

Rye tried to press. "Who would?"

Claudia just shook her head. "They'll kill me." Tears were streaming down her face, but Rye wasn't sure if they were fear or pain.

"Did Jodi know who these guys were, too?" Rye thought of the envelope Wanda had given the sheriff. Hardy had talked her out of opening it. Maybe her father had guessed that it might contain something like this—information that would put her in danger.

Claudia nodded. "She said she did. She said I could still get clean, that she would help me."

"Jodi did that sort of thing, I hear." Rye craned her neck, trying to see if an ambulance had arrived.

"The night she died, a girl down on the first floor was getting a beating. She was screaming. I can still hear her." Claudia closed her eyes. Rye gave her a gentle shake, and the other woman winced. "Jodi came flying down the stairs. I was on the third-floor landing. She was so focused. She didn't realize how slick it was from the rain, and when she ran past me, she slipped. She was right there, and then she wasn't." Claudia met Rye's gaze. "She didn't even scream, you know. I thought she hit her head, that she was just unconscious. It was my chance."

Rye slowly put the pieces together. "You're saying you went to her apartment to find whatever evidence she had on you instead of checking on her?"

"Her door was wide open, but I couldn't find anything. I thought maybe she'd made it up, that she didn't have any photographs or notes about what she'd seen." Claudia sniffled. "I went home after that. I didn't even know she'd died until it was in the paper."

"You walked by her body and didn't call for help?"

"I took the back stairs. I could still hear that girl down on one, and I didn't want to..."

"Help her? You didn't want to get involved." Out of the corner of her eye, she saw Daniel, his face a mask.

Claudia glanced past Rye and saw him, too. She sneered. "And you, thinking you were so smooth. We all knew why you were here. Jodi was so proud of her brother, always bragging about what an incredible PI he was, how he should join the police force. With you sniffing around this week, everyone here had to keep their noses clean."

"Doesn't seem like that worked," Daniel replied, gesturing to the flashing lights.

"Madeline got spooked," Claudia said. "She thought you were watching her side gig. She didn't know anything about the drugs, but she paid for protection. Then the big boss showed up tonight. Said he had taken care of the police, that they would be too busy to come around here." She shook her head. "I thought he was the real deal. Scary as...but then he shot his own foot? Madeline's never shot a gun in her life. I guess you figured that! She got in over her head."

"Why grab my dad?" Rye asked.

"The boss wanted you here. You and Wanda. Who better to take to bring both of you right to Madeline's doorstep?"

"But why?"

"How should I know? To bribe you? Threaten you? We weren't talking about crime while braiding each other's hair." Claudia coughed. "Madeline asked me to keep this one busy for a while." She gestured to Daniel. "I was hoping for more fun than weed, but beggars can't be choosers."

Rye turned at the sound of her father's voice. He was being led out of the apartment, his arm in a sling. She wanted to run to him, but her whole body felt numb. Daniel flagged down the medic and asked him to hurry.

The medics returned and eased Rye's grip on Claudia's wound. Claudia was strapped into the stretcher, but she batted the attendants away to grab Rye's shirt and pull her in close. Her face was pinched with pain, but her eyes were clear.

"I pushed her down the stairs," Claudia whispered so softly, Rye might have imagined it. "That confession just now? Not catching her in time? A performance that will guarantee me a lighter sentence." She paused, her lips a breath away from Rye's ear. "I wanted you to know. Let's see how well you sleep at night now."

The medics carried her away, and Daniel gently lifted Rye to her feet, letting her lean on him as the blood rushed painfully back into her extremities. Claudia's words were still ringing in Rye's head, but all she cared about was seeing her father. Together she and Daniel limped down the stairs to where Hardy sat at the edge of an ambulance bay. Wanda had her arm around him, speaking into his ear. Lance and Stephen were there, too, looking more excited than frightened.

Confessions had been blurted out by at least some of the parties involved. Arrests had been made. The documents Jodi had mailed herself appeared to be detailed evidence with photos to corroborate what she had seen, so the state police would follow up on arrests outside of Stone Ridge. It was a victory, and that was enough said.

Even Ryan had his moment, sternly informing Wanda and Daniel that he had Mike Nifterick's fingerprints on Wanda's prayer sheets and his credit card on record for purchasing stink bombs from a fireworks shop across the New Hampshire border that would have closed the whole operation without all their grandstanding.

When Hardy saw Rye, he opened his good arm, and she fell into him, the smell of his aftershave anchoring her to the reality that he was going to be okay. Rye would get to take her father home—if she could convince Wanda to let him go, of course.

46

WANDA DID NOT FEEL WONDERFUL IN THE MORNING, but she knew that whatever bruising she had would not be helped by lying in bed. Besides, Wink was not going to wait for her all morning. He had bushes to pee on and breakfast to scarf down before he went in for his nap on Stephen's bed. She let her dog lick her face until she laughed. It felt good to laugh.

After she had taken care of Wink and Figgy, she peeked in on both boys. They were sound asleep and seemingly none the worse for wear after last night. She had listened to them complain for about an hour after they'd gotten home that they had missed all the "good stuff." Wanda pointed out that if they hadn't, they would both be on a flight to Heathrow by this afternoon, which shut them up.

She took a hot shower and got dressed. She had a date for breakfast in a lovely hotel just outside of town. The contrast from the night before could not be more dramatic. Yesterday's events at the Cedars felt like a dream…except for the part with Hardy. She had been so scared for him. She shook her head.

When she reached the hotel, the ambiance was elegant. She had put on a gray clergy blouse with a collar, black skirt, and small silver earrings. She met Father Paul in the lobby. He was her oldest and closest friend among the clergy in town, and she often went over to his rectory for a Sunday evening movie or game of Scrabble, but this was serious. They needed to help this couple make the right words out of the tiles they had been dealt and keep their family together.

Jorge Santos met them and brought them into the dining room, where Aline was already drinking a cup of coffee and writing some notes. Wanda prayed a blessing over their coffees and pastry tray. Ana and Camila's parents seemed a bit surprised.

Wanda spoke first. "I brought Father Paul with me because he offered to share his faith's understanding of the current situation, which is the same as our Protestant one."

"I understand that you were concerned with the couple's eagerness to be together and start a family." Father Paul began at the core of the issue. "I do understand this couple's love overcame…conventional doctrine, but they were already committed to each other. Reverend Wanda and I support their going forward to the ceremony that names a marriage of what is already true."

"We understand this is a challenging situation for you," Wanda said. "But—"

"The wedding is still on," Aline interrupted. "We've discussed it at length, and we have agreed that Jorge was being hasty in the way he responded to Ana and Tyler's news."

Wanda hid her smile at the woman's strategic use of the word "we." Aline might present a united front with her husband in public company, but it was clear who called the shots behind closed doors. "This is wonderful news."

Father Paul nodded. "My friends, I do not tell everyone this, but I was once a married man. After my wife died, I received my call to the priesthood. I was never blessed with children of my own—that was not the path of God's call for me—but I do understand many of the struggles of the modern family in our church. You have chosen a path of forgiveness. May God bless you as your family expands."

Jorge practically glowed at the priest's words, and Aline looked satisfied that the wedding would go on. Wanda prayed it would do so without another hitch.

In the afternoon, Wanda dropped her professional persona and was thrown back into visions of the night before. She remembered wiping the blood off of Rye's hands. She knew vaguely that it had taken a lot of wet wipes, and that every time one had gotten too dirty, Lance had handed her another. She'd experienced enormous relief upon learning that Hardy did not need to stay overnight at the hospital, but she could see that Rye was feeling protective, and so she had left the two of them to debrief together.

Lance, Stephen, and Wanda had discussed what to tell Mickey and Rob. Lying was considered but discarded. He and Stephen hadn't been in danger, Lance reasoned, so there was no need to mention anything to them at all. Wanda rejected that idea but agreed that they would keep to minimum details.

It was a relief when Rye called with an update on Hardy.

"Wanda, are you free to come over? I need to go out for a few hours, but I'd rather not leave my father alone that long. He's a terrible patient. I found him trying to feed the chickens when I got up this morning." She paused. "You could bring the boys."

"I'd be delighted to come. Lance and Stephen are expected at Nicole's for pizza, but I think I can handle a difficult patient on my own. Should I pick up dinner on the way?"

"If I'm not back in time, you can order something. Dad also has a full freezer if you want to heat a meal up."

Wanda smiled. Rye sounded like a mother leaving an only somewhat reliable babysitter in charge. "Leave the door unlocked. I'll be there soon."

When she arrived, she could hear Rye arguing with her father in the kitchen from all the way down the hall. It sounded like Hardy was not going to take his recovery lying down, figuratively or literally.

Wanda walked into an incredible scene. Rye was at the stove checking a pot of what looked like stew. Hardy was tossing an arugula salad one-handed. On the counter were fresh-baked rolls, from the smell of it, just out of the oven. In the center of the table was the most beautiful cake Wanda had ever seen in real life.

"Is that the cake from *Recipes for Love and Murder*?" Wanda gasped. It was decorated with fresh flowers, presumably from Hardy's garden.

"The carrot, coconut, and pineapple cake that Tannie Maria makes in the first season, yes," Hardy replied. "I remember you mentioning you wished you could try it."

"He also insisted on making Tannie Maria's vegetable stew," Rye said. "He tried to sneak out to pick everything from the garden himself when I went to take a shower." She glared at her father.

"I wasn't sneaking!" Hardy protested. "This is a flesh wound! I'm fine!"

Wanda put down her laptop bag and came to take the salad bowl out of his arms. The table was set with delicate china Wanda had never seen before. Each plate and bowl had a different flower pattern, and every one of them was lovely. "What's the occasion?"

"Survival," Rye snorted.

"Get out of here, you tyrant," Hardy replied, pushing her out the door.

"Save me some cake!"

Hardy rolled his eyes. "Kids. Can't live with them—"

"Would die without them," Wanda finished.

"Exactly." Hardy pulled out a chair for her.

"Absolutely not," she said, and stared him down until he grudgingly sat. Wanda served them each a bowl of soup, then brought the bread and butter to the table. "Are these all recipes from the show?" The two of them had been watching it together, and Wanda always finished an episode starving.

"The rolls are my own recipe, because I know you love them, but everything else, yes."

Wanda's eyes were wide with delight. "This is the most incredible surprise!"

"After the month you've had, I figured it was time you got spoiled," Hardy said. "I feel like the only time I've seen you, we've been dealing with the case, or wedding drama, or last's night debacle."

"Is that what we're calling your kidnapping? A debacle?"

"You know I've been through much worse," he replied. "I was more concerned about Lance and Stephen. When I found out that Daniel was hiding them, I was so relieved."

"Me, too. When I heard you tapping, I knew Madeline had you, but I was also scared the boys were with you."

"Maybe you've managed to shake a little sense into them." They looked at each other and started to laugh. It turned into one of those fits where making eye contact sent them back into gales of laughter. Wanda finally wiped tears from her eyes and took a roll.

"I needed that." Her hands were still shaking, and she had to concentrate on buttering her bread. When she looked up, there was a ring box on the table between them. It was open to reveal a beautiful opal ring banded in rose gold.

"You will marry me, won't you?" Hardy asked.

Wanda had imagined, hoped, prayed for this proposal. She loved this man so much. He had become her best friend over the last year, the person she could argue with and still depend on completely.

"Wanda?" Hardy's tone had taken on a hint of anxiety.

"I thought you'd never ask." Then she was silent again, just long enough for him to look a little panicky. "Of course I will, with all my heart."

They were both silent then, as awkward as teenagers, until Wanda realized she was crying. She stood up and pulled him out of his seat with his good arm.

And they kissed.

Hardy whispered, "I look forward to making an honest woman out of you."

She considered the implications of that and decided the wisest response was another kiss.

47

THE LAST WEDDING OF THE SEASON WAS STUNNING. Ana wore her mother's dress. It was a tailor's dream—altered to fit her taller, less curvy frame, then altered again to fit her new curviness. Tyler began to cry the moment he saw Ana walking down the aisle, and stray tears kept running down his face from that moment until after they'd cut the cake.

Wanda and Father Paul alternated readings as if they did it at every wedding. The good priest even took Ana's bouquet and put it in Camila's hands when both twins forgot. Ana's brothers' wives were as lovely as expected, but the surprise was Sam—more elegant than any of the other guests. Her inner strength seemed to have come to the forefront overnight as she dealt with her mother's incarceration and rose to the occasion of becoming the matriarch of this branch of the extended family. Charlie chose to watch the wedding on Zoom, along with approximately half of the population of Brazil.

The kiss got spontaneous applause that must have been heard blocks away.

In the recessional, Ryan, as best man, walked behind his brother with a box of tissues someone had given him under one arm and the other arm entwined with Camila. The wedding couple looked as though they were floating ten feet above their guests, completely entranced with each other. The groomsmen forgot to return and dismiss the guests, as groomsmen so often did, and Father Paul had slipped out to lead Saturday mass, so Wanda waved in Hardy's help. They had agreed to keep their engagement a secret until after this wedding so that Ana and Tyler could enjoy the spotlight. They'd already discussed a December wedding with a honeymoon in England for the twelve days of Christmas.

At the reception, Wanda breathed a sigh of relief. Her wedding season was finally over. It was nearly the Fourth of July, and as she nibbled on the plate of cake her fiancé had brought to her, she wondered whether church members would decorate a pickup truck for the parade. Maybe Martha Snider would enjoy helping with it.

She was lost in thought, wondering whether she should call or email the older woman, when she realized Stephen had joined her. Wanda was so glad he had decided to stay until September, when his classes would start. Rob had been surprisingly calm when he heard about…well, everything. He had even seemed proud of Stephen's part in the case's resolution.

Rob and Mickey had been thrilled by the news of another family wedding on the horizon. Mickey might have jumped back on a plane to 'organize' it, except she was working a few afternoons a week at her local library. Wanda was deeply relieved.

Stephen was doing something with his hands. She watched him. "You are using ASL?"

"BSL. British Sign Language. And watch this." His hands shifted. "Now I'm using SSE. That's Sign Supported English. I talk, and the signs are for only some of the words, but they make the whole conversation easier."

Wanda continued to watch him. "I've never heard of SSE."

"I know. Lance told me you've been willfully resisting him," Stephen replied. "You probably also don't know that my studies focus on connecting people with disabilities in as many ways as possible to proudly be themselves without losing connection with people who do not happen to have a situation that includes a disabling condition."

She shook her head, amazed. "I had no idea."

"Your deafness is progressing, and *you* might want to make some progress to balance that fact. Lance has been going to ASL classes for months because he wants to learn with you. He wants to give you that gift, not just because he thinks you'll lose hearing beyond the assistance of the aids, but because he thinks you could use that to reach so many people, maybe in church, maybe in life."

"And I've been shutting him down."

Stephen nodded. "You can be as stubborn as Mickey in your own way." He paused. "The difference is that she isn't afraid to ask for help. You and Lance are both used to being the help-*er*."

"It's true," Wanda said. "I hate feeling so…vulnerable."

"Even with Lance?"

"Especially with Lance. He spent his whole life taking care of Mickey. I don't want him to fall into that role with me."

Stephen reached out and took one of Wanda's hands. He squeezed it gently. "You aren't your sister. This isn't the same."

Wanda didn't want to have to make another trip to the bathroom to fix her makeup, but the tears had other plans. She blotted them as carefully as she could with a cocktail napkin. When she could finally speak, she said the only thing she could think of. "Thank you."

RYE WAS THRILLED THEY COULD HOLD ANA AND Tyler's reception outside. She never got tired of garden weddings, especially since all the rain they'd had this summer meant the blooms were thick and fragrant. She could get lost studying the flowers bouncing gently in the breeze, a glass of champagne in one hand and the sound of friends and family laughing drifting over her.

It had been a busy week. Rye had spent more time at the station and caring for her father than at work, but Gerard had covered for her, laughingly admitting that she had a long history of doing the same for him. At night, she would stay up late doing paperwork, send it off, and fall into bed. In any spare time, she'd helped Camila, Ana, their cousins, and their friends with wedding prep. She dyed shoes, advised on hair and makeup, and chauffeured out-of-town guests around to nail appointments and dress fittings.

Wanda had brought Lance and Stephen over for dinner almost every night, although none of them would allow Hardy to cook until his arm healed. Rye was especially grateful that the boys were so helpful in the garden and kitchen, and that they took Hardy's direction without their usual countersuggestions. Her father was in surprisingly good spirits for being treated like an invalid. Rye didn't question that good fortune.

Having Wink and Figgy around also helped Rye shake off the nightmares she had been having since Claudia confessed. She never felt better than when she was sitting on the porch with Wink in her lap or Figgy's head under her hand. Co-regulation, her therapist called it, saying that animals were even better at the technique than people. Rye wouldn't mind a dog of her own if she were ever home. For now, though, having these good pups around each evening was a balm for her soul.

A hand touched her arm, and Rye startled. She wondered how long her half sister had been standing beside her, a plate of food extended. "Thanks, Kara." Rye followed her to the closest table, empty now that everyone was on the dance floor.

"It feels strange to go to two weddings in barely a month," Kara mused as she forked a bite of cake into her mouth.

"Especially for people you don't even know," Rye replied. "I appreciate you being my last-minute plus one. I've been meaning to text, but it's been…busy."

"It's okay. We don't need to stay up all night talking about our crushes to qualify as sisters," Kara said. She twirled a finger through her curls—a near exact match to Rye's own whiskey-shaded locks.

"Is that an option?" Rye asked. It sounded nice.

Kara looked up in surprise, and then a smile creased her normally serious expression. "I'm free tonight."

"Me, too." Rye glanced around at the party in full swing around them. "Eventually." She ate a few more bites, studying her half sister's face. She could see a bit of their mother there, but both of them took after their fathers except for the hair.

Rafael wandered over as Rye finished her dinner. "I'm bored. Have you seen Lance and Stephen?"

"They were working on a surprise for the happy couple." Rye checked her watch. "They should be ready soon." She admired Rafael's look for a moment. He wore a navy suit tailored for his narrow frame. He'd paired it with a pale sage shirt and had left a few buttons open at the top. "The haircut looks amazing!"

Rafael beamed. "Thanks for getting me that appointment! I'm sorry you couldn't come with us, though." He ran his hand through the long, sideswept front bangs, all the more striking in contrast to the buzz cut on the sides and back. Just behind his right ear, the barber had shaved three little stars, one each for Rafael, Andy, and Crystal.

Rye wasn't about to tell him that Andy had asked her not to come to the appointment, to allow it to be something he and his new wife could do to show Rafael their support. Rye hadn't minded at all. Some things meant more when done with family.

"I'm sorry I missed it, but Andy sent some pictures of your shopping trip afterward. I can't wait to see all the new clothes," Rye replied. "By the way, this is Kara, my half sister."

Rafael was practically bouncing through a retelling of his trip into the city when the lights went out. A panicked gasp went up from the crowd, but then the music started up again, softer this time, and above them, fireworks went off. The three of them joined the crowd at the edge of the dance floor, marveling at the gift Wanda and the boys had managed to pull off at the last minute.

Rye felt a hand slip into hers, and she glanced down, then up at Camila. She and Ryan were standing arm and arm, staring up at the sky. Rye squeezed Camila's fingers back, a happy tear slipping free as she turned to watch the show.

AUTHORS' ACKNOWLEDGMENTS

Our deepest gratitude goes to Ben Miller-Callihan for his gifted guidance as our agent for this fourth book in the Rev and Rye Series. Five years ago, he picked our manuscript from the pile, and he has been with us every step of the way. We are grateful to Courtney Miller-Callihan and the Handspun Literary Agency community of writers, where we feel at home. In addition, we are resourced by many authors, writers' groups, readers, and friends, as well as the wonderful world of "Sisters in Crime."

Our beta readers are the best! Jeff Deck, Nadine Donnell, and Nancy Hardy ask questions, spot the inconsistencies, and even fix the dawdling commas. We are ongoingly grateful to the team at Brain Mill Press for the care and guidance of each book, as well as the sifting of many small issues that make the fictional town of Stone Ridge, Massachusetts, come alive. Their personal support has meant so much.

Thank you to our faithful readers! Making connections is the reward for all our plot-twisting and comma chasing. We're so pleased you invite these characters into your homes time and time again. Special appreciation goes to Katherine Thornton, the charity auction winner of the "your name in our next book"—thank you for gifting your daughter's name to one of our villains!

Finally, to Donald, to Matt and Julia, to David and the boys—you are the best! Thank you for your support and encouragement when we are glued to our computers or insist on driving a one-hundred-mile round trip to a book talk in a storm that limits the audience to five! Your cheer, patience, and love are the fuel that keeps us going.

ABOUT
THE AUTHORS

MAREN C. TIRABASSI'S FORTY-FIVE YEARS' EXPERIENCE in mainline ministry shape Wanda Duff's professional life (but not her personality). In addition to the three previous Rev and Rye mysteries, Maren has published twenty-two nonfiction titles, one book of short stories, and two books of poetry, as well as poetry and short stories in fifteen anthologies. She is a former Poet Laureate of the city of Portsmouth, New Hampshire, and the recipient of the 2023 Lifetime Achievement Award from the New Hampshire Humanities Council.

AFTER TEACHING AND WORKING IN EARLY EDUCATION for a decade, Maria Mankin has published six books with Pilgrim Press, in addition to first three Rev and Rye mysteries with Brain Mill Press, and she has contributed essays to several anthologies. She is also a coauthor of *Circ*, a mystery set in Skegness, England, published by Pigeon Park Press, and *Pitching Our Tents: Poetry of Hospitality*. She is a regular contributor to Living Psalms, a collection in which the Psalms are reinterpreted in poetry and art as a reflection of God's work of justice and compassion. In 2024, Maria received an Impact on Education Award for her work with elementary grade students and staff.

* 9 7 8 1 9 4 8 4 5 5 9 9 5 9 *